I0655754

THE HOUR OF MERCY

THE HOUR OF MERCY

A NOVEL BY
Mary Anne Mulholland

Halo
PUBLISHING
INTERNATIONAL

PUBLISHING INTERNATIONAL

Halo Publishing International
7550 W IH-10 #800, PMB 2069,
San Antonio, TX 78229

First Edition, May 2025
ISBN: 978-1-63765-749-2
Library of Congress Control Number: 2025903964

Halo Publishing International is a self-publishing company that publishes adult fiction and non-fiction, children's literature, self-help, spiritual, and faith-based books. We continually strive to help authors reach their publishing goals and provide many different services that help them do so. We do not publish books that are deemed to be politically, religiously, or socially disrespectful, or books that are sexually provocative, including erotica. Halo reserves the right to refuse publication of any manuscript if it is deemed not to be in line with our principles. Do you have a book idea you would like us to consider publishing? Please visit www.halopublishing.com for more information.

This book is dedicated to
the priest who baptized me,
the priests who have heard my confessions,
fed me the Body and Blood of Jesus in the Eucharist,
and guided me on my spiritual journey.

CONTENTS

PROLOGUE

So teach us to number our days that we may
get a heart of wisdom.

—*Psalm 90:12, Revised*
Standard Version

Father James Collins pulled back the drapes, rested his head against the windowpane, and watched the sun as it quietly slipped behind the barren trees and disappeared. He had just administered the last sacrament Father Brendan Murphy would ever receive and was using this moment to collect his thoughts. Father James was familiar with the final hours and minutes people spent on this earth, and they were not always peaceful exits. But today there was a quiet stillness, a holy aura to the room.

He stepped back to see the reflection of a lighted candle in the window and thought of how Father Brendan had been a light for him during his darkest moments. Father Brendan's fatherly advice and spiritual guidance over the past six years had helped him navigate the role he played in the life of the parish.

Father James had lit that candle an hour before and placed it on the nightstand that held Father Brendan's breviary, its pages worn thin from years of prayer, and his reading glasses.

The flickering light created a warm glow in the room that held the hearts of four dear friends.

Father James's thoughts were a mixture of joy and sorrow. *Your departure is a well-deserved beginning of a new life with the Lord, but your going will impact the lives of those you leave behind.*

He bent down and touched the shoulder of the dying priest as if to glean a final bit of wisdom from his friend and mentor. He then turned his attention to Marge Gallagher, who was praying at her brother's bedside in anticipation of his departure from this world and entry into eternal life. Her love for Father Brendan was evident to anyone who had met the pair.

"He seems to be holding on," she whispered, "like he's waiting for something."

Sam, Marge's husband, stood behind her and tenderly squeezed her shoulders.

Father James sighed and said, "Marge, I'm going to church to help Father Mateo with confessions. I'll be back as soon as I can. Do you need anything before I go? I could bring you and Sam a cup of tea."

She raised her eyes. "You look exhausted, James."

Sam added, "Don't worry about us. I'll go to the kitchen and get something for us to nibble on in a few minutes. You take care of the parish now."

Father James bent down and kissed Marge's forehead, then motioned for Sam to follow him out of the room. "Sam, I left the wreath on the porch. Please hang it on the door if Brendan passes before I return."

Father James went to shake his hand, but Sam pulled him into a shoulder bump and a pat on the back and said, "You've been a good and faithful friend to Brendan."

Father James took a deep breath, descended the stairs of the rectory, and entered his office. He picked up his purple stole, kissed it, and placed it around his neck as his eyes came to rest on the framed calligraphy Maggie had penned for him last Christmas:

I can do all things in Him who strengthens me.

He suppressed the lump in his throat, grabbed his coat from the hook, and crunched across the snow-covered parking lot. The cold evening sky gave him no solace.

As he entered the church, Father Mateo led the congregation in prayer. Organ music filled the air as Father James made his way to the confessional. His heart was still at Father Brendan's side, but his parishioners needed him to restore their relationship with God through the sacrament of Reconciliation. He prayed:

> *O Lord, look at the crowded church tonight. They've come to ask for Your forgiveness to celebrate the birth of Jesus and welcome Him into their hearts this Christmas. I need You to lighten the dull ache in my head so that I may offer sound spiritual guidance.*

Father James knew the importance of this sacrament since it supplied the repentant sinner with much-needed grace. He assured everyone who left his confessional that God loved them despite their transgressions.

As the evening progressed, the crowd dwindled, and the steady flow of penitents subsided. Father James lowered his head, and in the silence of this small space where sins are forgiven, he drifted off to sleep. Soft organ music gently seeped into his dream.

***

I see Brendan walking toward a bright light. I try to follow him, but I can't seem to move. Slowly, Brendan turns, approaches me, and places a key in my hand—

***

A voice roused Father James from his dream.

"Bless me, Father, for I have sinned. It's been six months since my last confession."

He slowly lifted his head and, for a moment, felt liberated from the anguish surrounding his soul as he acknowledged the request, "May God, who has enlightened every heart, help you know your sins and trust in His mercy."

He opened his eyes to focus on the dark-haired woman who was kneeling on the other side of the screen that separated the priest from the penitent. He leaned closer to hear her confess the reason she had come. It was clear that she was there to be forgiven by God for things she had failed to do.

There was something oddly familiar about the woman... Or was there? He knew his parishioners, but this one baffled him. Was it the sound of her strained, almost-hoarse voice? Did she suffer from a cold, or was she crying?

The dull ache swelled in his head as she spoke, and his heart began to pound. When she finished her confession, he only managed a few words of encouragement, gave her a penance of three Hail Marys, and asked her to make a good Act of Contrition. He then raised his hand in a blessing and asked God to give her peace and absolve her sins. He watched through the screen as she rose and pulled back the curtain to leave.

Before she exited, he heard four grateful words, "Thank you, Father James."

He was going to respond, but the curtain closed. He bent down, placed his fingers on his temples, and massaged them to relieve the pain. Only seconds after she left did he notice the tiny red-and-black insect slowly crawling across the pages of his breviary. He sat up with a start, took a deep breath, and held it. He rubbed his head again, trying to hold on to the déjà vu moment, but it slipped away, allowing an imprisoned memory to surface. He tried to block it out, to keep the memory buried in the recesses of his mind where he had the power to control it. Instead, it erupted like a burst of thunder and forced its way into his heart.

His mind catapulted back to June when Hurricane Agnes had devastated the town. The superstorm had taken the lives of two teens, Maggie and Kevin, who had often approached him for spiritual guidance. Ironically, their acceptance of difficult circumstances inspired him to accept his suffering humbly. They had become like family to him.

Kevin died the night of the storm, and Maggie disappeared. Her loyal dog had also vanished. Father James buried his grief for Kevin and the agony of Maggie's disappearance deep in his heart. It was the only way he could bear the sorrow. With Father Brendan's passing, there would be one less person to share his sadness.

But he found comfort in how the woman who had left the confessional moments before had said his name. Then he remembered what Maggie had said long ago—"*You can tell when someone loves you by how they say your name.*"

He stared blankly at the picture on the confessional wall; it depicted Jesus raising Lazarus from the dead. The ladybug was now making its way along the top edge of the frame, and hope burst from his heart, much like Lazarus emerged from the grave.

Can it be?

Father James flew from his seat, opened the confessional door, raced down the aisle, stopped, and looked around frantically. He noticed the startled stares on the faces of his parishioners and blurted out, "Oh, sorry!" as he raced to the front door and hurried down the aged stone steps. His heart furiously beat, and sweat covered his forehead despite the frigid air. He looked up and down Saint Paul Street, but she was not there. His heart suddenly turned as cold and vacant as the empty road.

Have I allowed grief and exhaustion to confuse my mind?

His knees turned to jelly, and he slumped to a sitting position on the bottom step. His prayer was always the same. "Lord, please bring Maggie home." He placed his head in his hands and tried to block out the events of that stormy night, but the memory was too strong.

***

On Wednesday, June 21, 1972, Hurricane Agnes struck Ellicott City with a disastrous blow, and the Patapsco River swelled and flooded the valley. The raging river ripped up trees, destroyed bridges, and sent torrents of water to smash homes and buildings, killing people and animals along its path.

Maggie and Kevin had left the church only moments before the eye of the storm struck, but neither ever made it home. In the morning, a rescue crew found Kevin's lifeless body pinned under a fallen tree, and the search for Maggie intensified. It was never clear why anyone would be off the road in a heavily wooded area during a violent storm, and there was no trace of the graceful, golden-haired teen.

***

Father James believed he was the last to see the pair together, and the burden weighed heavily on him. He shivered as the cold air penetrated his body and replaced the short-term adrenaline rush. He forced himself to his feet and walked around the church building, grateful for the solitude.

When he reached the snow-covered garden, he slowed his step. The dark-haired woman from the confessional stood beneath the Blessed Mother's statue. The Christmas lights gently swayed and gave the garden an animated quality. She slowly turned as the clouds in the night sky drifted apart, and the light from the full moon illuminated her features.

Father James came to a standstill, unable to move as confusion replaced his sadness. *Is this possible?* He shook his head to clear it. *Am I seeing a ghost?*

Mascara-stained tears ran down the teen's cheeks.

No, this is no ghost. There is no mistaking those eyes.

She reached up and pulled a black wig from her head, exposing her golden-blonde hair.

He caught his breath, put his hands on his head, and whispered, "Maggie?" He could see her attempt to smile.

"Yes, but no one can know I'm alive, at least not yet."

CHAPTER 1

It is ours to offer what we can,
His to supply what we cannot.

—*Saint Jerome*

Six years earlier
Easter, April 10, 1966

The familiar rumble of the early morning Baltimore and Ohio train offered a soothing rhythm for Father James as he prayed in the garden outside Saint Paul Church. The sound brought to mind the evenings he had spent as a child praying the rosary with his family after dinner. He remembered how the train chugging in the distance had set the cadence of their Our Fathers and Hail Marys. It was a simpler time, surrounded by a family who loved and protected him. Today, the train engine echoed through the woods and helped calm his anxiety. The whistle confirmed his amen as he closed his breviary.

The train's vibrations slowly died away, making him aware of a less comforting sound. *Do I hear a child crying?* He rose from the bench and walked around the garden wall to enter an adjacent garden that boasted a life-size statue of the Blessed Mother. This area was adorned by a prayer bench and slate-paver paths lined by clay pots filled with flowers.

A young girl stood on her tippy-toes, which enabled her small frame to stretch over the retaining wall and cling to the statue's base. She had buried her head in the crease of her right elbow and held a spindly bunch of wildflowers. Her other hand was caressing the statue's right foot, which depicted the Blessed Mother crushing a snake's head. Easter blossoms filled the two-tiered garden and surrounded the child in a cloak of color, giving Father James the impression that the Blessed Mother was wrapping the child in her mantle. He wondered where the little girl could've come from at such an early hour.

Father James was about to speak when he noticed a large dog sitting on the second tier of the garden wall, just above the child. The dog keenly fixed his gaze on Father James, so he moved no closer, but asked, "My child, why are you crying?"

She looked up, sniffed, and turned to face him. Tear-soaked eyelashes accentuated her crystal-blue eyes, and a long, tousled braid fell across one shoulder of her loose-fitting blouse, which was too large for her small frame.

The sun's rays peeked over the wooded hills surrounding the church and reminded him that the joy of Christ's Resurrection was on the way, yet here was one of Christ's little ones crying beneath a statue of His Mother.

She did not respond to his question, so he tried again, "My name is Father James. What's your name?"

She wiped her nose on her sleeve. "Mary Magdalene," she responded between sniffles, "but everyone calls me Maggie."

Is she serious?

Yes, he could see her expression was serious. The irony that he was standing in a garden with Mary Magdalene, who was crying on Easter Sunday morning, was not lost on him. He doubted that seven demons plagued her, but, clearly, something was troubling the child.

24

He repeated his question, this time addressing her by name, "Maggie, why are you crying?"

"I picked these flowers for the Blessed Mother"—the tears began again—"but I don't have a vase."

"Ah. Yes, I see a vase would be helpful. Can you come with me? I'll help you pick one from Mrs. Gallagher's cupboard. She has quite the collection."

When he opened the church's side door, the massive dog leaped down from the wall and attached himself to the little girl's side. Father decided not to prevent the canine's entry, so all three filed into the area behind the altar that led to the sacristy. Maggie held on to the dog's collar, Father James suspected more for her comfort than to keep the dog in line. He shuddered to think of Mrs. Gallagher's reaction had she witnessed an animal enter this sacred space.

He watched Maggie as she observed the brass candlesticks, gold chalices, and Communion paten lined up next to the neatly pressed linens. She pointed to the thurible hanging on a stand and said, "I've seen smoke come out of this at my church back home, and it smelled good."

Father James lifted the lid. "That's because of the incense the priest puts in here."

"What's this?" she asked, examining all sides of an object.

"It's called a monstrance. The priest places a consecrated host, the Body of Christ, right in the center of the gold sunburst; then he puts it all on the altar."

She tilted her head to one side. "Why?"

"So that people can come and pray before Jesus. We call it adoration," he explained as he opened an old wooden cupboard, its hinges creaking slightly.

She let go of the dog's collar, and her eyes popped wide at the selection of ceramic and glass vases that filled the shelves.

The dog, meanwhile, sniffed every corner and crevice of the room, then sat down and stared at Father James.

He was about to ask her dog's name when Maggie asked, "Where did you get all these?"

"Well, people bring flowers to the church but seldom return to claim the vases. A good thing, so you can pick any one you want to hold your beautiful bouquet."

Maggie looked at the simple offering in her hand and decided on a small white vase for her flowers.

Father James took it from the cupboard and filled it with water from the faucet used to clean the sacred vessels after the celebration of Mass. He said, "This is no ordinary sink."

"How come?"

"The plumber did not hook it up to a pipe, so anything that flows through it goes directly into the ground. That way, remnants of the Body and Blood of Jesus on the vessels will fall right into the earth."

Maggie bent over the sink to look down the drain. "I can't see the ground."

Father James smiled and handed her the vase filled with water. He was impressed with her attention to detail as she positioned each flower. He noticed a ladybug sitting on one of the petals and saw how carefully she handled that particular bloom as she whispered something to the little creature.

He broke her concentration. "Maggie, will your family come to Easter Mass this morning?"

She slowly spun the vase to inspect it from all sides. "I'll be here." Then she lowered her eyes. "I'm not sure about Uncle Mitch though. He's not much for church." She carefully lifted the vase. "I'd better get home. I left before he woke up, and I don't want him to worry."

Before Father James could ask about her uncle or where he lived, Maggie slipped out of the sacristy with the precious arrangement and her watchful companion.

26

He caught up with them outside in the garden, where she set the flowers on the wall beneath the statue of the Blessed Mother. The dog took his place above her as she stepped back and knelt. Her small offering may have seemed odd, but it rested comfortably among the large azaleas, rhododendrons, and lilies. Father James thought her little bouquet appropriate for the Blessed Mother, who herself was the humble handmaid of the Lord.

He overheard her heartfelt prayer as Maggie whispered, "O Blessed Mother, today is my mom's birthday, and I know she will celebrate Easter with you and Jesus and all the angels and saints. Please tell Mommy how much I miss her and that I brought you these flowers to share with her. I could not find the daisies she likes, but I'll bet Daddy found some up in heaven for her."

Maggie stood up, wiped her eyes with her hand, and headed up the stone stairs in the garden wall as the dog watched her every move. She gave him a pat on the head as he wagged his tail and followed behind her.

The dog looked back at Father James as if to say, "I've got it from here."

CHAPTER 2

*And every day, when your heart especially
feels the loneliness of life, pray.*

—*Saint Padre Pio*

Father James watched the pair run up and over the hill. *How responsible can this Mitch character be if a young child can slip out unnoticed early in the morning?* He shook his head and walked to the rectory.

The tantalizing aroma of freshly brewed coffee filled the hallway, and he inhaled deeply. He savored the fragrance and allowed it to replace the homesick feeling in his soul. He entered his office, sat at a desk that still felt foreign, and reached for a framed photo of his parents. It was one of the few personal items he had brought on this unexpected assignment at Saint Paul Church. They had passed away within a month of each other, less than a year ago, and he missed them terribly. The smiling faces in the frame consoled his heart.

His peaceful moment was disturbed by the sound of clanging pots and pans from the kitchen, Marge Gallagher's domain. He knew he would not be welcome this early, but would love some coffee. He replaced the photo that held the happy faces of the two people who had given him life and reached for his journal. He opened to the last entry and found the sobering words he had written in his neat Palmer penmanship:

In my heart, I question my vocation. I know this transfer has not helped my fragile state of mind. Change is difficult for me—new faces in the congregation, new surroundings, and new customs. Father Brendan is a holy priest, but his sister, Marge, is a force not to be ignored. She has made that quite clear.

Then there was Vatican II—it felt like the changes hijacked the sacredness of the liturgy. My head still reels from the revisions.

Turning forty this year has added to my unrest. This "midlife crisis" took me by surprise. The Bible uses the number forty to signify something different is on the horizon—a time of preparation for something new. For example, it rained for forty days and nights to cleanse the world of wickedness back in the days of Noah. Moses stayed on Mt. Sinai for forty days before receiving the Ten Commandments. Jesus stayed forty days in the desert while Satan tempted Him before He began His public ministry. There are many more examples—I wonder what forty means for me.

Leaning back in his chair and resting his head against the wall, he indulged in thoughts ill-suited for a joyful Easter morning. His encounter with the child, Maggie, made him wonder if finding a vase was really what she needed. *I could have been more help if I wasn't so wrapped up in my gloominess. I hope she got home safely.*

Father James's misery was clouding his mission, and he had been like this for a while. The culture had shifted, and the flock he cared for too often caved to worldly enticements. Free love was all the rage. The crucifix on the wall proved that love was never free and required sacrifice.

Popular music frothed with sexual overtones or the wonder of drugs. There seemed to be a lack of respect by the youth, and their "devil may care" attitude plagued his soul. He cringed as loose morals seeped into society like a virus, and the virus was everywhere.

This month, a magazine cover asked, "IS GOD DEAD?" in big, bold letters. The question made him nauseous. Newspapers revealed images of Vietnam protests in the streets of Washington, DC, and President Johnson tripled the number of troops sent to war. Father James felt deep regret for the young men who lost their lives in a battle he believed could not be won. He offered counsel to families impacted by loved ones killed or injured in the war, but felt his efforts were ineffective. There was too much unrest in the world and his own heart. He didn't believe he could make a difference anymore.

The demands of parish work were numerous and left very little time for him to work through this hopeless feeling, so he had requested permission from the bishop to take a sabbatical. His appeal was denied, but with the promise that, in six months, the bishop would revisit the request.

He couldn't explain the prompting to spend more time reading Scripture, in addition to praying the Liturgy of the Hours from his breviary, but he believed that this was how the Holy Ghost would help him through this difficult time.

Father James's thin office walls absorbed the sounds and smells of the kitchen across from it. Mrs. Gallagher's voice reverberated down the hall as she slammed the oven door with an "Alleluia!"

His stomach responded, and his thoughts turned to the meal Mrs. Gallagher was preparing to mark the end of Lent. Easter brought him back to his senses, as this was a day of celebration, not a day to be self-absorbed. He stood up, dropped the journal on his desk, and headed to the kitchen, determined to at least glom a cup of coffee.

He hesitated when he reached the door and stuck his head in just far enough to see Marge pouring batter onto a pan. He recognized her as a driving force in the parish. She kept things in order, scheduled appointments for the pastor, and often tidied up the church when she disapproved of its appearance. She was Father Brendan's sister, but had served Saint Paul Parish for ten years before her baby brother arrived for his last assignment before retirement. Her husband, Sam, helped around the church as a handyman and tended the lawn and gardens.

Marge was very protective of her brother after he had a heart attack. Father Brendan was one of her favorite topics, and Father James knew he would never measure up in her eyes. From her childhood stories, he had learned that the six-foot-tall priest was quite popular, and he crushed many high school girls' dreams when he entered the seminary. She and Father Brendan were entertaining with their lively discussions, and Father James could tell their relationship was solid, built on love and trust.

"Happy Easter, Mrs. Gallagher." His voice sounded strained, even to him.

"Is that you, Father James?" Her eyes were fixed on the spatula as she quickly flipped a pancake with precision.

He knew darn well she knew it was he who had greeted her.

"I'm preparing a tray for Brendan. Go see if he's awake."

"I'll check on him." He took the stairs two at a time.

Father Brendan quickly opened the door when Father James knocked. He had already shaved and dressed in his clerical clothing; his usually pale face was filled with color.

"Good morning! You look great!" Father James exclaimed.

"I'm feeling well and hope to celebrate Easter Mass with you this morning."

"Well, your sister will be excited to hear this! She was fixing a breakfast tray for you."

"No need. I will surprise her."

As they descended the stairs, Father Brendan chuckled. "Perhaps celebrating the Resurrection of Jesus is the reason for mine."

"Well, he has risen!" a joyful voice bellowed from the kitchen door. "Happy Easter, Brendan." She hugged him. "Now, you sit yourself down and make sure not to overdo it today. Did you take your medicine this morning?" He rolled his eyes and winked at Father James as she rattled off more instructions while fixing his plate.

After she had fussed over every culinary aspect, she turned to Father James and said, "You can fix your own plate, right?" She shoved an empty dish into his hands, wrapped most of the casserole and griddle cakes on a serving tray to take home to Sam, and headed out the door.

Father James looked perplexedly at the breakfast scraps left on the counter and then at his empty plate.

"Pay her no mind, James. It takes her a while to warm up."

CHAPTER 3

Trials, tribulation, anguish, anxiety are
permitted by the very One who gives peace.

—Archbishop Fulton Sheen

M itch Hartman woke with a strong sense of Len's presence. In his dream, they were walking together. She wore a flowing white dress and had flowers in her hair. As the vision faded, reality seeped in, and that old familiar ache returned. It was Len's birthday. She would have turned thirty-five today.

As he dressed, he remembered it was Easter Sunday. *Maggie will expect me to go to church with her. I'm not up for this today.*

On his way to the bathroom, he noticed Maggie's open door. He looked in. "Maggie?" No answer.

He went downstairs. "Maggie? Blaise?" he called louder as his stomach started churning. He rushed to the back deck, but it was empty. He stopped by the mudroom and balanced on one foot, then the other, putting on his sneakers while hopping through the house and calling her name. He bounced through the front door and practically fell onto the bottom step of the porch while trying to pull his left shoe over his heel. His hands shook so much he could hardly tie the laces.

"Maggie! Blaise!" he yelled still trying to form a bow.

This time, a *woof* answered his panic-stricken plea. He looked up to see Maggie and Blaise running down the hill toward the house. Maggie's smile was as bright as the sun, and her cheeks were flushed. She arrived out of breath, Blaise panting happily by her side.

"Maggie, where have you been?" he asked with a furrowed brow. "What are you doing out so early in the morning? It's not safe!" As Maggie's smile clouded over, he asked, "What could be so important?"

She started crying. "It's Mom and Aunt Len's birthday. Did you forget?"

Her answer knocked the wind right out of him. No, he hadn't forgotten. He held her close as his anger slipped away.

Mitch prepared breakfast while Maggie ran upstairs to put on her Easter dress. Blaise stayed in the kitchen, sniffing the bacon-scented air.

After they had eaten, Mitch and Blaise walked Maggie to church.

"Uncle Mitch, come to Mass with me. Please."

"Sorry, I have to catch up on my work. I'll be here to meet you when church is over."

"But it's Easter."

"We've been over this before. I'm way behind in my work and have bills to pay. Hey, where are you going? The church entrance is this way."

"I know, but I want to go in the side door by the garden." She checked to see if her gift of flowers was still beneath the statue as Blaise trotted up the garden steps and lay down behind a bush.

"Come on, let's go, Blaise. We'll be back in an hour to get Maggie. You can't stay here."

Blaise didn't budge.

Mitch climbed the stairs. "I know where you're hiding." He pleaded again, "Let's go home. I'll give you a treat."

An elderly gentleman who had been watching him called out, "Are you okay, son?"

Mitch felt the heat rise in his face and his cheeks turn red. "What? Yes, I'm, just trying to get my dog." By now, a few others had gathered in the garden area just below the Blessed Mother statue. *I must look like the village idiot!*

He lowered his head and turned for home. As he walked, he thought of how different his life was from what he had intended. *Life is what happens when you're busy making plans.* He missed the life he and Len had planned together.

When he approached the front porch, he noticed the wild dogwood tree in full bloom. It was beautiful. He remembered how Len had insisted that he keep the tree when he built the house. She had told him, *"Just build around it."* She said it with such conviction and made it sound easy. Len always made life easy.

He thought of the first time he saw her, sitting in a circle of students outside the campus library.

***

He got close enough to hear a heated, one-sided discussion about the case under consideration by the Supreme Court, Brown versus the Board of Education. He noticed her because she sat calmly and peacefully among the angry and agitated undergrads. Those around her argued that desegregation would corrupt the educational system of America. The circle of students stated their views and pumped each other up with self-importance.

Len gathered her books and stood. She looked down at her fellow students with sad eyes and said, "I believe all men are created equal. Our Creator endowed everyone with certain inalienable rights. Among these are life, liberty, and the pursuit of happiness. That would include the same opportunities in education that you and I enjoy. I also believe that everyone should be allowed to sit at a lunch counter and order food, regardless of the color of their skin. We are all made in the image and likeness of God." She looked around. "We should remember *that* basic truth."

By now, more students had gathered and were standing around the group of debaters. Len was hard-pressed to find a place to exit the circle of stunned students as they sat staring up at her. She found a spot where the students, now embarrassed more than self-righteous, had moved apart to let her pass.

It reminded Mitch of Moses parting the waters. He was so captivated by her passion that he failed to move as she made her way through the crowd and bumped right into him.

"Oh, I'm so sorry. I didn't see you there," she said.

"That's okay," Mitch replied as she hastily threaded past him.

Go after her! But he couldn't get his feet to move. He watched her disappear behind a building. He thought, *That's the girl I would love to spend the rest of my life with*...but he had no idea how to make that happen.

A week later, he saw her sitting in the campus coffee shop. She had a textbook open on the table, and the place was swarming with students, but she was alone.

Here's my chance. What will I say? Um, I'll say how impressed I was that she stood up for her beliefs and that I agree with her views. Yeah, that is what I'll tell her.

He stood in line, paid for two coffees, took a deep breath, and turned in her direction. Len looked up, saw him, and smiled. His heart pounded at the thought that such a beautiful person, inside and out, would notice him. Just then, a guy slid into the booth and playfully kissed her on the cheek. Mitch did a one-eighty, handed his coffees to a surprised coed in line, and slipped out the door like a deflated balloon.

What was I thinking? Of course, she has a boyfriend, or she may be engaged. Why did I believe she would even notice me?

Mitch spent the rest of the semester admiring her from afar. He had seen her in the cafeteria, surrounded by others, laughing and having a good time, or walking to class with people who always wore a smile. She brought out the best in everyone.

His buddy Fred noticed that he always had an eye out for someone and finally figured out who it was. "Mitch, she's out of your league and older than you. Do you think that a girl that beautiful would even look at guys like us?"

"You don't understand, she's not like most coeds on campus. She's kind and compassionate—"

Fred interrupted, "And here she comes now!"

Mitch froze. *What will I say? Oh, come on, don't be tongue-tied now.*

"She's looking at us and smiling," Fred said with surprise.

Just as Mitch was about to speak, a group of girls came out of nowhere, like a gaggle of geese, and swept her away.

"You handled that well," Fred joked as he slapped him on the back in a friendly gesture. "You hardly date. How are you going to ask her out?"

"All I know is I would love to spend the rest of my life with her. I realize it could never happen, but let me enjoy my fantasy."

Then, one evening during finals, he sat in the library, cramming for an economics exam. This course frustrated him, and his fear of failure had become oppressive. He was tired and anxious and rested his head on his notes in hopes that he could feed his brain through osmosis. Instead, he fell asleep and had that foreboding dream in which he was taking the final exam without ever attending any classes or completing any assignments. He awoke with a jolt and almost fell out of the chair. He rubbed his eyes, looked up, and could hardly believe what he saw. She was sitting across the table from him with the sweetest smile.

"You know," she said, "the semester is almost over, and you haven't said hello."

A month later, Mitch discovered the guy who kissed her in the booth at the coffee shop was her cousin Teddy. When Mitch met him for the first time, Teddy said, "So you're the guy willing to put up with a virtuous, 'I will not go to a party if there are drugs or stay out past curfew' kind of girl? With all those boring traits, do you know I still have guys bribing me with beers to set them up with my cousin? You know, the one with the enchanting blue eyes." He said this last part as he mimicked his gawking schoolmates.

Mitch just smiled.

After graduation, Mitch started working for a small architectural firm in Howard County, Maryland, close to the school where Len was teaching. The firm loved his portfolio, and he soon acquired a reputation as the go-to guy for innovative designs.

Mitch and Len were hardworking and very frugal. They saved up for a small wedding and used the rest of their money as a down payment on land in Ellicott City. Len stipulated that the house be surrounded by trees and close to a Catholic church, so they built their home a stone's throw away from the Church of Saint Paul.

Mitch designed a house modest in size but filled with homey touches. His favorite was a stone-hearth, two-sided fireplace that graced the center of the living space. He had gathered the stones from the woods and riverbed nearby and placed each with precision and care. They loved dining by the romantic, crackling fire on winter nights and ending the evening on the other side of the stonework, enjoying the fire's glow in the den.

Mitch had built a sturdy bookcase in the den to match the desk they had purchased at an antique store on Main Street. The bookcase held Len's religious books and his collection of books about famous architects. He loved to work at his drafting table and watch her twirl her hair with a red pencil as she graded papers.

The television sat in the corner, as an afterthought, to make room for a rocking chair, a small table with a candle, and a crucifix, in front of which Len had prayed that this room would someday hold a playpen, toys, and children.

The floors boasted wide-planked Georgia heart pine. The kitchen was set apart by a raised bar, topped with butcher block, so Len could see into the living room. She imagined their children would paint or color on this bar and said, "I can easily oversee homework as I cook."

She had requested that Mitch build bunk beds to resemble a castle in one bedroom. The top bunk had a crenelated parapet that held a mattress accessed by a side staircase. A child could sleep there without the risk of falling off. A second bed rested inside the castle with a built-in desk and toy chest. Len had said that a fairy-tale bedroom would spark the imagination of children. The other side of the room was reserved for a crib and changing table.

Large picture windows adorned each room to take in the beauty of the landscape. It was a place for love to grow surrounded by God's creations. They had their lives all planned out.

Then, with one horrific medical diagnosis, it all fell apart.

CHAPTER 4

A man's mind plans his way,
but the Lord directs his steps.

—*Proverbs 16:9*

F ather James filled his plate with the leftovers after Marge Gallagher absconded with most of the casserole. Even the scrapings smelled delicious, and his stomach gurgled with anticipation. The first bite dissolved the forty-day sacrifice of his favorite foods, and he savored each morsel. He swallowed another bite of blueberry pancake and said, "Brendan, your sister is a culinary artist!"

He sipped his coffee and peered over the rim of the cup. "I found a young child in the garden this morning, crying at the foot of the Mary statue. She said her name was Mary Magdalene, but she went by Maggie."

Father Brendan was about to take a bite of egg casserole but halted his fork in midair. "My goodness, James, was she pulling your leg? Mary Magdalene in the garden, crying on Easter morning!"

"That was my reaction, too, at first. She was upset because there was no vase for a handful of wildflowers she had picked for the Blessed Mother, who was to share them with the child's mother in heaven. It was very touching."

Father Brendan cut off a piece of pancake. "What did she look like?"

"Well, she looked about eight or nine years old, thin but not a weak thin. I believe she was athletic by the way she moved about the garden. Her blouse was far too big for her, like a hand-me-down. She had a long blonde braid and the bluest eyes I have ever seen. There was this huge—and I mean huge—brown dog sitting on the wall, and I could tell he was eyeing me suspiciously, and—"

He stopped mid-sentence because Father Brendan was smiling at him. "What?"

"This sounds like a hallucination. Maybe your empty stomach created an illusion," he said with a hint of amusement.

Then Father James remembered, "She said she had to get home so her Uncle Mitch would not worry."

Father Brendan wrinkled his brow. "I don't know any child in the parish that fits that description."

They finished eating, went to the study for prayer, and did a last-minute reflection on the readings.

On their way to church to greet parishioners, Father Brendan reminded the younger priest, "There will be a lot of 'C and Es' in attendance today. By the time Mass begins, it will be standing room only."

"Ah yes, our Christmas and Easter Catholics." He prayed that the liturgy would touch their hearts and hoped his sermon would do the same.

They put on their vestments and greeted people at the front entrance. Father James fought another homesick feeling when an elderly couple walked hand in hand into the church. They reminded him that this was his first Easter without his parents.

Marge and Sam Gallagher walked up. Sam shook Father James's hand while Marge brushed past him to hug her brother. Sam noticed the snub and gave his hand an extra shake.

***

The bells chimed, and the priests and altar servers processed up the aisle. Father James opened with prayer, read the Gospel, and delivered the sermon he had been contemplating all week. It focused on Mary Magdalene, and he wondered if Maggie was somewhere in the crowded nave. He took a deep breath and asked, "How many of you think you are rational human beings?"

There was murmuring in the room. Father James knew the congregation was deciding whether his question was rhetorical or if he wanted a show of hands.

"Take a close look at Mary Magdalene. She knew Jesus died on the cross because she was there. She knew His followers placed Him in a tomb, and a huge boulder sealed the entrance. There is no way Mary could get into the tomb, yet she sets out while it is still dark." He paused to let this scene settle in, then asked, "Is this a rational thing to do?"

The congregation did not murmur this time but waited for him to answer the question. But he left them hanging when he noticed two young brothers in the second pew giving each other the elbow. Father James stared at them until they realized his eyes were on them. They immediately sat up straight, trying to look serious, as their faces turned beet red. Father James smiled.

"Why would Mary Magdalene go to the tomb, knowing that Jesus is dead and she cannot see Him?" He paused, then remarked, "She does it out of love for Jesus, to be near Him even in death. True love is not rational. Holy Week proves that to us. Is it rational that our all-powerful and omniscient God would suffer and die on the cross for us? Does it make sense that this is how God chose to save us? No, in human terms, it's illogical. Mary Magdalene going to the tomb is senseless, maybe not even safe. Yet her irrational love led her to the resurrected Christ. She is a great model of irrational love for us." He paused. "Do you want to love irrationally?"

This time, unexpectedly, several hands went up.

"I extend an invitation to everyone to attend adoration on Wednesdays. Just like Mary Magdalene, you can seek Jesus and experience His presence. If you spend time with the Lord, you will discover God's depth of love for you. Then you will learn to love beyond what the world expects." Father James left the ambo and waited for Father Brendan to begin the renewal of baptismal promises.

Father Brendan slowly rose from his chair, instructed the faithful to stand, and asked, "Do you renounce Satan and all his works? Do you believe in Jesus Christ, who was born of the Virgin Mary, suffered under Pontius Pilate, died, and was buried and rose on the third day? Do you believe in the Holy Ghost, the Holy Catholic Church, the communion of saints, the forgiveness of sins, the resurrection of the body, and life everlasting?"

To all these questions, the people responded, "We do."

Father James helped Father Brendan down the steps as an altar boy walked beside him, carrying a brass bucket, called an aspersorium, that held holy water. Father Brendan dipped an aspergillum into the aspersorium and flicked his wrist, forcing the blessed water out of the aspergillum. The droplets of water fell like gentle rain upon the people who then made the sign of the cross. When he approached the two brothers who had misbehaved during the sermon, he gave them an extra, playful sprinkle. The congregation chuckled.

He reached the last pew, stopped, leaned over, and froze in that position. The aspergillum dripped rather than sprinkled the precious water. He brought his left hand to his chest.

Father James couldn't determine if the look on Father Brendan's face was one of pain or fear. He panicked and gripped the arms of the presider's chair. *Oh Lord, he's having another heart attack. Maybe this blessing was too much for him.*

Suddenly, Father Brendan straightened up, flicked his wrist to dispense the holy water, and blessed the people in the pew. As he moved on, Father James recognized the figure over whom Father Brendan had hovered. It was Maggie.

***

The Mass continued, and Father James called on the Holy Ghost to consecrate the bread and wine and perform the transubstantiation that changed them into the Body and Blood of Christ, as he prayed the ancient Eucharistic prayers. When the consecration was complete, the congregation approached the priests for Holy Communion. Father James noticed how reverently Maggie received the host, looked up at the crucifix, and made the sign of the cross.

To end the Mass, Father James announced, "Go in peace to love and serve the Lord. Alleluia, alleluia."

The people answered, "Thanks be to God. Alleluia, alleluia."

The final hymn, "Jesus Christ is Risen Today," filled the air with horns and trumpets, rallying the choir to a new crescendo. The two priests stood at the front door, eager to speak with departing parishioners.

Maggie spotted Blaise when she exited the side door. He stealthily rose from his concealed spot in the garden.

A little girl called out, "Mama, look. It's a bear!"

The mother froze, but Maggie laughed. "No, he is my dog, and he's very friendly." Maggie hugged Blaise, and the little girl clapped.

"Blaise, do you see Uncle Mitch? He said he would be here." She stood at the edge of the parking lot and looked up College Avenue, but didn't see him. She hesitated, remembering how upset he had been that morning. After all the cars had left, she decided to walk home.

***

When the priests returned to the sacristy to disrobe and hang their vestments, Father James commented, "I noticed your reaction when you saw Maggie during the baptismal blessing."

As Father Brendan hung his vestments on the hook, he whispered, "Remarkable."

"What'd you say?"

He turned to face Father James. "I was amazed. That child could easily be a young version of Len Hartman. When I raised the holy water for the blessing, I heard a voice inside my head say, 'Mitch needs you,' and it was Len's voice." Father Brendan rubbed his chin. "I guess I froze for a moment."

Now it was Father James's turn to kid the older priest. "Maybe you imagined it. Perhaps the girl was a vision and the voice a piece of undigested blueberry pancake."

Father Brendan's rosy complexion faded, and he lost his balance. Father James reached for his arm to support his friend, who slumped onto a pew, puffed out his cheeks, and exhaled.

"Who is Len Hartman?"

"Len was married to Mitch Hartman, and she passed away a few years ago. When you mentioned Uncle Mitch this morning, it didn't ring a bell. After Len died, Mitch left the church and became a recluse. I reached out to him, and others did as well.

His anger toward God made him inconsolable; he refused help and told us to leave him alone. I made several attempts after that, but he never responded." His voice quavered. "After a while, I just kinda forgot about him. I got busy with parish activities and caring for the ones who did show up."

Father Brendan looked down at his hands. "Maggie must be related to Len. She was beautiful, with the same blonde hair and clear-blue eyes. Len was very involved in the parish, and everyone loved her. She volunteered in our religious-education program until she became ill. Her death was a sad blow to all of us." Father Brendan took out a handkerchief and wiped his forehead. "I met Len's sister, brother-in-law, and their little daughter at her funeral. Her sister was her identical twin. I only learned at her funeral that Len was short for Magdalene."

Father James commented, "So Maggie must be Len's niece."

Father Brenden nodded. "And it makes sense that Maggie can show up here with ease. Mitch built their home just over the hill on College Avenue." Sadness seeped deeper into his voice as he continued, "They were very much in love and wanted lots of children. She had several miscarriages and was finally diagnosed with cardio- or -pathy something or other. The doctors said it probably entered her system through a virus and slowly took its toll on her heart. Her body was too weak to carry a baby to term." Father Brendan rubbed his eyes. "Then, without warning, the ailment reared its ugly head, and her fatigue and shortness of breath made it impossible for her to teach. She was determined to push through it, but within a few months, her heart gave out."

Father Brendan's eyes teared up. "I performed the apostolic blessing a day before she slipped away. She remained faithful during her sickness and confided in me that she had offered up her pain in the hope that Mitch would one day have the children he desired. She never once felt sorry for herself, but was concerned for Mitch. She didn't think he would handle her passing well, and she was right."

Father James wondered out loud, "So why is Maggie here under the care of a recluse who has abandoned his faith?"

"Well, perhaps this is where you and I come in. Maggie has shown up here without Mitch, so maybe God and Len are trying to get our attention through this child and remind me of my lack of charity toward Mitch by leaving him alone all these years. It's time to perform my pastoral duties again. I should give him a call."

Father James helped the older priest to his feet, and Father Brendan leaned on him as they headed to the rectory.

"I'm thankful you're here, but sorry the bishop denied your sabbatical. He will grant it once another priest becomes available to fill the vacancy."

"Perhaps the Lord has another plan for me right now," Father James said, wondering if Maggie might also be a message for him.

CHAPTER 5

*It is with the smallest brushes that the artist paints
the most exquisitely beautiful pictures.*

—*Saint Andre Bessette*

The front door swung open, and Maggie and Blaise bounced into the living room. Mitch's eyes shifted from the drafting table to his watch. *Oh no! I lost track of time.* Dropping the pencil on the table, he put his hands in his pockets and lowered his head. "Maggie, I'm so sorry I forgot to meet you after Mass. It will take time to get used to our new life together. I shouldn't have been so hard on you this morning."

"Blaise and me, we were fine walking from church. It's not far at all."

"Still, I meant to be there, like I promised. We're a team now, you, me, and Blaise. I know we'll get better at this." Mitch turned back to his drawing. "How was the Easter Mass?"

"It was wonderful! I wish you had been there. Two priests were on the altar. One was Father James. You know, the one who found the vase for me."

"Yes, I remember."

"The other priest was kinda old. I think someone called him Father Brendan."

Mitch's mind drifted back to his last months with Len. He leaned on Father Brendan, who was a great source of comfort. His bedside manner brought Len peace, and he never once preached about how she would soon be in a better place. Mitch could grieve without being judged.

There was, however, a twinge of guilt on Mitch's conscience as he recalled that, a few weeks after Len's funeral, he told everyone, including the priest, to leave him alone. He'd grown tired of perfectly manicured single women showing up at his door with a homemade meal and bottle of wine. He didn't want to be consoled or pampered by anyone. So much so that he had removed the WELCOME sign Len had him hang over the front door, rolled up the welcome mat in his heart, and closed the door on the world. The only people he had allowed in were Len's family.

Maggie interrupted his thoughts. "Uncle Mitch, are you okay?"

"What? Yes, of course. I was remembering Father Brendan."

"I prayed for Mom and Dad while I was at Mass. Mommy always prayed for Aunt Len. She said we should always pray for those who have died."

Mitch put down his pencil again and looked at this childlike version of Len. He cleared the swelling lump in his throat with a cough and said, "Maggie-doodle, that was sweet of you to keep everyone in your prayers."

"I pray for you too, Uncle Mitch…that you'll come to church with me just like you used to go with Aunt Len."

"Uh-huh," he replied and changed the subject. "Hey, do you know what this is?"

"Don't be silly. I know it's a basket."

"It's not just any basket. There was a note attached that said the Easter Bunny hid twenty-four eggs outside and something for Blaise too."

He was relieved to put an end to the former conversation. He didn't want to disappoint the child, but if he never set foot inside a church again, it would be too soon. *She'll learn that prayers are a waste of time. God doesn't listen to prayers, any more than the Easter Bunny hides the eggs.*

"When you finish collecting eggs, we'll have ham and potato salad for lunch. I even got a carrot cake for dessert." *I do not feel like celebrating, but the cake will compensate for my forgetfulness.*

Maggie ran up the stairs to her castle room and changed into her mother's oversized blouse. As she descended the staircase, Mitch noticed her smelling the blouse's collar and hugging her arms. This was the blouse she had told him not to wash. When she reached the bottom step, she jumped off, grabbed the basket, and headed for the door, with Blaise in close pursuit.

Mitch thought of her unauthorized morning visit to the church and called from the den, "The bunny stayed in the yard."

She gave him a thumbs-up signal as she opened the door.

Mitch wasn't sure if Maggie knew he'd hidden the eggs and didn't want to spoil it for her. As he left his drafting table and walked through the dining room to the living room window to watch the two search the yard, he thought of Len. *She should be here, watching our children search for eggs.*

The huge picture windows were Len's idea. She had wanted the children to feel as if they lived in a giant tree house and were a part of God's creation. That was Len, always thinking of ways to make God real. *Well, God was real…a real disappointment!*

Mitch watched from the window. *Maggie, how are you feeling inside? You and I are two peas in a pod. We'll always have that deep connection of losing the most important people in our lives.*

He would never get out of his mind the torture of that first night after Maggie's parents' fatal accident.

***

He and Blaise had been like bookends on either side of her as she fitfully slept on the couch while his mind spun out of control. The sight of Maggie curled up next to Blaise on the couch picked at the scab that covered the wound on his heart. He had no strength to handle this, but would have to find it anyway.

The funeral Mass for Maggie's parents, Mary and Joe, had been handled by their many friends and the pastor. The cathedral's beauty had been wasted on Mitch as he sat dazed and angry at God. After Communion, he noticed Maggie's eyes fixed on a tiny ladybug sitting on the pew where she knelt. Maggie put her hand next to the bug, who willingly climbed aboard. She smiled for the first time since he arrived.

They traveled silently in the hearse to the graveside. Maggie leaned into Mitch and only opened her eyes once or twice to look at the ladybug nestled in the palm of her hand. At the graveside ceremony, Maggie was handed flowers by the funeral director, and she placed a mum on her father's casket. Then she took a daisy and held it next to the ladybug who had accompanied her from church. The little creature climbed off her finger and onto a white petal. Maggie tenderly placed the daisy on her mother's coffin with all the other flowers. He could hear the sobs of mourners as she turned, took his hand, and walked away.

There was a small reception at the home of Grace, who was Mary's best friend. Mitch knew her from his many visits. She took Mitch's hand and led him to the kitchen for privacy. She placed her hand on his shoulder and looked him in the eye.

"You are Maggie's godfather and the only person in the world who shares the family she lost. You'll always have that special bond. Maggie once told me she loves you because you always have time for her when everyone else is busy being adults. I'm not making that up. Those were her words."

Grace could see into the living room and teared up when she saw Maggie and her daughter, Annie, huddled together on the sofa. Annie whispered in Maggie's ear something that made the child smile.

"Mary always spoke highly of you. It was obvious to her and Joe how much you loved Maggie, and they were thankful for your care of Len during her illness. I know you're wondering how to handle this new life with Maggie. Just put one foot in front of the other, and you'll create a new path together."

Her words were like a life preserver thrown to him as he floundered in a sea of grief.

During their first week at home in Ellicott City, Maggie pored over the family photo albums. She chose several pictures that Mitch then had blown up. He took special care in framing each one to hang in the castle bedroom that now belonged to Maggie.

They had spent a day painting one of her walls sky blue. He remembered smiling when she said, *"Pink is my favorite color, but we had better paint the wall blue because I'm gonna be growing out of pink pretty soon."*

She put her puzzles and board games, books, and acrylic paints on her shelves, and the family Bible on her desk.

An Etch A Sketch, Chatty Cathy, and Winnie the Pooh were placed in the toy chest.

In the space originally intended for a crib, Mitch went to work on building a guardhouse for the castle. He painted "BLAISE" above the door in bold letters. Of course, Blaise preferred to spend the night curled up next to Maggie's castle bed.

Maggie's mom had given her a tapestry of Mary Magdalene greeting Jesus outside the tomb. Mitch held it up to view it, and Maggie tearfully gasped. "What happened to my tapestry when it was in the box? It's a jumbled mess! Look at those ugly black threads! How did they get knotted together?"

"No, that's the back. Here's the front." He turned it around to show her. "It's hard to believe the mess on the back could produce such a beautiful picture on the front," he said with amazement. "Shall we hang it over your bed?"

"Yes, I'll see it when I say my prayers."

And Maggie prayed for everyone. Mitch knew the Our Father and Hail Mary, and she had introduced him to the Guardian Angel Prayer and Saint Michael the Archangel. Even though Mitch did not believe in the efficacy of prayer, he humored this child in need of comfort.

Sounds of Maggie crying in her sleep had often wakened him. The routine was always the same. He'd come into her room to find Blaise resting his head on her pillow. His furry face calmed her in a way the Pooh bear or he could never do. Mitch then quietly returned to his empty bed and longed for Len. His sleepless nights were plagued with questions. *How can I raise a little girl? I don't know how to fix her hair, buy her clothes, or teach her to become a woman.*

***

He was now two months into his new role as guardian and needed Len more than ever.

"Yahoo!" Maggie hollered and danced as she triumphantly lifted the twenty-fourth egg above her head. Her twirls around the yard pulled him back to the present moment and lightened his mood, as did Blaise's victory lap with the bone between his teeth.

Blaise was a mix of Chesapeake Bay retriever and Chocolate Lab, with a bit of mastiff mixed in somehow. He weighed about ninety pounds and stood twenty-eight inches tall. His webbed feet were perfect for swimming, and his muscular body demanded a lot of dog chow. His fur was thick and dense, and Maggie brushed him once a week.

Maggie burst through the door and dumped the basket of eggs on the bar. Blaise lay down next to her, gnawing on his treasure. She opened the eggs as Mitch made lunch. As he watched her, he remembered that Len had said she could prepare meals while the kids did their homework at the bar.

He heard a gentle whisper say, "This is your time."

He stopped slicing the tomato. "Did you say something?"

"I said I'm having a fun time."

Some eggs held jelly beans and chocolates. Three eggs contained crisp one-dollar bills, and one had a beautiful ladybug pin. It was bright red with little black hearts instead of the usual spots. Glass specks decorated the wings and looked like little diamonds.

"Oh, Uncle Mitch, I love it. I've never seen anything like it. Thank you."

"Well, I wasn't sure if you were too old for the Easter Bunny," he said with a smile, "but I figured not too old for surprises."

"Can you pin it on Mommy's shirt collar?"

As he did so, he said, "I saw it in the window of Caplan's Department Store the day we strolled Main Street. Remember when I sent you to buy us two cones from the ice-cream truck? That's when I ducked into the store and got the pin. I thought it would be special for you."

"Gosh, you're the best!" She hugged him, and he felt the wound in his heart begin to heal.

"I need change for one of the dollars."

From the kitchen cupboard, he retrieved the jar filled with his pocket change. He then watched Maggie count the coins and place a dollar bill into the jar.

"Maggie, when you buy something at a store, you don't have to have the exact amount. The cashier will give you change."

"I know. I need thirty cents to put in the poor box at church."

Mitch was amazed! *She's tithing her Easter windfall of three dollars! Here's a child who lost everything, yet still thinks of those less fortunate. Every day, I learn something new about you, Maggie.*

He would have prayed for guidance if he had faith that God listened.

CHAPTER 6

*Holiness consists simply in doing God's will
and being just what God wants us to be.*

—*Saint Thérèse of Lisieux*

Mitch started to sweat even though the air was cool on this sunny April morning. He slowed his pace and half listened to Maggie chatter incessantly as they walked, and he was glad for the distraction. She would not understand his apprehension as they approached the rectory porch. Feelings of guilt rattled his brain for having rejected Father Brendan's help after Len's death; they were compounded by his failure to reach out to the priest after he had suffered a heart attack. When he received the call that Father Brendan wanted to meet Maggie, he'd hesitated then agreed. He figured he could use this opportunity to see if there was room for her at the parish school. These things consumed Mitch's thoughts as he lifted his hand to knock but then paused.

"Aren't you gonna ring the bell?"

"Well, yes. Of course, I'll ring the bell. I'm just thinking for a moment." He wiped his hands on his khaki pants and looked down at Maggie's smiling face. He half smiled back, then cleared his throat.

Ding-dong.

The doorbell rang!

He shot Maggie an annoyed look as her smile turned into a sheepish grin. "Oops. Sorry. I thought I'd save you the trouble."

The door swung open, and Marge Gallagher's face lit up with a smile. "Well, bless my soul! Mitch Hartman, it's so good to see you."

Mitch had not seen Marge for three years and felt awkward when she hugged him. He noticed that white strands had woven into her jet-black hair, which she wore in a tight bun. Only a few wrinkles framed her penetrating eyes, and her confident, commanding presence was at odds with the apron she wore.

"And this must be Miss Maggie. How do you do?" She bent down to shake Maggie's hand.

Mitch thought the greeting rather formal, but Maggie was not to be outdone. "Very well, thank you."

A jovial command echoed through the hall, "Well, Marge, don't keep our guests standing on the porch. Come in, come in. It's so good to see you, Mitch." Father Brendan gave him a firm handshake. The priest's genuine affinity relieved Mitch's uneasiness.

Then he leaned over to shake the hand of the small figure smiling up at him. "Well, Maggie, it's so good to have you here too. I suspect we will become good neighbors living so close by."

"Yes, I suspect we will."

Everyone laughed at her frankness.

Father Brendan invited Mitch to his office, and Marge said, "Maggie, would you like to come with me to the kitchen? I just made some chocolate chip cookies. They are warm, and the chips are melty."

"Can I, Uncle Mitch?"

"Of course. I'll come to get you when Father Brendan and I finish."

Marge and Maggie went to the kitchen as Father Brendan and Mitch walked down the hall to the office. "It has been a while. Please have a seat. Would you care for a cup of coffee?"

"No thanks, I'm good."

"Mitch, I'm so sorry I have ignored you these past years—"

"Father Brendan, please," he interrupted, "it was my fault." He blushed a little and continued, "I should've returned your calls. I'm sorry about your heart attack. I may not be at church, but the word does get around."

"Yes, I know too well. Sometimes I feel like I live in a fishbowl," Father Brendan answered with a chuckle. "So Maggie is your niece?"

"Yes, and as I mentioned on the phone, she came to be with me quite unexpectedly."

Father Brendan leaned forward.

Mitch hoped he could tell the story without breaking down. "Maggie's parents were headed home from a party. Maggie had spent the night with her best friend, Annie, since they were rehearsing for an Easter play at school. She loves to act and can be quite a ham sometimes."

Mitch hesitated and thought of how Maggie never got to act in the play. He cleared his throat and pulled out a handkerchief to dab his eyes. "A drunk driver ran a red light and T-boned the car. The impact killed Joe, and Mary died in the ambulance." He wiped his eyes again and blew his nose. "The drunk driver walked away unharmed."

Father Brendan sat close enough to place his hand on Mitch's shoulder. "I'm sorry, Mitch. It's heart-wrenching and quite a responsibility to be placed suddenly on your shoulders."

Mitch could hardly get the words out. "She lost her whole family in the blink of an eye. I lost my connection to Len."

Father Brendan tightened his grip. "Maggie is your connection to Len, and I'm still here. I know it is not the same, but you have a whole community in the parish to help if you want it. How has it been so far with Maggie coming to live with you?"

"Not easy. We've had a few rough spots. Maggie seems to be a combination of her parents, sensitive like Mary but feisty and strong-willed like Joe. Assertive yet humble, if that makes any sense. I think, because of her, I'm beginning to feel whole again. Maggie has filled an ache I have had for a long time. You know Len and I always wanted children." He blushed again and lowered his head. Mitch could feel the priest's eyes on him.

After a pause, Father Brendan remarked, "You stopped short of saying maybe God has answered your prayer."

Mitch straightened up with pursed lips, clenched his fists, and blurted out, "What a cruel way to answer a prayer!" Mitch was flustered, and it annoyed him that Father Brendan remained calm.

"Life has taken a turn for you and Maggie."

Another uncomfortable pause ensued and lingered like a heavy cloud.

"Mitch, I know you have abandoned God because you think his ways are unjust. But the truth is that God has not abandoned you or Maggie. You have each other."

Mitch turned his head. He didn't feel like listening to empty platitudes.

Father Brendan continued, "There is an old aphorism; I think it was Saint Teresa of Ávila who said, 'God writes straight with crooked lines.' Perhaps this is one of those times."

A knock on the door broke the tension.

"I didn't mean to interrupt. I wanted to meet you, Mitch. I'm Father James."

Mitch stood up to shake his hand. "Maggie hasn't stopped talking about you. Thank you for finding her the vase. You must think I'm irresponsible. We are still figuring out this new arrangement and trying to be a team."

"I was happy to help. Please don't let me disturb you. I'm going to get a cookie with Maggie. I can smell them all the way upstairs."

Father James left the room, and Mitch remained standing. He collected himself and addressed the reason he had agreed to meet. "I know you invited us here because you wanted to meet Maggie. Thank you for welcoming her. Since I'm here, I wonder if I could enroll her at Saint Paul School. I'm sure Mary and Joe would want her to continue her Catholic education."

"Well, of course. I see no reason not to, even though the school year is winding down and, speaking metaphorically, the children have already left the building. But this might be a good transition for Maggie—no pressure, just getting to know the children and the routine. What grade is she in now?"

"She's in the fifth grade. Her principal had recommended she keep up with her classes. She said it would provide a bit of normalcy and security for the child whose whole world had turned upside down. So I waited until the Easter break to bring her back to Maryland."

"I'm sure we can find a spot for her. Let me check with Sister Anne Patricia, the principal, first. She would know better than me if it would benefit Maggie. I'll have her contact you directly."

"Thanks. I'll go collect Maggie from the kitchen."

"Before you go, can I ask a favor?"

Mitch hesitated and could feel his body tense up. He wanted desperately to leave, but answered, "Sure, how can I help?"

"You may remember that we hold adoration here at the church every Wednesday."

"Yes, I remember."

"An elderly lady, Mrs. O'Brien, is the committed adorer for the three-o'clock hour. Her children are moving and taking her with them next month. It's a difficult spot to fill since that's the hour school lets out, and parents are involved in car pools and getting kids off to practice for sports. I remember that you work from home sometimes and wondered if it might be possible for you to be a committed adorer for that hour. It would only be until I can find a permanent replacement."

Mitch looked past the priest as the invitation reverberated in his head. *Come to adoration every Wednesday and sit with Jesus! Why would I want to do that? Len used to come, and look at what happened to her! But wait; maybe that is a good idea. I could let the Savior of the world know how disappointed I am with a God who takes the love of my life away and leaves Maggie an orphan. I'll ask Him—no, I'll demand an answer. What kind of a God allows such terrible things to happen to good people?*

The uncomfortable silence that had punctuated the meeting returned.

Father Brendan added, "Maggie is welcome to join you. You don't have to answer right now. Take your time to think about your decision."

Father Brendan had barely finished his sentence when Mitch replied, "Yes, I would love to take the three-o'clock hour, and I'll bring Maggie too." He abruptly turned on his heel, left the room, and walked down the hall to the kitchen.

Father Brendan stood almost paralyzed, blinked his eyes, and shook his head. *Did I hear correctly? I thought this would be the last thing Mitch would want to do. The Holy Ghost must have prompted me to ask him.*

***

Meanwhile, Father James had slipped into the kitchen and sat in the chair across the table from Maggie.

"Oh boy! I was hoping I'd see you again." Maggie's face was beaming.

"Well, it's just about impossible to ignore the smells from the kitchen when Mrs. Gallagher has produced another culinary delight." Marge, who was retrieving another batch of cookies from the oven, turned to face him. He quickly added, "You'll not find a better cook in all of Ellicott City."

"Is that true?" Maggie asked with admiration.

Marge's expression went from stern to cordial. "Well, I bake my bread and cakes from scratch."

"Can you teach me?"

"Well, first, how about you finish your cookies and milk."

Father James and Maggie conversed easily about all sorts of things, such as why the sky is blue and whether cats really have nine lives.

"What about guardian angels?" Maggie asked.

"What about them?"

"Well, are they real? Johnny Phelps from my old neighborhood said they're not. He said that's just a bunch of BS, and anybody who believes in them is plain stupid. I don't know what BS is, but Johnny shouldn't call people stupid."

Marge's eyes grew round as silver dollars, and Father James covered his smile with his hand. He kept his mouth hidden but separated his fingers enough to ask, "Well, what did you say to Johnny?"

"I chased him out of the playground and said, 'Don't come back here until you apologize to your guardian angel.'"

"Well"—Father James cleared his throat—"let's see if Johnny's right. Mrs. Gallagher, is that your Bible by the refrigerator?"

She handed him the holy book, and he opened it to the Gospel of Matthew, chapter 18. "Maggie, can you read verse ten to me?"

Maggie read slowly, "See that you do not despise one of these little ones; for I tell you that in heaven their angels always behold the face of my Father who is in heaven."

"So what do you think? These are the words of Jesus."

"But Johnny said there's no such thing as guardian angels because we can't see them."

"Johnny is correct. We don't usually physically see them, but we see with eyes of faith."

Father then stroked his chin to show he was thinking. After a while, he asked, "Mrs. Gallagher, what makes bread rise?"

She happily expounded on the qualities of yeast fungi, "The yeast comes to life when warmed by hot water and starts to eat the sugars in the flour, which creates gas bubbles and causes the dough to rise."

"There, you see?" He asked.

Both Maggie and Marge shook their heads.

"That's the point. You can't see what is happening to the yeast to make the bread rise, but we know it does its job. Just because we can't see our guardian angels doesn't mean they're not watching over us. Ask your guardian angel to take care of you every day."

When he finished his explanation, Marge unceremoniously placed a glass of milk on the table.

"Thank you. I worked up quite a thirst talking about angels."

By the time Mitch made his way down the hall and entered the kitchen, he found them in a contest to see who could dangle a spoon on their nose the longest. Father James's spoon crashed onto the plate, hit a chocolate chip cookie, and flipped it off the dish into the air. His mouth was open in surprise, and the cookie landed smack dab on his tongue. He chomped down on the cookie and chewed it, making it look like a planned performance. He then downed his glass of milk, purposely leaving a thick white mustache on his upper lip.

"Do it again; do it again." Maggie laughed as she nearly fell off her chair with the spoon still dangling from her nose, which added to the hilarity.

Marge submerged a giggle that elevated to a snort and blossomed into a full-blown belly laugh. She even had tears running down her cheeks. Mitch laughed too.

Father Brendan heard the joyful noise ring through the hallway. He walked to the kitchen and asked, "What's so amusing?"

His sister told him, "Believe me, you had to be here to appreciate this one."

Father Brendan observed Mitch, a man who had divorced himself from the world and carried a grudge against God, but was now willing to sit with the Creator of the universe at adoration. He witnessed his sister's prim and proper exterior dissolve as she tried desperately to suppress another snort. He knew she'd been anxious since his heart attack, and it felt good to see her laugh. And Father James, who had been wrestling with a decision of great importance, was enjoying the impact his milk mustache had on everyone. Father Brendan recognized, at once, the joy this child had brought to this small kitchen and smiled.

No, big sister, you are mistaken. I do appreciate this one.

It occurred to him that God does indeed write straight with crooked lines.

CHAPTER 7

The value of life does not depend upon
the place we occupy. It depends upon
the way we occupy that place.

—Saint Thérèse of Lisieux

An important meeting had been scheduled for Mitch on Maggie's first day at Saint Paul School, so Marge offered to take her. He loaded the back seat with his drafts, Maggie climbed in the front seat, and Blaise jumped in after her.

"Oh no, Blaise, you need to get out."

Mitch was in a hurry, but the stubborn dog wouldn't budge.

"Maggie, Blaise can't go to school with you."

"I know, but it feels good to have him with me."

Mitch let out a huff and drove over the hill to the church. Marge opened the rectory's kitchen door when Maggie knocked, then shrieked at the sight of Maggie's strong-willed companion.

Mitch was apologetic. "We didn't mean to scare you, Mrs. Gallagher."

"Sorry," Maggie said, "he wouldn't stay home."

"Well, my lands," said Marge with a harrumph in her voice, "I've never had a dog in my kitchen, and I don't expect to start now, especially one as big as a bear!"

With that, Blaise sat down with a harrumph of his own as the door closed.

"Maggie, I've made pancakes and scrambled eggs. Are you hungry?"

"Kinda, but I hope the butterflies in my stomach will make some room."

"Don't be nervous. The children will love you, and the sisters who teach there are kind."

"I'm not nervous that way; it's just that..." She burst into tears.

This poor child. Marge handed Maggie a tissue.

"I have a best friend back home—Annie. We had planned to go to high school and college together. We love to write stories and then act them out. I miss her." Maggie lowered her head and played with her fork as a few more tears ran down her cheeks.

Marge cupped Maggie's chin and dabbed her cheeks with the tissue. "Perhaps it's time for you to make new friends."

"My mom once told me I had to let go of *my* plans to free my hands for *God's* plan."

"That was wise advice," she responded with a note of compassion. Then Marge added, "How about you call me Aunt Marge?"

Maggie's eyes lit up. "I'd love that!"

"All my children went to school here and made some life-long friends."

"You have children? I thought you were the housekeeper."

Marge chuckled. "Sam and I have six children. Three girls and three boys. They are all grown now. We also have nine grandchildren and one on the way. Our children live in other states, but the two youngest, Peter and Paul, live in Washington, DC. They are our Irish twins and have gotten into politics, God help us."

"What is politics? Is it like the ticks we pull off of Blaise?"

"Yes, that's just what it's like."

"I always thought it would be fun to be a twin," offered Maggie. "My mom was an identical twin. Are your twins identical?"

Marge smiled. "No, dear, Irish twins are called that because they're born close to each other. Peter was born in January and Paul in November of the same year."

"Oh." Maggie looked puzzled.

Marge quickly changed the subject. "When is your birthday?"

"I was born July 22, 1956."

Marge did some calculating as she dried a dish. "So you'll turn ten this year."

"Yep, people think I look young for my age."

"It's always good to look younger. You'll appreciate that when you reach my age." Marge stopped drying the dish and said, "July 22, that's the feast day of Saint Mary Magdalene."

Maggie took a bite of pancake. "It seems the stars all lined up for my name the day I was born. My mom's name is Mary, and her twin sister is Magdalene, but she went by Len. Aunt Len was married to Uncle Mitch."

"Yes, I remember your Aunt Len. She was a lovely, faith-filled lady."

"Well, when I was born, they figured it was a sign that I should be named Mary Magdalene. Cool, right?"

"Yes, very cool. Now, finish your breakfast before it gets cool. You shouldn't be late on your first day of school."

Maggie continued, undaunted by Marge's prompting, "I learned a lot about Mary Magdalene. Did you know she was the first to see Jesus after He rose from the dead?"

"Why yes, I did know that."

"The Bible says that Jesus expelled, that means got rid of, seven demons from her. She had a sad past, but Jesus cured her. Then, she became a special follower of Jesus. Neat, huh?"

"Yes, it shows us the mercy of Jesus," Marge interjected.

"She loved Jesus very much, and so do I."

Maggie finished the last few bites of breakfast just as the two priests arrived for theirs.

"Your meal is in the oven. Maggie and I are off to school," Marge announced over her shoulder as she closed the kitchen door behind her.

Father Brendan said, "Well, this is a first. With Maggie's arrival, maybe I won't get the third degree. Like, did I remember my medicine? Are my ankles swollen? Et cetera."

"Well, did you? And are they?" Father James inquired in jest.

"All right, James, enough! Can you grab a pot holder and retrieve our breakfast?"

***

As they hurried next door to the school, Blaise followed behind them.

"Oh no, boy, you're not allowed in school." Maggie knelt to console him with his face in her hands. "You need to go home. I left a bowl of water for you on the porch. Go home now, Blaise; it'll be okay. I'll be back this afternoon." They were nose to nose until Blaise lowered his head, turned, and walked away.

Marge said in amazement, "I think he understands you."

Marge left Maggie in the hands of Sister Anne Patricia and walked back to the rectory. Her eyes teared up so much that she felt foolish. *Marge, how silly! You just met this child, and you're acting like you dropped off one of your own —*

Her thoughts were interrupted. "Oh my lands, what are you doing here?" she addressed Blaise as he lay in the shade by the kitchen door, his chin on the ground. "Well, I guess you're more attached than I am. Okay, boy, you can stay and wait here for Maggie. I'll get you a bowl of water." She wiped the corner of each eye with her apron and added, "Maybe the good priests have left you some scrambled eggs."

CHAPTER 8

Eucharistic Adoration is the greatest powerin the universe,
Capable of transforming us and changing
the face of the world.

—*Saint Maximilian Kolbe*

Some of the girls wrestled for the ball on the playground, while others gathered around to witness the commotion.

Sister Bridget hurried over.

Beverly grabbed the ball from Maggie. "I'm telling Sister Bridget that you're being bossy!"

"I'm not bossy, just practical."

"Whoa, whoa. What's the problem here?" Sister Bridget asked as she approached.

Beverly put one hand on her hip, and the other hand held tight to the ball. "Maggie said I couldn't play kickball."

Maggie corrected her, "No, I asked if you would keep score."

"Okay, girls, settle down. Maggie, can you come and sit here with me, please?"

Maggie walked over, sat on the bench, and watched the girls get on with their game.

"Maggie, why don't you want Beverly to play? I think you hurt her feelings."

"I didn't mean to hurt her feelings. It's just that…"

"It's just what?" Sister Bridget asked.

"I didn't want Beverly on my team because she's the worst player, and we would lose. So I suggested she keep score."

"I see. You've only been here a month and have already determined who has talent?" She looked at Maggie with sympathetic eyes. The child couldn't control much in her life, but Sister Bridget understood her attempt to control the kickball game. "Beverly doesn't want to keep score. She wants to play."

"I know." Maggie's eyes were downcast. "But my idea is better because I'm saving Beverly from embarrassing herself when she makes us lose the game."

"Maggie, look at me." After Maggie raised her eyes, Sister continued, "You need to consider your motives and show a little mercy to Beverly. Was your aim to spare her feelings, or were you primarily focused on winning?"

Maggie looked down again and moved the dirt under the bench with her black-and-white saddle shoe. "I guess… maybe…a little of both."

Sister Bridget knew that was a turning point for Maggie. She prayed for guidance from the Holy Ghost and chose her words carefully. "You know there are more important things than winning a ball game."

Maggie looked away.

"Maggie, you should be aware of God's mercy. You may not understand it now, but someday you'll look back on these years and realize God takes care of us even in the worst circumstances. We must be willing to open our arms and hearts to welcome His gift of mercy and then be merciful to others."

Maggie teared up, and Sister Bridget put her arm around the child. "God forgives us when we make amends. He is a

God of mercy, forgiveness, and love. The next time you play ball, I want you to choose Beverly for your team. That will help make up for what happened today."

Maggie softly agreed, "Okay." Then her eyes lit up. "I know! I'll invite Beverly to my house and practice kickball with her!"

"A splendid idea." Sister Bridget smiled.

***

Mitch was grateful for his ordinary windup travel alarm clock. He'd started using it after he forgot to meet Maggie at church, and it had become integral to his daily routine. The new system relieved his stress by helping him remember his many responsibilities. There had been a doctor's appointment for Maggie (she was in good health), a dentist appointment (no cavities), and a visit to the veterinarian for Blaise (he needed his shots). He was grateful to learn Aunt Marge could take care of Maggie's split ends (something foreign to him). He would write these appointments on his calendar, but the travel alarm clock was his saving grace.

The new method was working well, and the alarm at two forty-five would ensure that he was on time for Maggie's three-o'clock school dismissal. Blaise excitedly waited at the door so he and Mitch could walk up the hill together.

Today, he took too much pleasure in pounding the alarm's Off button. It was a way to release tension before heading to church for his first Wednesday adoration commitment. He questioned his sanity in consenting to such an arrangement.

He took his new 1966 Ford pickup. Driving it made him happy, and Blaise jumped in to sit beside him. Unfortunately, a song about a lost love who went to heaven came on the radio, and he hit the button to change the channel so hard that he jammed his finger. *Great, just great. God has a warped sense of humor!*

Maggie met him outside of school, and they walked to church. The pews were nearly empty, but he still had trouble deciding where to sit.

A gray-haired man exited a pew, knelt in the aisle, and humbly lowered his forehead to the floor for several seconds before he rose, blessed himself, and departed. Mitch shook his head, irritated at such a display. He had agreed to this hour not to adore Jesus but to rebuke Him.

Maggie left his side and walked silently to the front of the church. She placed her schoolbooks in the pew, knelt, and opened her arms to the monstrance. Mitch's eyes teared up at the sight of her devotion, and he slipped into a back pew. Refusing to kneel, he stared blankly at the gold monstrance designed to imitate a sunburst with rays emanating from the consecrated host in its center. It was time to deliver his disappointment to God.

Len had a compassionate and loving heart, and You, God, chose to attack her heart! He hardened his jaw and asked, *Why would You take a good and caring woman away from a world that needed her tenderness? What kind of God would take the parents from a little girl, leaving her an orphan?*

Mitch responded to his flurry of questions, *I'll tell you what kind of God. A heartless God. A God that I want nothing to do with ever again. The fact is that I'll come and sit in Your church, but I refuse to keep You company.* His face reddened, and he clenched his teeth. *I've come to remind you of the disappointment you are as God.*

Then, in the depths of his soul, he heard these words:

Be My companion in place of those who do not bother to sit in My presence because they're lukewarm. You have grown cold, but I desire your company.

That's ridiculous! How could I have such a thought? Mitch quelled a sob to avoid disturbing Maggie or other adorers trickling in and out during his hour. He kept his head down, looked at his watch, and frowned as time stood still. Fatigue overtook him, and he placed his arm on the back of the pew in front of him, rested his head, and closed his eyes.

What seemed like a moment later, Maggie was shaking his shoulder. He looked up and saw her with her pointer finger to her lips in a shushed position. She nodded toward a couple who had entered as the church bells chimed four times. She whispered, "I think they have the next hour."

Mitch nodded, sleepily stumbled to his feet, and followed her out of the church. He was at odds with those who came to worship the God he chose to criticize, and Maggie's reverence annoyed him.

Blaise greeted them at the bottom of the stone steps. He wagged his tail, dropped a stick, and fixed his gaze on the piece of wood until Maggie picked it up and tossed it.

Mitch tried to think of something to say and finally fell back on an easy topic. "So what happened in school today?"

She hesitated. "Well, you know, the usual stuff."

Mitch didn't respond.

"I got a hundred on my spelling test and a ninety in science," she said with enthusiasm.

"Uh-huh." He wasn't listening.

"The school caught on fire, and we had to run for our lives!"

"Well, those things happen."

"I kinda got in trouble at recess today."

"That's nice."

Mitch's mind was far from anything Maggie was sharing. He opened the door to the truck. "Maggie-doodle, have you ever been to adoration before today?"

"No, that was my first time."

"What made you open your arms when you knelt?"

"I dunno; I think it was something Sister Bridget told me at recess."

"And what was that?"

"She said we must open our arms and hearts to God's gift of mercy, so I did. I felt warm all over, like when the sun hits your face on a cold day. I had seen that gold sunburst before when I came here on Easter Sunday and Father James showed me the cupboard with the vases. It was sitting on a shelf, but the center of the burst was empty. He had told me what it was for, but I didn't understand it then. But now I think I do."

"What do you mean?"

"Well, when the monstrance was empty, I didn't feel anything. Today I felt cozy and warm when I opened my arms to God's mercy, forgiveness, and love, just like Sister Bridget said."

"A God of mercy, forgiveness, and love," repeated Mitch disparagingly as he pulled the truck into their driveway.

"What did ya say, Uncle Mitch?"

"Oh, nothing important. You think that's what God's mercy is like?"

"Yeah. It's hard to explain, like a giant hug."

How can you feel such tenderness from God?

When they reached the porch, Maggie sat down on the porch swing. Mitch joined her.

"Then what happened?"

"Sister Bridget taught us that Jesus proved His love for us when He suffered and died for our sins. The Bible says Jesus died at the ninth hour, which is three o'clock in our time. That's why the three-o'clock hour is the hour of great mercy."

"Huh, the three-o'clock hour," Mitch grunted and thought it interesting that Father Brendan asked him to cover that particular hour. He knew that Maggie could accept all this with the innocence of a child. He got up from the swing and placed the key in the front-door lock.

I know that someday she'll discover that God doesn't answer every prayer, and it will break her heart.

As the door swung open, he felt rather than heard another voice in his mind:

> *Behold, I stand at the door and knock; if any one hears My voice and opens the door, I will come in to him and eat with him, and he with Me.*

Mitch had an inexplicable sensation that he would soon need to open another door and cross a threshold of trust in the mercy of God, and he didn't believe that such a thing existed.

CHAPTER 9

We all have a vocation.
We believe that God has placed us in this life
to fill a special need that no one else can accomplish.

—Saint Francis de Sales

"Maggie, Blaise! We want to get an early start before it gets too hot," Mitch bellowed from the front porch as a mother bird flitted past his head. He watched her land on a branch of Len's dogwood tree and disappear into the leaves. He tilted his head to listen for Maggie's reply, but the chirping of the baby birds filled the air. "Well, Mama Bird, I'm glad you know where to find your little ones. Where *is* that child? Maaaggeeee!"

Maggie was busy behind the house. "Blaise, look at this!" She had stumbled upon an overgrown garden surrounding a butterfly bush. It was dense with coneflowers, black-eyed Susans, Queen Anne's lace, wild honeysuckle vines, and weeds. Butterflies flitted around the bush, creating a kaleidoscope of moving colors. She quickly picked a handful of flowers from between the weeds and then ran to the front porch.

"Uncle Mitch, look what I found! We can put these on Aunt Len's grave! Aren't they wonderful?"

"Yes"—his impatience dwindled—"they are beautiful. I'm sure she'll love them."

"I found an old garden out behind the house. We should fix it up."

Mitch had forgotten about Len's garden just inside their property line. "I'm surprised it's not overgrown by now. That sounds like a good fall project." He had no desire to resurrect the garden. That had been Len's passion, not his.

They visited Len's grave, as they often did, before taking to the trails next to the river in Patapsco Park. Blaise's energy and fondness for the water kept them busy throwing the tennis ball into the river for him to retrieve.

Maggie loved to walk on the swinging bridge that stretched across the river and connected Howard County to Baltimore County. It felt unstable and rickety since its construction consisted of ropes and wood, but that was part of its charm. The swaying motion created the feeling of floating above the water. Maggie often stopped in the middle of the bridge and looked down, mesmerized by the water swirling around rock formations.

"It's so neat how the water from this river flows downstream and will mingle with water in the Chesapeake Bay, and that water will flow into the Atlantic Ocean. Then the water in the Atlantic Ocean keeps going, and going, and… Gosh, it's like rivers connect the world, like we are all joined together somehow."

Mitch rested his arms on the ropes of the bridge as she continued, "A river can be strong enough to wear a path through a mountain or calm enough to house little tadpoles. I find that fascinating. I wonder what it'd be like to jump in and go wherever the river takes you." She leaned over one side of the bridge to drop a small stick into the water, then peered over the other side to watch it float downstream.

That night, Maggie dreamed she was strolling a path next to the river with Mitch.

***

A woman in a white, flowing dress floats in and tries to take Mitch's hand, but he ignores her. He is busy stomping on seeds that lie on the path.

The woman picks up the seeds and attempts to plant them, but the soil is too rocky or full of weeds. She finally finds some rich soil and reaches for Maggie's hand.

Maggie realizes the woman is her Aunt Len, and together they pat the seeds into the fertile ground as a shower of rose petals falls around them.

***

Maggie opened her tear-filled eyes to see the sun peeking through the window. *I wonder what that dream meant. It made me sad to see Uncle Mitch ignoring Aunt Len.* She stared out the window at the shimmering dew on the leaves. "I miss my mom. I would love a dream about her." She buried her face in her pillow.

"Maggie, time to get up. I have a deadline," Mitch called upstairs.

She slowly rose, washed up in the bathroom, and headed downstairs. "Is something burning?"

"Oh gosh darn it!" Mitch ran to the kitchen. "I forgot the eggs!" He turned off the stove but couldn't salvage the omelet. "I'm sorry, Maggie. I'm a little out of sorts this morning. How about peanut butter toast?"

"What's wrong?"

"A demanding customer who keeps making changes to the design. Can you hang out with Marge since I'll be gone most of the day?"

"Sure, we already had plans to bake cookies for the church bazaar. She's even invited Beverly and two other girls from my class to help."

"That sounds like fun. I'm sure she'll have something for you to eat."

***

After morning prayer, Father Brendan handed Father James a letter. "It's from the cousin of our parishioner Andy Lakatos."

Father Brendan walked away as Father James opened the letter penned by a shaky hand.

> *Dear Father James,*
>
> *Thanks for you hearing my sins. I know my English not good. I live most my life in Hungary, behind Iron Curtain, and now escape to America. There were not many priests left in my country due to religious persecute. We could not go to Mass or Confess. When I come to your Mass and hear the words "This is My Body given for you. This is My Blood poured out for you." My heart overflow with joy. When I hear you say, "Your sins are forgive," it brought me great peace. I want to thank you for being priest. God bless you.*
>
> *Norbert Lakatos*

Father James silently folded the letter and placed it between the pages of his breviary, wiped his eyes, looked up at the tabernacle, and bowed his head in prayer. Christ's presence filled him with peace. "Thank You, Lord, for letting me know that You have chosen this place and time for me."

He heard a coin clank in the candle-offering box and opened his eyes to find Maggie lighting a prayer candle, then kneeling to pray.

So, Lord, You've sent another little reminder of why it's good for me to be here.

When Maggie stood up, Father James said, "You're here early."

"I'm helping Aunt Marge bake cookies for the bake sale."

"I'll have to come by the kitchen and do a taste test after Mass." He smiled, but she didn't respond. "Something on your mind?"

"I had a dream, but it makes no sense. I think my Aunt Len was trying to tell me something."

"Would you like to share it with me?"

Maggie relayed her dream as best she could remember.

Father James said, "Interpreting a dream can be challenging. It could be your subconscious trying to work something out, but I would not dismiss the possibility of someone trying to convey a message to you. Have you ever heard of Saint Thérèse of Lisieux?"

"Who?"

"Saint Thérèse. She is sometimes called the Little Flower of the Child Jesus."

"Gosh! My dream had a lot to do with flowers."

"Before Thérèse died, she promised to send down a shower of roses from the heavens, and spend her heaven doing good on earth. My mother loved Saint Thérèse and taught me to pray a novena to her when my father was very ill. We prayed together for nine days, and I still remember the prayer:

> *O Little Thérèse of the Child Jesus, please pick for me a rose from the heavenly gardens and send it to me as a message of love. O Little Flower of Jesus, ask God to grant the favors we now place with confidence in your hands: to restore Joseph to good health. Saint Thérèse, help me to always believe as you did in God's great love for me so that I might imitate your 'little way' each day.*

Then we said an Our Father, a Hail Mary, and a Glory Be."

"What did she mean by her little way?"

"She believed God's love could work through her actions, no matter how small."

"What happened to your dad?"

"A few days after we finished the novena, my mom and I were going to the hospital to see my father. The driver of a white truck put his arm out the window, indicating that he needed to get in our lane. My mom waved him over. When he got in front of us, we saw his license plate—RED ROSE."

"For real?"

"For real. I'd never seen a license plate without numbers, and my mother told me you had to pay extra for them."

"What happened to the truck?"

"It turned, and we never saw it again. When we got to the hospital, my father was sitting up in a chair and eating pudding with the biggest smile on his face."

"That could have been a coincidence."

"Yes, it could have been. Or maybe it was a God moment. God moments occur all around us if we have the ears to hear and eyes to see them."

"I'm gonna pray that novena for Uncle Mitch."

***

Father James opened his Bible to chapter 8 in the Gospel of Luke and meditated on the parable of the sower. He felt that Maggie's dream vividly expressed this Gospel's message. The seed in the parable represented the Word of God that Mitch had abandoned after his wife's death. Could Len be reaching out to Maggie to help Mitch return to his religious roots? God works in mysterious ways. He recalled that Father Brendan said he heard Len's voice the first time he encountered Maggie at the Easter Mass. Father James knew there was a thin veil between heaven and earth.

Father James saw Maggie's dream as a calling. God sought her help to find the fertile layers of Mitch's heart to plant the seeds. Father James was beginning to understand that God's Words were the seeds, the kernels of hope, that inspired the soul.

CHAPTER 10

*The crucible is for silver, and the furnace
is for gold, and the Lord tries hearts.*

—*Proverbs 17:3*

Weeks later…

"Maggie, long-distance call. Annie's on the phone."

Maggie rushed down the stairs excitedly and nearly knocked him over. "Oops!" She put her hand over the mouthpiece. "I bet she's gonna wish me a happy birthday and invite me for a visit!"

Mitch watched her expression turn from delight to disappointment. "When?"

Mitch knew Annie's father had accepted a new position, but didn't know how soon the family would move.

"Two weeks!" Maggie shrieked.

Now, he knew the California job had opened up sooner than expected. Mitch watched as tears rolled down her cheeks.

Her only words were, "Miss you too," as she hung up the phone, ran upstairs, and collapsed on her castle bed.

Mitch knocked on her door, entered, and sat next to her. "I'm sorry, Maggie. I know this is difficult news for you."

Maggie raised her head to look at him. "I miss her, and now I don't know when I'll see her again." She looked at him with pitiful eyes, then buried her face in the pillow.

I should have taken her right after school let out. We needed to visit her mom and dad's graves, but I was busy getting her settled and meeting my deadlines. It's been three months, and I'm still playing catch-up. Fortunately, it's summer, so she can attend morning Mass.

"Why don't you get dressed, and I'll walk you and Blaise to church."

He left her room and cursed the situation. *Well, thanks a whole heck of a lot! Maggie thinks You're so wonderful. How hard could it have been to hold off on Joe's transfer just one more month, Almighty God?*

They walked to church in silence. "I'll meet you here after Mass, and I promise we'll do something special today." After Maggie hugged him, she headed toward the rectory. He took a deep breath and hurried home.

When Marge opened the door, she exclaimed, "Oh dear Lord! Whatever is the matter?"

Maggie tightened her lips and closed her eyes to hold back the tears. "Annie called me today, and I thought she wanted to invite me to her house this summer. I miss her so much."

"Well, what happened?"

"She's moving to California in two weeks. Annie and her brothers are being sent to camp while her parents get everything ready, so there's no time for me to visit."

"Oh dear, that's terrible news. Come in, poor child, and sit down." Marge comforted Maggie by gently patting her back. "There, there. You go ahead and have yourself a good cry."

She let loose all the pent-up sadness surrounding her young life and cried like the first night she learned the tragic news about her parents. "Aunt Marge, why are all these things happening to me?"

"You know, Maggie, there's an old saying: young oak trees bend and grow strong in tempestuous winds. If we only experience joy when we are young, we'll never grow into brave and strong adults. I think the Lord desires you to be brave and very strong."

"But it's not fair! I don't want to be brave and strong. I want my parents back. I miss my mom so much, and I can't tell Uncle Mitch because he's trying hard to make me happy. I know he misses Aunt Len, and it's all so sad." She broke into tears again, and Marge held her until she regained her composure.

"Now, let me cool your face with some cold water." Marge wiped Maggie's eyes and cheeks with a wet towel, then held her close. "Maggie, you will survive this tragedy, but it'll never go away. It will always be painful and always be a part of you. Do not run or hide from it. Instead, embrace it and make it a prayer. I know you don't want Mitch to know how you're hurting, but it's unhealthy to keep your feelings bottled up."

She looked into Maggie's eyes. "This morning, while you're at Mass, I want you to offer your broken heart to Jesus during the offertory. Will you do that?"

Maggie nodded.

"You tell Him how much you hurt. I know you are devoted to the Blessed Mother, so tell her about the ache in your heart. After Holy Communion, you thank God for listening and being so close to you."

Maggie's tears subsided.

"You can always come to me when you need to talk or cry, okay?" Marge wiped another tear from Maggie's cheek with her thumb. "Now, if you want to be on time for Mass, you better skedaddle." After Maggie hugged her, Marge bent down to kiss the top of her head and whispered, "Be happy, Maggie; it's your birthday."

Marge opened the door and watched her walk away. *Lord, please watch over this child.*

Just as Maggie chose her usual spot up front, genuflected, and entered the pew, the church bells rang, and everyone stood as the priests proceeded up the aisle and ascended to the altar. Since it was Mary Magdalene's feast day, they opened with a beautiful prayer about how Jesus had entrusted Mary Magdalene with the honor of being the first to announce the great joy of His Resurrection.

Father Brendan's homily was about how death no longer existed because Jesus destroyed it when He rose from the dead. Father Brendan said, "Our death is not a death at all. It is nothing more than the beginning of the fullness of life."

These words penetrated Maggie's heart, and she remembered her ninth birthday when her parents had taken her to the beach. Her dad had bought her an ice cream cone. It was the best she had ever tasted. She and her mom savored three different snowball flavors. They played in the surf, and Maggie thought that up in heaven, you could probably go to the beach anytime you wanted.

She gave Jesus her aching heart at the offertory, just as Marge had suggested. Then she asked the Blessed Mother to help her see that everything happens for a reason and that one day she would understand why.

Father Brendan ended Mass with a blessing and encouraged everyone to go in peace. The priests came down from the altar and stopped next to Maggie. Father Brendan motioned for her to come into the aisle.

"Ladies and gentlemen," he announced, "we have a special occasion to celebrate today, on the Feast of Saint Mary Magdalene. Today is Maggie's tenth birthday."

Everyone clapped and cheered, and she was amazed to see Uncle Mitch on his way up the aisle with an armful of red roses and a huge smile. Aunt Marge and Sam were there, beaming with delight, and a few of her classmates, their parents, and many of the school's sisters were also there.

Then Father Brendan announced, "You're all invited back to Maggie's home for cake and ice cream and some games for the kids."

Maggie stood overwhelmed as Mitch bent down to kiss her cheek and hand her the roses.

***

Mitch and Sam had decorated the house with streamers and balloons everywhere. She wondered how all this happened without her knowing about it. Uncle Mitch and Aunt Marge never let on that anything was different.

The cake was a homemade creation from Marge in the shape of a ladybug with strawberry icing, blueberries for the spots, and black licorice for the legs and antennae. The girls played musical chairs and Pin the Tail on the Donkey while the boys entertained Blaise with a ball.

Beverly, now Maggie's best friend, gave her a journal. "I saw it had a giant ladybug on it," Beverly said. "I told my mom it would be perfect for you."

Sammy said, "Remember you taught me how to suck the juice out of the honeysuckle flower? When I sniffed this perfume at Reed's Pharmacy, it smelled just like the honeysuckle tasted!"

Marge and Sam gave her a beautiful crystal rosary blessed by Father Brendan. If the sun hit it just right, it created small rainbows on the wall. The priests gave her a book about the rosary; it told the story of the Blessed Mother's appearance at Fatima in 1917.

The sisters from school gave her a small ceramic stable that housed the Blessed Mother, Saint Joseph, and Baby Jesus. Sister Anne Patricia remarked, "This is your family, Maggie. Keep them in your heart wherever life takes you, and stay close to the stable in Bethlehem."

Maggie thanked everyone for her gifts and the wonderful surprise. The roses she received from Mitch sat boldly on the dining room table. The roses meant that God had heard her prayer through the intercession of Saint Thérèse. She didn't know how or when He would answer it, but she knew it would be in God's time, not hers.

***

The two priests returned to the rectory with Sam and Marge, who said, "What a fun birthday party!"

Father James commented, "It's obvious how much Maggie is loved. She had no clue about the party and seemed humbled by all the attention."

Marge sarcastically added, "Humility—not easy to come by these days."

Father James was sure that she had directed that statement at him.

Father Brendan said, "There's something unique about Maggie. She brings out the best in people, especially Mitch. I see a real change in him. He's beginning to look like his old self again."

Once inside the rectory, Father Brendan wiped his brow and headed for the stairs. "I'm going to lie down for a bit."

Marge patted his shoulder. "I'll have Father James bring a lunch tray up to your room. You have a good rest." She then turned abruptly and, in the voice of a drill sergeant, said, "Father James, help Brendan up the stairs."

"I don't need help up the stairs! And no more of that rabbit food you keep trying to convince me is good for my heart."

The phone rang, and Marge ran into Father James's office to answer it. She turned to Father James. "It's the bishop for you." She shoved the phone into his hand and walked away.

When she heard him say, "Thank you for getting back to me. Yes, things are going well here," she stormed off to the kitchen in a huff. *It has been almost six months since he requested that sabbatical. Now, the bishop will give it to him. Father James is prideful. He thinks only of himself and doesn't care about Brendan's poor health.*

Marge returned in a few minutes with the lunch tray. She stopped outside Father James's door to eavesdrop on the conversation.

"Well, Vatican II weighed heavily on me. Many of my brother priests were abandoning the priesthood, and sisters were leaving their convents. I was having a tough time."

Marge's hands started to shake in anger, and she feared the rattle of dishes would give her away. She leaned against the wall for support and listened to Father James whine about himself.

His voice became strained. "When the altars were reoriented to face the people, I found it difficult to meditate and offer prayers of the congregation up to God. I miss the Communion rail and the veils worn by women. I felt like the reverence and sacredness of the liturgy was lost."

There was another pause as Father James listened to the bishop. Then, "Yes, I appreciate how it benefits the people and helps them understand the Mass when they hear it in English." Yet another pause, and then James said, "In my head, I understood, but it took a while for the message to get to my heart. I believe all these things added to my uneasiness."

Marge shook her head. *I hope the bishop isn't buying any of this.*

"Then, as you know, my parents passed away just before my transfer. I know this may sound childish, but I didn't get to celebrate my fortieth birthday with them or receive a pair of socks from my mom this year." Father James laughed. "It's those small things that mean so much."

He paused before responding, "Thank you for attending their funerals. Your support was and is much appreciated. This past year has been challenging." Another pause as Father James listened. "I've spent time in prayer, which has proved helpful."

Oh boy, here it comes. He'll go on sabbatical and leave Brendan even though he's treated him like a brother!

Father James continued, "The past six months gave me time to adjust to the new Mass. Father Brendan has been a wonderful companion during my time of discernment. I know you went above and beyond for me, so thank you. I now realize the Lord has asked me to be patient, to wait for His direction, and to know that I am where He needs me right now." Father James was silent a moment, then said, "I'm sure. I don't need a sabbatical."

Marge's eyes grew wide at this last statement.

There was more silence before Father James repeated the bishop's question, "How is Brendan doing? He tires out easily but still manages his pastoral duties."

There was another pause, and then Father James chuckled. "Yes, she's quite a handful. She worries about her brother, but nothing interferes with her helping wherever needed." Father James took a breath as he listened, then answered, "No, really, I see her with parishioners, and she's got a kind, compassionate heart." Another pause. "Yes. She helps with clothing drives and bake sales and is great with kids. The parish is lucky to have her. She keeps Father Brendan and me in line. We depend on Mrs. Gallagher a lot."

Marge slowly backed away from his door as if she were seeing her reflection in a mirror. Her hands started to shake again, this time not in anger but in an awkward sense of shame. She had judged Father James unfairly. She decided to deliver the lunch tray herself.

She examined her conscience as she slowly ascended the stairs and recognized her behavior had been harsh and disrespectful. She was a bully, and he had humbly accepted her criticisms. She reached Father Brendan's room, placed the tray on his lap, and burst into tears.

"Jesus, Mary, and Joseph, Marge! What on earth is the matter?"

She wiped her eyes on her apron and said, "I need you to hear my confession."

Chapter 11

Do not say, "I will repay evil";
wait for the Lord, and He will help you.

—*Proverbs 20:22*

The day after Maggie's party, Father James was in his office listening to pots and pans clanging in the kitchen. *Mrs. Gallagher is here early. She doesn't usually show up until lunchtime on Saturday.*

Within a few minutes, he noticed her standing in the doorway with a large breakfast tray in her hands. Her expression was one of a sergeant demoted to private. She hesitated before entering and placing the tray containing eggs, bacon, toast, coffee, and a miniature chocolate-frosted cake with a lit candle on his desk.

"Mrs. Gallagher, I don't—"

"Please call me Marge," she said, her voice quavering. "I realized yesterday that we failed to celebrate your fortieth birthday after you arrived."

He sat there in shock.

"Father James, I am so sorry for how I've treated you since you arrived here. I've been cold, pigheaded, and horrible."

She pulled her apron up over her face. "I'm so ashamed. Can you ever forgive me?"

She began to cry, so he stood up and came around the desk to do…what? He wasn't sure. *Should I hug her? No, better not.* So he placed his hands on her shoulders and tried to look into her eyes, but she wouldn't remove the apron.

"There now, don't be so hard on yourself. I know you are stressed, worrying about Father Brendan and keeping this place running smoothly. Then this new priest shows up needing a lot of attention." He chuckled, but she wouldn't be consoled or take the apron away from her face. "Mrs. Gal—uh, Marge, all is forgiven. Thank you for this wonderful breakfast. Is this one of your famous homemade chocolate delicacies?"

She peeked above the apron. "Yes, with chocolate pudding in the middle."

"Ah, how wonderful." He leaned over, blew out the candle, and knew he was finally home.

***

Maggie's surprise birthday party launched Maggie and Mitch into a new social circle. They accepted invitations to cookouts, birthday parties, and picnics. Maggie joined a parish-sponsored softball team, and Mitch volunteered to coach. This flurry of activities meant that, once again, he would have to dodge sporadic flirtatious single women, but he had become adept at that. Mitch had no intention of starting a new relationship or finding a wife. He felt fulfilled and happy taking care of Maggie.

Maggie and her new friends played together all summer. They rode bikes, went swimming, roller-skated, and played hopscotch in the church parking lot since its surface was perfect for such activities. They breathed new life into the garden

Aunt Len had planted many years ago. They volunteered to help the priests with Vacation Bible School for the little ones. Maggie taught her friends to pray the mysteries of the rosary, and they often hung out in Mary's garden. Aunt Marge supplied them with home-baked cookies and, on the hottest days, made sure Blaise's water bowl never ran dry.

***

The lighthearted summer months gave way to new seasons of growth around Mitch's little home. Saint Paul School provided friendships that helped Maggie's grieving over the loss of Annie subside. Her activities added to Mitch's hectic schedule. He had little time for himself as he chauffeured Maggie to her events and worked odd hours to keep his deadlines. He had come to terms with the notion that Father Brendan never tried to find another replacement for his three-o'clock adoration. Ironically, this hour had become a place for him to slow down and rest. He often felt the Lord's presence even though he tried to ignore the gentle whispers.

Do not be afraid to allow Me to fill you with joy. I can heal your heart.

Mitch admitted to himself that he had grown tired of his one-sided feud. It expended way too much energy. One day, while at adoration, he closed his eyes but had the mystifying sensation that he could still see. He looked down at his hands and was surprised to find they held his bruised heart. He envisioned himself standing up, walking from the back of the church to the altar with his barely beating heart, and placing it before the monstrance. The large crucifix loomed overhead. He laid his battered heart on the altar. He gave it to the Lord.

As he turned to leave, however, he had second thoughts. *How can I live without that old familiar pain and sadness? How can I even think of abandoning my heart to Jesus, who did nothing to save Len or Maggie's parents?*

He quickly turned around to snatch his heart from where he had laid it at Jesus's feet. What he saw astonished him. Jesus had bent down from the cross to draw Mitch's battered heart to His breast. Mitch gazed into Jesus's compassionate eyes. He felt the Savior's words more than heard them.

I cannot hold and heal your heart if you will not let go and surrender it to Me.

Mitch drew in his breath and opened his eyes to find himself still sitting in the pew at the back of the church. He had not moved from his spot, and Christ still hung upon the cross. Everything was in its place. He lowered his head and covered his ears to quiet the sound of two hearts beating in unison.

CHAPTER 12

It is only we who brood over our sins.
God does not brood over them.
God dumps them at the bottom of the sea.

—*Saint Benedict*

F ather Brendan extended his hands over Maggie. "Father in heaven, we ask Your blessing over Your child, Mary Magdalene, also known as Maggie. Keep her safe in her travels, true to Your commandments, and dedicated to her faith. May she call on the Blessed Mother to guide her, and may Saint Frances de Sales intercede for her as she begins high school." Both priests made the sign of the cross above her head.

Marge pulled her Kodak Instamatic camera from her purse. "I'll have copies made for everyone." Then she handed Maggie an eraser and said, "Mistakes are only mistakes if you don't learn from them." They hugged.

Mitch wiped the corner of his eye, grateful for this extended family. He even allowed himself to be thankful to Jesus for establishing the priesthood.

The priests and Marge waved goodbye as Mitch and Blaise drove Maggie to school. When they arrived, Mitch leaned over for a hug. "I guess I'll have to stop calling you Maggie-doodle now that you're in high school."

"It's okay, just not around my friends."

He watched her through the rearview mirror as she greeted other students and disappeared behind the wooden doors. "Well, she's growing up. I'm not sure I like the idea. How about you?"

Blaise tilted his head, one ear up and one down, then turned to look out the back window.

Mitch put the car in gear. "Ya know, Blaise, it seems that life is a series of endings or beginnings, depending on how you view it. My head sees this as a new beginning. I've got to get my heart on board. I guess I better get you home."

Mitch had dreaded this day. Maggie was growing into a beautiful woman, like her mother and Len. He knew dropping her off at the high school would be emotional for him, so the empty feeling in his heart didn't surprise him. *I wish Len were here.*

After dropping Blaise off at home, he had a compelling urge to visit the church. *I'll sit quietly before the tabernacle for a little while. That's what Len used to do when she was feeling down.*

He walked to the first pew, genuflected, sat down, and closed his eyes. He felt Len's presence and heard her voice in his head.

We used to sit together in this pew and pray for a child. God answered your prayer. Why are you so glum?

This thought came from deep within, but it was Len's voice. He answered, "Maggie's growing up, and I'll have to let her go."

Have you ever let me go?

"No."

Have you ever thanked the Lord for the gift of Maggie?

"No."

Have you ever thanked the Lord for the years we had together?

"No."

Perhaps it's time for you to grow up too.

Mitch lowered his head and waited for Monday-morning Mass to begin.

The church bells rang, and Father James walked up the aisle and onto the altar. When he turned to face the congregation and saw Mitch, a look of surprise filled his eyes.

Mitch felt conspicuous. *I'm just as amazed as you.*

Father James made the sign of the cross. "Let us begin. In the name of the Father, and of the Son, and of the Holy Ghost. Amen."

Father James read the Gospel and delivered his short sermon:

> *Trust, that is all the Lord asks of us. The Creator of our bodies and souls knows our limitations and our weaknesses. Jesus healed the physically paralyzed man in today's Gospel. He can heal those paralyzed by anger, fear, or a hardened heart.*
>
> *In the Gospel, the friends who lowered the paralyzed man through the roof had faith in Jesus's ability to heal. This reminds us that having faith-filled family and friends around us is a blessing. Jesus indeed healed the man after forgiving his sins.*

Father James slowly closed the Bible. "The only question left is...are we willing to be healed, to take up our cross and follow Jesus?"

The sermon cut Mitch to the quick. He needed to trust the Lord and stop hiding behind his grief and pride. He had used them long enough as an excuse to close the world out. Mitch was aware of his strained relationship with God, so when it was time for Communion, he approached Father James, lowered his head, and crossed his arms over his chest. This meant he was there, not for Communion, but for a blessing.

Father James raised his hand over Mitch and blessed him with the words, "May the Lord Jesus be above you to bless you, below you to support you, before you to guide you, behind you to protect you, and beside you to give you strength."

Mitch answered, "Amen," returned to his pew, knelt, and prayed, *Lord, please forgive me for my inability to forgive You. Thank You for sending Maggie to me. She has enriched my life in a way I can hardly believe. I'm grateful that Len was my wife. We shared a lifetime of love in those short years.*

He straightened up and looked right at the tabernacle. *From now on, I promise to trust You, no matter what size cross You ask me to bear.*

He waited after Mass and asked, "Father James, would you have time to hear my confession?"

"Mitch, that would give our Lord great joy." He kissed his green stole, placed it around his neck, and entered his side of the confessional.

Mitch lifted the curtain on his side and knelt.

Father James began, "May God, who has enlightened every heart, help you to know your sins and trust in His mercy."

"Bless me, Father, it's been almost six years since my last confession." Mitch poured out his remorse for being prideful and despairing. He was sorry for abandoning God, the community, and the church, for taking the Lord's name in vain, and for working on Sundays instead of making it a day dedicated to the Lord. He ended his confession with these words, "Lord, I am so sorry for all the times I was not grateful for Your blessings."

"You have made a humble confession, recognizing that you have hurt your relationship with the Lord. God the Father forgives you and welcomes you home. Do you remember the story of the prodigal son in the Gospel of Luke?"

"Yes, I do."

"Good. For your penance, read and meditate on it before you go to sleep tonight. Now say a good Act of Contrition."

"Oh my God, I am heartily sorry for having offended Thee, and I detest all my sins because of Thy just punishment, but most of all because they offend Thee, my God, who are all good and deserving of all my love. I firmly resolve, with the help of Thy grace, to sin no more and to avoid the near occasions of sin. Amen."

When Mitch drew back the curtain, it was as if scales had fallen from his eyes. The church seemed brighter than he ever remembered. He put his hand to his face to shade it from the radiant light that shone through the stained-glass window depicting the Transfiguration of Jesus.

A voice came from behind him. "Would you like to receive Communion now?"

Mitch turned and raised his eyebrows in surprise. "I have missed Mass every Sunday since Len's death. I've been angry and abusive and hateful to God. You just heard all my sins. How can I receive?"

"Mitch, God is true to His word. He has cleansed you and forgiven your sins. He remembers His promises but has a short memory of our failures. We just prayed Psalm 32 at Mass this morning. 'Blessed is he whose transgression is forgiven, whose sin is covered. Blessed is the man to whom the

Lord inputs no iniquity, and in whose spirit there is no deceit.' Take these words to heart. The Lord desires you to have food for life's journey. Follow me."

Mitch stepped up on the altar as Father James opened the tabernacle door and genuflected. Mitch knelt as Father James took out the ciborium that contained the consecrated hosts, held one up, and said, "The body of Christ."

Mitch responded, "Amen," and received the host on his tongue as a tear slipped down his cheek.

Father James comforted him, "We expect harshness for sins, but God offers eternal life. Rest in His presence and stay as long as you like."

Mitch, to this day, cannot tell you how long he knelt on the altar, resting with the Lord. Time had no bounds; the eternal God was within him.

The next Sunday, Mitch dressed in a collared shirt and shoved a tie into his pocket. He walked with Maggie and Blaise to church, stopped in the usual spot, pulled the tie from his pocket, and looped it around his collar.

"Uncle Mitch, what are you doing?"

"I'm putting on my tie for Mass."

"You're coming to Mass with me? For real?" She hugged him.

"Absolutely!" He took Maggie's hand. "I want to apologize for resisting this for such a long time. Thank you for being patient and for your prayers. I now understand how wrong I was to criticize Jesus when He is so good. I truly believe that He brought you into my life."

CHAPTER 13

Woman, the child of so many
tears shall never perish.

—*Saint Ambrose to Saint Monica*

Kevin leaned out the window of the car as it sped down Ilchester Road. The car slowed, and Kevin raised Chuck's baseball bat. His timing was perfect. He swung the bat through the cool autumn air and knocked over a mailbox with one shot.

"Another home run!" he exclaimed as all the guys in the car whooped their approval.

Jimmy hollered, "Do another one!"

"I'll have to wait because my arm is still tingling from the impact," Kevin admitted.

"Hey, I need you guys to get something for me at Reed's Pharmacy." It was not a request, but an order from Chuck, the ringleader of this little band of vandals.

When Chuck told them what he needed, Ben said, "Not that again."

"Yeah, Ben, and get me as much as your chubby little arms can hold."

When Jimmy and Ben left the car, Kevin said, "So you're going after Diane because she shut you down."

"So what's it to you?"

"Nothing. This will get her attention, but not in a good way."

Jimmy and Ben came running out with their arms full of toilet-paper rolls.

"Open the door and take off," yelled Jimmy.

They were being chased through the alley by the store manager, who slipped and fell face-first into a pile of trash as the thieves sped away. The manager returned to the store out of breath and with a scraped elbow, only to find Cheryl, the cashier, resting against the brick wall of the pharmacy, puffing on a cigarette.

"So what happened?" he asked.

"When I realized they were not gonna pay, I yelled at 'em, but the one with the chipped tooth hollered back that they didn't have time to pay 'cause they were late for a diarrhea party."

"I'm not amused. That chipped-tooth hoodlum has been in here before causing trouble. Last month, I saw him knock over a display and blame it on a small kid. When I confronted him, he got angry and tried to punch me! I almost caught that little chubby guy today, but I slipped," the manager said, pressing a handkerchief to his bleeding elbow.

***

"Frances, whatever is the matter with you today? You've put the pajamas in with the winter coats!" Marge was worried about her friend.

"Oh, have I? I'm sorry. Let me fix it," she said as she sorted the items. "I guess my mind is elsewhere."

"Maggie, can you and the girls sort the last few bags of clothing? Mrs. Jackson and I are going to the rectory for a little break."

"Sure thing, Aunt Marge."

Fran sat at the table as Marge poured coffee. "Fran, we've been friends forever, and I know when something's wrong."

Fran's lip quivered. She tried to sip her coffee but then put the cup back on the table. "It's Kevin. I had to go down to the police station yesterday. He shoplifted record albums from Caplan's Department Store."

"Oh my."

"When I questioned him, he was very flippant and told me it was no big deal and that it was the first time." She stared at the coffee cup. "I said, 'Do you mean the first time you stole or the first time you got caught?' He slumped down in his chair and wouldn't answer." Fran started to cry. "Marge, you know how I worry about my grandson. Kevin acts like his mother, Katie, and you remember how that turned out. He won't come to Mass anymore, doesn't care about school, and his grades show it."

Marge sat down and put her hand on Fran's. "Have you ever told him the story?"

"No, I didn't have to. You know how a small town talks."

"Yes, there's not a lot of mercy for an unwed teenage mother."

"Katie tried to care for him, but she couldn't handle the shame. She's gone. I'll sometimes receive a birthday or Christmas card, but that's all the correspondence in the last twelve years. I stopped crying for Katie when I started shedding tears for Kevin."

"Fran, I know it's been difficult since Glen died, and you have to deal with this alone. Kevin and Glen were very close."

"Yes, he was a wonderful grandfather. The only father figure Kevin ever had." Fran took a sip of her coffee. Her hand shook as she set the cup down in its saucer. "They'd go fishing or to ball games. Glen loved the Orioles. He showed

Kevin how to make things too. I still have the birdhouses they built in the backyard…" Fran stared blankly into space. "He's been in trouble with the sheriff too. He wrapped a house in toilet paper instead of going to the library to study."

"How did the sheriff get involved?" Marge asked.

"The house they chose to wrap was two doors from a deputy's home. Kevin was the only one caught, and the deputy took him to the sheriff's office for questioning. He wouldn't give up any of his accomplices. The sheriff, Billy Wilson, drove him home. He did it as a courtesy to me since Billy's mom and I were good friends. We taught together before she passed away. Kevin's punishment was to clean the toilet paper off the house the next day after school."

Marge said, "That seems like the punishment fit the crime."

"The sheriff told me that Kevin's next stop will be juvenile court if he doesn't shape up. I don't know any of his friends, and he's out later and later at night. Marge, I don't know what to do. There's been a lot of vandalism around town, and I hate to think Kevin's involved, but that's where my mind goes."

Marge handed her a tissue. *Poor Fran. She's a good woman, and this is such a heavy burden.*

"I've noticed the garage filling up with things. He has no money, so I fear he's stealing more than record albums."

"I know you've taken good care of him, Fran."

"Yes, but something is missing between us. He told me he doesn't know where he belongs."

"I remember when you and Glen surprised him with the banana bike with the mustache handlebars. He rode it around like he was on a motorcycle, with such a smile. How old was he then? About ten?"

"Yes, but when Glen passed, something died inside him."

Marge stood up and opened the cabinet to replenish the sugar in the bowl.

Father Brendan appeared in the doorway and said in a cheerful voice, "Hello, wonderful church ladies. How's the clothing drive coming along?"

Fran looked at him and burst into tears.

He looked at Marge, who motioned for him to say something. "Oh my goodness, Frances. Is the drive going that poorly?" After Marge gave him a look of disapproval, he quickly sat down next to Fran and took her hand. "There now, tell me what's wrong."

She put the tissue to her mouth and couldn't speak, so Marge interjected, "Brendan, it's Kevin. Seems he's getting himself into trouble."

"Oh no. What kind of trouble?"

So Fran collected herself and repeated the story as Marge poured Father Brendan a cup of coffee and reheated Fran's cup while he listened and sipped his coffee.

A loud screeching noise outside the kitchen startled them as Sam's ladder scraped across the window frame.

"Jesus, Mary, and Joseph! What's Sam up to now?"

Marge answered, "He's trying to prune that huge bush. He says it blocks the sunlight from coming into the kitchen. Look at him, all scraped up and bruised, wrestling with that shrubbery." She made a *tsk-tsk* sound with her tongue as she watched him through the window.

"Now, Fran, did you say you know the sheriff?"

"I knew his mom years back. That's our only connection."

Marge looked at Father Brendan and asked, "What are you thinking?"

Fran asked him, "Can you talk to Kevin? Maybe he would listen to you."

Father Brendan replied, "I was thinking of something a little more subtle."

Sam raised the clippers to trim the bush, and Marge read her brother's mind. She turned to face Father Brendan, took her pointer finger, and traced it across the base of her neck.

But Father Brendan paid her no mind. "Fran, could you get the sheriff to tell Kevin that if he wants to stay out of juvenile court, he has to report here for community service? We could use a strong young man to help Sam with his projects." He ignored Marge as she threw her arms up in exasperation. "Maybe just being here with Father James and me would help get him straightened out. It'd be community service at first, but if things work out, we can pay him a little to keep his head in the game."

"Oh, Father Brendan, thank you so much." Fran hugged his neck and practically skipped out the door.

As soon as she was out of earshot, Marge exploded. "For the love of God, Brendan, what are you thinking? Sam can't babysit Kevin! He might pull those pranks around here! Sam already has his hands full. Just look at him."

Father Brendan went over and opened the window. "Sam, maybe you could use some help?"

"You think?" Sam responded sarcastically.

Father Brendan turned toward Marge with a smile. "I rest my case."

CHAPTER 14

A saint is a sinner who keeps trying.

—*Saint Josemaria Escriva*

"Thank you, Sheriff Wilson."

Kevin's ears perked up.

"I'll see that he gets this." Granny closed the door, holding what appeared to be an official document. "Kevin, it says here that you are to report to Saint Paul Church on October 12, 1971, at 4:00 p.m. That's tomorrow!"

"What!" Kevin grabbed the paper from her hand and scanned the document. "It says it's for community service in reparation for delinquent behavior in Howard County, Maryland."

Granny wrinkled her brow. "Oh no." She sounded sympathetic. "But, Kevin, this has to be better than ending up in juvenile court."

Kevin crumpled the paper into a ball, threw it to the floor, stormed into his bedroom, slammed the door, and gritted his teeth. "Now, everyone will laugh at me, and I'm sure Jen and Brenda won't hang out with me anymore. None of the girls will. Community service at the church will ruin my reputation!"

He plopped down at his desk and looked at the photo of his grandfather and him proudly displaying the fish he had caught. His eyes teared up.

"I need a cigarette." He got up and opened his chest of drawers. "Damn!" He crushed the empty wrapper in his fist and knocked his Little League trophy off the bureau, breaking the arms that held the bat.

***

The high school bus pulled up, and Blaise waited patiently to greet Maggie. They walked to the church, and Maggie sat on the prayer bench to study. It was a warm autumn day, and she took advantage of the sun-drenched crimson and gold garden surrounding the Blessed Mother statue. Winter would soon prevent her from such a luxury.

As she read her American history, she sensed someone watching her. Blaise raised himself from his relaxed position to sit at attention, pinning his ears back and making a low, guttural growl. She turned to follow his gaze.

Above her in the garden, next to the Blessed Mother statue, stood a young man balancing a shovel over his shoulders, both arms hanging over the shaft. It reminded her of the early Pilgrims' pillory punishment for those who had committed a crime. He stood motionless, a cigarette dangling from his lips.

"Hello," she said, "what are you going to do with the shovel?" and waited a moment for him to respond. When he didn't, she offered, "Has the cat got your tongue?" It looked as if he was about to answer, but then he repositioned the shovel on his left shoulder instead. *This is weird.*

"Ya know, smoking is bad for your health."

Finally, he replied, "Huh, yeah. I mean, I'm not worried." As he talked, the cigarette bounced up and down on his lips.

He shifted the shovel from his shoulders and placed the blade on the ground.

"Are you planting something in the garden? It's a little late in the season unless you're planting mums or pansies."

He removed the cigarette. "Huh, no…um…I'm not…um…here to…um…plant anything."

"Then what are you here to do?" she asked politely with a hint of amusement at this tongue-tied teen.

"Oh, um, I'm here to help Mr. Gallagher spread mulch. At least that's what Father Brendan told me to do, but I can't find him. I've never met him, and…"

Maggie waited for him to finish his thought.

He shifted the shovel to his right shoulder and flicked some ashes into the garden.

Her amusement faded. *How annoying! I need to get rid of this guy.* She said, "There was a mulch delivery to the rectory's side yard yesterday."

He just stood there, shifting his weight from one foot to the other and flicking the ashes off his cigarette.

Blaise became perturbed by this motion and moved from sitting to standing.

Maggie put her hand on the dog's head and advised, "If you don't get there soon, he'll finish the mulch job without you."

The boy took one more puff, dropped his cigarette into the garden, and crushed it with the toe of his shoe. "Yes, maybe you're right." He turned and strolled across the parking lot as if he had all the time in the world.

"Blaise, have you ever seen such arrogance?" She walked up the garden steps, held her nose, and picked up the cigarette butt with a tissue. "I wonder if he will be a frequent visitor around here. I sure hope not." She picked up her books. "Although he is kinda cute…but way too pretentious if you ask me."

***

Kevin, you're so pathetic! He criticized himself as he made his way over to Sam, *You looked like such a half-wit! Cat got your tongue? But how could I help it? There was something so enchanting about her. No, it was more than physical beauty, more like magnetism.* He stopped dead in his tracks. "I should've asked her name." *Kevin, you've never been shy around girls. What the heck?!*

He turned around and saw the girl was about to enter the rectory. "Hey," he called out, "my name's Kevin. What is your dog's name?" *Really! That's the best you got? You don't care about her dumb dog!*

Maggie hesitated, then answered, "His name is Blaise…and mine's Maggie." She then entered the rectory, and Blaise gave him a menacing look before he followed her inside.

Maggie found Marge adjusting her hat in the mirror. "I just had the weirdest experience," she said as she threw the tissue and cigarette butt in the garbage.

"Maggie… Sorry, honey, I'm in a hurry and late for the Catholic Daughters meeting. See if you can get Father Brendan to take his medicine. He's so darn obstinate."

Blaise had learned that he was welcome in the rectory as long as he stayed out of the kitchen, so he and Maggie trotted down to Father Brendan's office and found him working on his homily.

He peered over his glasses and beamed with delight when he saw her. "I thought you were Marge coming in here with more instructions," he said as he winked at her.

She sat in one of the comfy, leather-upholstered chairs a parishioner had willed to the rectory. The cushions enveloped her, and she looked small even though she was now a sophomore.

Maggie visited Father Brendan often, and he was always up for a theological discussion or ready to listen as she read to him. They were currently reading *Kristin Lavransdatter* by Sigrid Undset. He often drifted off to sleep and was amazed to find her content to sit in the chair and wait for him to wake. He was grateful for this child who was quickly growing into a young woman. He had once commented, "It's not often we have the blessing of a parishioner whose sole purpose is to spread joy."

"So what is going on today?" He asked. "Anything new to discuss?"

"I need to write an essay on what freedom means to me."

"What are your thoughts?"

"Freedom means no person or government should enslave another. Everyone should be able to do what they desire as long as it does not infringe on someone else's freedom."

"Very good. Suppose I sum it up by saying that freedom allows us to do what God calls us to do." He sat back and adjusted his glasses.

Maggie nodded.

Father Brendan added, "When God is the center of your life, and your relationship with Him the purpose of your life, you find that criticism doesn't tear you down, and, conversely, accolades or approval don't puff you up. Always trust that God has a plan. That is the recipe for freedom."

Maggie smiled and said, "The greatest freedom is to have the right relationship with God."

"That's the ticket!" Father suddenly felt exhilarated and sat back in his chair and smiled. His usual afternoon slump had vanished.

Maggie stood up as if she intended to leave, but then lingered while tracing her finger up and down the doorjamb.

"Okay, what's on your mind?"

"I met a boy in the garden today. He said his name is Kevin."

"Ah yes, Kevin is here to help Sam. He's had a rough time of it lately. You remember Mrs. Jackson from the clothing drive?"

"Sure, she's a sweet lady."

"Well, she's Kevin's grandmother." *Uh-oh, it never occurred to me that Maggie would be the least bit interested in him.* "Maggie, you'll be a good influence on him. You may talk with him, but I do not want you to go anywhere with him."

"You mean like on a date?" she asked with a theatrical gesture mimicking a heart attack.

"Well, yes, maybe... I mean, no..." Father Brendan was flustered. "I mean..."

Maggie giggled and placed her hands on her hips. "Father B., I have no intention of going out with some boy I know nothing about, except that he has a sweet grandmother. You don't have to worry. I have no time anyway. I'm fifteen now and will start work at Caplan's Department Store a few days a week for the Christmas rush. Beverly's mom works there and put in a good word for us. I start next month."

She made a whimsical curtsy. "Oh, and by the way, Aunt Marge said you're free to take your medicine." She flashed a smile, skipped out the door, and barely escaped being hit by a wad of notepaper that Father Brendan had launched in her direction.

Blaise intercepted the paper ball, chewed, and swallowed it.

***

Sam entered Brendan's office. "Hello, Sam, how's it going with the mulch?"

"It would be better if Kevin hadn't given me the third degree about Maggie! He must have asked a million questions. 'What kind of music does she like? Does she have a boyfriend? What sort of things does she like to do?' I tell you, Brendan, it was nonstop!"

"Well, what did you say to him?"

"I told him she was only fifteen and too young for him. Then he said he was seventeen, and two years wasn't a big deal. I wanted to tell him he wasn't good enough for her, but I held my tongue and told him to stop yapping and go to the shed to get the clippers. I needed a break!"

"Maggie was in here asking about him too. Do you think this is going to be a problem? I didn't foresee this happening at all."

"I don't know. Maybe."

"Let's just keep an eye on Kevin when Maggie's around. Between you, me, James, and Marge, we ought to be able to handle this. Maybe tell Mitch as well. I told Frances we would give her grandson a try. Let's give him a chance."

"Okay, boss, but I remember being seventeen and…"

"Stop, Sam. I remember being seventeen, too, but I don't want to hear anything about you and my sister!"

But Sam knew Maggie was in a different league than this cocky kid. He had already formed his opinion, and only a miracle could change Sam's mind.

***

Mitch had the embers on the charcoal grill red-hot when Maggie brought the prepared hamburger patties to the deck and handed him a cold soda.

"Thanks, Maggs."

"Uncle Mitch, do you think I'm old enough to go on a date?"

Mitch had just taken a swig of his drink, and it went down the wrong pipe. He coughed and sputtered, "Oh. Gosh darn!" Then, he stepped back to unsuccessfully keep the soda spraying from his mouth off his clothes. He bumped the grill and put his hand out to steady it. "Ouch! That's hot!"

"Are you okay?" she asked and giggled.

"I'm fine. You just surprised me with that question. Let's see; you'll be twenty-five in ten years. Hmm…" He smiled.

"Uncle Mitch, I'm serious."

"I know, I know. Next year you can picnic in the front yard with a guy if I approve of him."

"Uncle Mitch!" Maggie huffed. "This is the 1970s, after all."

"Look, keep going to school dances and teen club, but with a group. You're already having a fun social life. Let's both agree you need to be at least sixteen before you go on a date. Okay?"

"Okay," she replied half-heartedly.

"Until then, don't try to grow up so fast. Being an adult isn't as easy as I make it seem." He sucked his burnt thumb.

They both burst out laughing.

CHAPTER 15

*Heaven is filled with converted sinners
of all kinds, and there is room for more.*

—*Saint Joseph Cafasso*

"I'll tell ya what. The first time I met Kevin, he was a pain in my…"

"Sam!" Marge exclaimed.

"Gluteus maximus," Sam said as he sat at the breakfast table with Father Brendan, Marge, and Father James. "When I sent him to collect the trash from the school, he took a smoke break! I told him not to smoke at work. Do you know what he said? 'Okay, Mr. Gallagher, I was thinking of quitting anyway.' Then he threw the whole pack in the trash!"

"You mean he quit right there on the spot?"

"I haven't seen him light up since. At first, he would take his sweet time getting here after school, so I told him he had to be here fifteen minutes after the final bell."

"So what happened?" asked Father Brendan.

"He said, 'Sorry, Mr. Gallagher, I'll do better.'" Sam shook his head. "At first, he was bold and opinionated, telling me how I should run the grounds. Within a week, he shaped up and did everything I told him to do. But I didn't expect him to be competent. It makes me wonder where he could have acquired such skills. He's a natural."

"That's true," Father James replied. "The crack in the sacristy wall disappeared once he had plastered, sanded, and painted it."

Father Brendan looked around the table. "I can think of only one plausible reason."

They all replied in unison, "Maggie!"

***

Kevin saw Maggie and Blaise in the parking lot, so he ran to Mary's garden and hid behind a shrub. She entered, pulled out a rosary, and made the sign of the cross. He could see her lips moving while running her fingers delicately over each bead. He was intrigued by her devotion to prayer.

Blaise's ears perked up when Kevin adjusted his position. *Uh-oh, Blaise heard me.* He stood up and caught Maggie's attention.

"Kevin, I didn't know you were here." She made the sign of the cross and placed the beads in her pocket.

"Oh, sorry, I didn't mean to disturb your prayers."

"I try to pray a rosary every day."

"Boy, that's devotion."

She pulled out a textbook. "It's a way to walk with Jesus through the eyes of His Mother, Mary."

"That's what you do when you pray a rosary? Walk with Jesus?"

"Some think it is nothing more than repeating the Our Father and Hail Mary prayers, but it's much more. Praying the Joyful Mysteries reminds me to be humble and obedient. The Sorrowful Mysteries help me be more patient when life gets tough and to remember all Jesus endured to save us, and—"

"Whoa, whoa, this is way too much information. I don't believe in a man-made religion."

"Oh yeah, me either." Maggie turned her attention to her schoolbook.

She had surprised him with her comment, and he felt emboldened. "I don't see why we're supposed to go to Mass every Sunday. I can talk to God anytime and say prayers in my room. I don't have to go to church for that."

She looked up from her book. "Oh, do you sing hymns of praise and read Scripture in your room?"

"What? No!"

Maggie drummed her fingers on her book as she pondered the situation. "Hmm, I know you're not receiving Communion in your room or hearing any sermons. You know, the apostles started doing all of that from the very beginning. They handed on what Jesus taught them. It was Jesus who set up the Church."

"And just how do you know that?"

"It's in the Acts of the Apostles, chapter 2." She set her book down, walked over to the wall, and picked a yellow mum from the garden.

Kevin scratched his head and leaned on the rake.

"Jesus chose twelve apostles, gave them the power to forgive sins, and consecrate bread and wine into His Body and Blood." She held the flower above her head and twirled it against the blue sky. "He told them to make disciples of all nations by Baptism. He used people to spread His message. It wasn't just everyone sitting in their room praying. They came together on Sundays to worship God, not because God needed it, but because God knew men needed it. People need to be a part of a community. It's healthy. Mass is Christ's gift to us. He didn't just leave us with a message. He established a body of believers and then sent them out. If you're a Catholic, that is your mission too."

Kevin stared down at her with a confused look on his face.

Maggie continued, "Jesus wanted everyone to belong to His family as part of His body through the Church."

Kevin folded his arms over his chest. "Yeah? Well, maybe I don't feel like I belong."

"Kevin"—Maggie reached up and handed him the flower she had been twirling—"believing is belonging." She gathered her books, smiled at him, and walked up the hill to go home.

He wished she had stayed because he liked listening to her, even though she perplexed him. He put the garden tools away, stopped at the Dairy Ranch on his way home, and ran into Chuck and the guys.

Jimmy said, "Hey, Kev, where've ya been? We've missed you after school these past weeks."

"I've been busy. You know my grandmother needs my help with stuff around the house."

Chuck said, "We need you tonight. We're gonna wrap Stephanie Quinn's house. She's such an annoying—"

Kevin said under his breath, "Another girl unimpressed with you?"

"What did you say?"

"I said my grandmother has the flu. I gotta get home."

"C'mon, Kevin, you're the only one who can throw the roll over the house."

"What can I get for you, Kevin?" A friendly Dairy Ranch employee disrupted their conversation since he was next in line at the takeout window. It was Betty from his geometry class.

Kevin turned his back to Chuck, and Betty flashed him a playful smile. "I'll have one of those delicious chocolate shakes you prepare and fries." Kevin flirted back to buy himself some time.

A voice came from behind him. "We're meeting at eight o'clock at the bowling-alley parking lot. Your grandmother should be in bed by then. I better see you there," Chuck warned.

Sam and Marge walked out of the restaurant and bumped into Kevin.

"Kevin, so good to see you," Sam said with a smile. "Grabbing some dinner?"

Oh jeez, I hope he doesn't mention my work at the church. "No, just a snack. I've gotta get home."

"So, Kev, we'll see you tonight."

Not if I see you first!

Kevin noticed Sam's smile fade as Chuck and his crew quickly moved away. Sam abruptly took Marge's hand and said, "Have a good evening, Kevin." They walked away, and Kevin noted that Marge had a look of disappointment on her face.

He turned back to Betty, who winked and said, "I put some extra chocolate in your shake."

He grabbed his food and got into the car. He drove off, annoyed that he'd gotten involved with Chuck and company. If he ignored them, perhaps they'd get the hint. He knew that was a dangerous plan. They had a lot of incriminating evidence against him. But Kevin knew that Chuck couldn't accuse him of burglary without implicating himself.

What would Maggie think of me if she discovered my past?

He was in a complicated situation, but despite Chuck's threats, Kevin felt safe, the way he did when his grandfather was alive.

Later that evening, Kevin looked at his watch. It was five minutes past eight. He knew his absence would anger them. He also figured they would abandon their plans to wrap Stephanie's house. They were just a bunch of cowards...dangerous cowards.

CHAPTER 16

All the darkness in the world cannot
extinguish the light of a single candle.

—*Saint Francis of Assisi*

C huck watched Kevin bolt out of class as soon as the bell rang. *I know Kevin's avoiding me. I'm gonna follow him to see where he goes every day.*

Chuck allowed a few cars between Kevin and him since his car was a repurposed state-police vehicle that his dad had purchased. The car stuck out like a sore thumb. He followed Kevin as far as Main Street, but lost sight of him when a delivery truck pulled out and stopped in front of his car. He hit his horn, and the driver gave him the finger. Chuck banged the steering wheel with his hand in frustration.

Oncoming traffic finally stopped and allowed him to maneuver around the truck, but Kevin was gone. "Which way did he go?" He banged the steering wheel again, turned right, and ended up on College Avenue.

"Well, well, well. Look who's up ahead." Chuck was talking to himself. "I recognize that dog, but what was the girl's name?" He drove past her. "Maggie, that's it."

He stopped the car and looked in his rearview mirror. "She sold me a ticket to the teen-club picnic a few years back. She was a little kid then, but she's not little anymore. Whew!" He rolled down the window. "Hello, Maggie. Where are you headed?"

Blaise moved between Maggie and the car.

She started to walk faster. "On my way home."

He stepped on the gas to keep up with her. "Can I give you a lift? Your books look heavy."

"No thanks, I'm almost there."

He eyed her cute figure and remembered her lovely smile, but she wasn't smiling now. "What grade are you in now?"

Maggie ignored the question and kept walking.

"I guess by your uniform that you don't go to Howard High." A car pulled up behind him and honked. "Well, gotta go. Maybe I'll see you around." Then he sped down the road.

Maggie's body relaxed. She knew his dad was the sheriff, but that knowledge didn't alleviate the unease he produced in the pit of her stomach.

***

Maggie quietly entered the church building and found Kevin scrubbing the wall behind the votive-candle display.

"I don't understand why people light these darned candles anyway. What good can they possibly do?" he complained.

"They bring a lot of comfort to people."

He jumped up and turned around to find Maggie suppressing a smile. Her blonde hair was in a ponytail with two curly tendrils on either side of her face. "Oh, I didn't know anyone was here."

"Clearly." She smiled.

"So tell me about these candles."

"Remember when I told you that Jesus founded the Church so that we would be a body of believers?"

"Yes."

"As believers, we are a family. We hold each other up and pray for one another. If a person is ill or needs encouragement, someone can light a candle for them. The candle is a symbol of prayer, but also of Christ, who is the light of the world. I like it when I see all the candles burning. It's a sign that people care about each other."

"What is this little slot for?"

"You put money in as an offering for the candle."

"Aha! Another way to make money!"

Maggie exhaled. "Kevin, you're such a cynic. I've heard Father Brendan say they lose money on the candles. You can still light one, even if you don't have a dime. Prayers are free. The neat thing is that, after you leave, the candle flame continues your prayer vigil."

He grumbled, "Just sounds like more baggage of an organized religion."

Maggie sat down in a pew. "Well, maybe it sounds that way. All I know is, when my parents died, I came here often to light candles for them." Maggie quietly focused on the tabernacle. "It helped me feel connected to them…you know, less sad."

Kevin's cynicism turned to shame. "Maggie, your parents are dead? I didn't know that. Gosh, I'm so sorry for saying that about the candles." When Maggie didn't respond, Kevin continued, "I never knew my parents. I don't know what happened to them. The kids would tease me at school when my grandparents showed up for Parents' Day. One kid told me his father said I was illegitimate." Kevin hung his head. "It was years later that I found out what that meant."

Maggie went over and put her hand on his shoulder. "So we are kinda orphans together. But we are so blessed, Kevin. You have your grandmother, and I have my uncle Mitch."

"You live with your uncle?"

"Yes, he's pretty cool and takes care of me."

"My granny takes care of me too. But I miss my grandpa."

"I have an idea. Let's light candles for my parents and your grandfather."

"Okay, but we're out of those wooden matches."

"That's not a problem," Maggie said as she picked up a candle. "We can use a burning candle to light ours." She turned a candle upside down, lowered it so the wick touched another flame, and it caught fire.

Kevin took a candle and did the same. It was a solemn moment.

"Did you notice that, Kevin?"

"Notice what?" he whispered.

"A candle loses nothing by lighting another candle, but it makes the world a little brighter."

***

Sam met Marge in the rectory kitchen and walked with her to their car. "I asked Kevin if he could help me with a gutter problem tomorrow. I'll talk to him about Jimmy and Chuck. I don't like that he's friends with those two."

"There was a time you wouldn't have cared about him. You've changed your opinion of Kevin."

"My first impression of him has softened. I guess we both had a bit of an attitude toward each other. Now that we've settled down, I would describe him as respectful and reliable." Sam opened the car door for Marge and said, "I believe he enjoys a sense of accomplishment in his work. I like the kid. He reminds me of Sam Jr."

"Really?"

"Yes, and I'd like to keep Kevin on the right path and advise him to stay away from Chuck and Jimmy. I remember Brendan had a run-in with them at a teen-club fundraiser a few years back. Money went missing, and Jimmy and Chuck were the last ones near the cashbox. No one accused them, but everyone suspected them. Brendan offered them several opportunities to help with other projects so he could keep an eye on them. They refused and never returned."

"Well, Sam, I'm glad you're taking Kevin under your wing. You've always been a good judge of character."

***

Sam had a ladder out and was staring up at the gutter that had come loose. "I think it just needs to be hammered back in place."

When Kevin inspected the wood, it crumbled at his touch. "We'll need to replace this section before we can reattach the gutter." He scraped off the rotted wood and pulled out his tape measure. "I can go down to the lumberyard and pick up a board."

"No need. I have a few boards in my truck."

They retrieved a handsaw from the shed, and Kevin cut the board to the correct length. He hammered the wood in place while Sam held the ladder.

"So what's your opinion of Johnny Unitas? Think he'll lead the Colts to victory this year?"

"Man, I hope so," Kevin responded between hammer blows. "He's a pretty awesome quarterback."

Sam added, "I'm still licking my wounds over the Pittsburgh Pirates beating the Orioles in the World Series."

"Yeah, I hear ya."

After a few minutes of small talk, Sam started his interrogation, "So how long have you been friends with Chuck and Jimmy?"

"What? No. We aren't friends. More like acquaintances."

"Uh-huh. Well, I suggest you avoid those acquaintances at all costs. You're a good kid, Kevin. You are smart, skilled, and strong. Hmm, any more words beginning with *S* to describe you?"

Kevin didn't acknowledge the compliment, and there was an awkward lull in their conversation. He finished nailing the gutter and came down from the ladder, but wouldn't meet Sam's eyes. He looked at his work and said, "I'll seal the seam tomorrow and paint it to match the other trim."

"Kevin, if you need help with those guys, just let me know. I'm here for you."

Kevin's face hardened. "Mr. Gallagher"—he clutched his hammer, looked down at the ground, and moved a twig with the toe of his shoe—"I know what I need to do. You really shouldn't interfere in my affairs."

Sam could see that Kevin was upset and hoped he hadn't overstepped and hurt their relationship. He felt as if they were finally getting along.

Suddenly, Kevin raised his hammer over his head and shouted something Sam didn't understand.

Sam lifted his arm to protect himself. *Oh my gosh, I've upset the kid!*

Kevin came down fast and hard with a well-placed blow and crushed the head of a copperhead snake that was slithering across the top of Sam's shoe.

Sam nearly jumped out of his skin. They both watched the dying snake as its tail flailed in the air.

"Mr. Gallagher, are you all right?" Kevin asked, breathing heavily.

"Well, if I could just get my heart to stop pounding, I might be." They watched the snake's last spasmodic twitch, and Sam said, "I just thought of two more S words for you—snake slayer."

Kevin blushed and hung the hammer in his pant loop, which made him look as if he were a gunslinger holstering his weapon.

"Here's one more S word for you. From now on, call me Sam."

CHAPTER 17

You must be holy in the way God asks you to be holy. God does not ask you to be a Trappist monk or a hermit. He wills that you sanctify the world in your everyday life.

—*Saint Vincent Pallotti*

"Enough pussyfooting around Kevin," Chuck demanded. "Ben, we'll follow him today in your car."

When they saw Kevin pull into the church driveway, they parked on the road adjacent to the parking lot, slithered down the embankment, and hid in the tall weeds on the far side of the property.

With the aid of binoculars, Ben could see Kevin digging in the garden.

As Maggie approached, Ben said, "Hey, I've seen that girl at teen club." Then he added, "When I used to go, that is, and look at the size of that dog. He's huge!"

As they spied on Kevin, Ben gave them a blow-by-blow description of what was happening. "He stops digging to say something to the girl."

Chuck ripped the binoculars from Ben's hands. "Her name is Maggie Hartman. She is good-looking. Whew!"

"How come I never see her at school?" Ben asked, squinting hard to see since Chuck had seized the binoculars.

"She goes to a Catholic girls' school in Catonsville."

"How do you know so much about her?"

"I have my ways."

Jimmy put his pointer finger in the air and enlightened the crew. "So this is why Kevin doesn't have time for us anymore."

Chuck rolled his eyes but kept them glued to the binoculars and watched every gesture Maggie made. He liked how her blonde hair fell around her shoulders, and her outfit complemented her slim figure. He saw she held a *Caplan's Guide for Employees* book in her arms and made a mental note. He studied her with the binoculars as she and Kevin conversed.

Kevin turned to watch Blaise stealthily cross the parking lot as if stalking a wild animal. "Where's Blaise going?"

"Oh, I don't know. He probably sees a deer in the woods. Blaise, come back here!"

"Holy cow!" exclaimed Jimmy.

Chuck moved the binoculars away from his eyes and said in exasperation, "What now, Jimmy?" Then he spotted Blaise. "Whoa!"

The boys scampered through the weeds and up the hill to Ben's car.

Blaise trotted back with a puffed-up chest.

Kevin asked Maggie, "So whatcha got under your arm?"

"Oh, this? It's just the things I need to learn about being a good and efficient employee. You know, between work and school, I haven't had much time to spend at church, so I'm going to make a quick visit before I head over to Caplan's." She entered the church as Blaise returned and lay down in his usual spot.

132

"Blaise, how can Maggie be so excited about her faith? She treats prayer like a steering wheel, and for me? Well, maybe it is a spare tire."

A half hour later, Maggie came out just as Kevin planted the last bush. "Hey, would you like to get a bite to eat when you get off work? I could pick you up."

Maggie lowered her head, but she had a smile on her face. "I'm not allowed to date until I turn sixteen. That's my uncle's rule."

"Well, do you get a break? I could bring you an ice cream, a hot dog, or something."

"I get a break around seven. Gee, a hot dog sounds great!" She looked at her watch. "Oh no...being on time is the first rule in the guidelines. I gotta go!"

Kevin hollered after her, "What about your dog?"

"He knows the way home."

***

Their encounters on the bench outside Caplan's Department Store became a ritual for Maggie and Kevin. He brought her ice cream or dinner. Sometimes, she surprised him with candy from the store. They sat and talked about many things and shared their greatest joys and deepest wounds. The friendship that began in the church by lighting a candle grew and strengthened the bond that tied their two orphan hearts together.

CHAPTER 18

It is the duty of every man to uphold the dignity of
every woman.

—Saint Thérèse of Lisieux

Kevin's homeroom teacher handed him his report card. "Good work, Kevin, you've improved in every subject. And thanks again for helping me tighten the drawer on the file cabinet the other day."

"You're welcome, Mrs. Green. I'm happy to help."

Chuck mimicked Kevin's voice in his head, *You're welcome, Mrs. Green. I'm happy to help. Come on, Kevin! What the hell is going on with you?*

Later that afternoon, the gang confronted Kevin in the school parking lot. Chuck, Jimmy, and Ben leaned against the door of his car.

"So where've you been, Kev? We've missed you."

"Working, if it's any of your business."

"Oh, tough guy, huh? We know you've been working up at the church," asserted Chuck.

Kevin leaned in Chuck's direction. "They need a lot of help up there. Mr. Gallagher is getting on in years and can't do stuff that needs attention."

"You're a real humanitarian, is that it?" Jimmy piped in. "Yeah, I'll bet you give that Maggie Hartman lots of attention."

"Shut up, Jimmy. You don't know what you're talking about." Kevin slammed his books on the hood of his car, then knocked Jimmy down with one push and stood over him. "Say one more word about Maggie, and I'll beat you to a pulp!"

Jimmy got up and started for Kevin, but Chuck grabbed him by his shirt collar. "Stop it, Jimmy; settle down. Everyone, settle down."

Kevin glared at Jimmy with his hand in a tight fist. He had never felt this way about a girl before and was ready to defend her honor.

"So, Kevin, we're going up to Enchanted Forest tonight. Jimmy's older brother got us some beer, and we're gonna hang out. Join us. I'll bet Jen and Brenda would come if they knew you'd be there."

Kevin hesitated, unclenched his fist, and, through gritted teeth, responded, "No thanks." He grabbed his books from the hood and got in his car.

The three watched him drive away. Chuck said, "If Kevin finds God, it won't be good for us." He was irritated that Kevin had lost interest in home invasions. He was the mastermind behind the money-making schemes. Jimmy and Ben were nothing more than clumsy oafs.

***

As Kevin drove to church, he contemplated his situation. *I should never have gotten involved with that band of future felons.* He was ashamed of his past and knew he was their enabler and the one who had led them into more serious crimes.

He arrived at church still feeling the sting of his soul-searching. He found Sam and Father Brendan looking through a religious catalog.

Father Brendan looked up. "Hi, Kevin, we were just thinking of you."

"You were?" Kevin asked in surprise.

"We were? Ouch!" Sam replied as Father Brendan's elbow jabbed his rib cage.

"Yes, I purchased these four-foot figures of the Holy Family from this catalog. Here, have a look."

"Pretty cool! You're gonna need a pretty big stable."

"Yes, and I want you to build it."

"What! Me?"

"It will need to be easy to assemble and disassemble every Christmas. I'd like it to fit inside the wall of the Blessed Mother Garden. Sam said you could build it."

"I did?"

Father Brendan shot him a look.

"Oh yeah, that's right."

"Gosh, I'm not sure I could build something so complicated and have it look good."

"Well, can you just think about it? Sam's confident that you can do it and has offered to help. I'll bet Maggie's uncle could work up a design. He's an architect."

"I dunno. It would take a lot of time, and I have other duties. There must be a carpenter in the parish who could do this better than me."

"Well, there may be, but I'm asking you."

Kevin shoved his hands in his pockets and looked away. *How can I be the one to build a stable for Jesus? I'm not worthy of such a project.* "I'll have to think about it. Right now, I need to mow the back lawn."

As he walked away, Sam said, "I see what you did there. You want to get Mitch and Kevin together. I don't think he'll take the bait."

"Oh, he will."

"And how do you know that?"

"I prayed a novena to Saint Joseph the Carpenter before I asked him."

Sam laughed. "You know it doesn't work that way."

Father Brendan opened the door to the church and turned to face Sam. "Oh ye of little faith."

***

Blaise barked at the knock on the door, and Mitch heard Maggie's voice.

"Kevin, this is a surprise."

Mitch walked into the living room and observed Kevin smile and blush.

"I know, but your uncle is expecting me. Father Brendan just called him."

Mitch came to the door. "Hi, Kevin. Come in; it's good to meet you."

At first, he had been wary of Maggie's exposure to someone with Kevin's reputation. But he trusted that she was in good hands with Marge and the others on the lookout, probably better off than most teens her age, and he knew that Blaise would always protect her.

They shook hands, and Kevin said, "This is a neat house."

"Uncle Mitch designed and built it himself," Maggie bragged as they all went into the den to see Mitch's draft of the stable.

"Wow, this is amazing, Mr. Hartman. I like how the boards fasten together with carriage bolts and wing nuts. That'll make it easy to reassemble each year."

"So you think you'll do it? I know Sam has a lot of confidence in you."

Maggie smiled. "It's special that Father Brendan asked you to build the stable."

Mitch noticed the chemistry between the two teens and was not surprised when Kevin answered, "Okay, I'll do it."

***

The following week, Sam and Kevin purchased the wood for the stable. Kevin wanted to get started even though Christmas was months away.

Maggie went to the back lawn by the shed, where Kevin was working on the stable.

When he saw her, he playfully asked, "What great book of enlightenment will you study today?"

"Botany," Maggie answered. Then she said, "Tell me everything you know about the sequoia tree."

"Well, I know the sequoia trees are the biggest in the world. They are large enough to drive a car through the ones with tunnels cut in the trunks."

She pressed on with excitement, "Do you know why a sequoia is so big and tall?"

"I guess it's just the nature of the tree."

"It's because the roots are not deep, but they spread way out."

"Is that so?" Kevin stopped hammering for a moment and looked at Maggie with a smile.

"Yes, and because its roots spread out, they entangle with roots from other sequoia trees, and this entanglement gives the trees stability."

"I see. And why this scholarly dissertation on the sequoia?"

"Kevin, we are like the sequoia." She was very animated. "The way we grow strong and become who God created us to be and to live the life He fashioned for us is to connect to Jesus and other people with the church as our foundation. That's why Jesus gave the Church to us. When people in our church family are rooted in faith, our lives intertwine, and we hold each other up, just like the giant sequoias." She was so excited to share her insight.

But her enthusiasm fell flat after Kevin's response. "Well, guess what? A lot of people in this church aren't like you. I know how many of them act, and you shouldn't count on them to hold anyone up. They're more like poison ivy than giant sequoias. They're hypocrites. Why should I be a part of something like that?"

"Really!" she said in an exasperated voice, hands on her hips. "You don't want to belong to the church because some people are hypocrites?" She furrowed her brow and tilted her head. "Isn't that a little like not going outside to enjoy the sunshine because the sun is shining on the good and the bad alike?"

"No, no, that's not what I mean—"

She cut him off, "If all the sinners decided to stay away from the church, you know what? The pews would be empty." She pointed to the church door. "Everyone who comes through that door is a sinner. Jesus said that He didn't come to call the righteous, but to call the sinners."

He fiddled with his hammer and then looked at Maggie with her hands on her hips and her face red with frustration. He lowered his head. "You make it sound like I could make a difference in someone else's life."

"Well, you've made a difference in my life. I know we haven't been on a date or anything, but we have a good time talking about things, don't we?" Her eyes pleaded for him to say yes.

He wanted to, but instead said, "Nobody needs me. Besides, I'm self-sufficient. I don't need anybody looking out for me either."

"But don't you see? Jesus doesn't expect us to be on our own. He knows we need help, so He instituted the Sacraments so we can receive grace. We receive grace at every Mass when we go to Communion." She continued, "It bothers me that you are so anti-Church."

"Yeah, well, I don't need church or any grace either."

Maggie clenched her fists at her sides and let loose her frustration. "Maybe your pride makes you believe you don't need the church. Maybe your attitude is that you can do it all yourself, on your terms, because you don't want anyone to point out when you're doing something wrong. That's convenient!"

He swung the hammer but missed the nail and hit his thumb. "God—" He didn't finish his swear, but clenched his teeth as his eyes watered.

"Kevin! I'm so sorry. I didn't mean for you to get hurt." She took his injured hand into hers. "I was trying to help you understand that everyone is important, and we are all connected and meant to help each other out."

Kevin was silent. *Don't blow it, man; don't be so stubborn. Look at her sweet smile.*

"Well, do you know what I'm going to do?" She brought his hand to her lips, kissed his injured thumb, and lifted her eyes to his.

Kevin, stop being pigheaded. Take her in your arms and kiss her. No! Don't do that. One of the priests, or Mrs. Gallagher, will see us. But wait, didn't she just kiss me? Kiss her!

He leaned in, anticipating the feel of her lips on his, and inadvertently let go of his hammer, which landed squarely on the toe of his sneaker.

"Ouch!" He hopped around on one foot while holding his thumb. Maggie started to laugh, and he couldn't help but laugh too.

"Kevin, I'm going into the church and pray that you feel as welcome as the rest of us. While I'm at it, I'll pray that you finish building the stable without any more injuries."

He called after her, "Yeah…well…go ahead. It won't help. I'm…"—then in a whisper—"doing great." But he knew she didn't hear him, and he was baffled that she cared so much. He winced as his thumb continued to throb, and his big toe ached.

She's so beautiful, both inside and out. I don't know what she sees in me. She irked and amazed him, probably because what she said made sense. *Honestly, I don't feel good enough for God or Maggie, so why even try? I bet she wouldn't care so much if she found out about the things I've done.*

He gathered his tools and took them to the shed. *But, Maggie, your words give me hope.*

On Sunday, he attended Mass with Grandma Fran, who was beaming. Kevin felt conspicuous, but calmed himself as he searched for Maggie in the congregation and saw her up front with her uncle. He tried to concentrate on the Mass but found his eyes drawn in her direction most of the time. He didn't go up to Communion. Maggie had said he should go to Confession first since he had skipped Mass, but going to Confession was a little extreme. *I can't tell all my sins to a priest. If they knew everything I've done, whew!*

He reached over and took his grandmother's hand.

This unexpected gesture of love surprised her, and then she noticed the direction of Kevin's gaze. Fran deduced he was there for Maggie and smiled to herself. *God can use any means to bring someone home, and I'm not one to question the Good Lord's tactics.*

***

It took him two months to build the stable because of his attention to detail. He created a star of wood, painted it a bright yellow, and outlined it with a string of lights. He hung the star on the roof he'd constructed of sticks to give it a thatched effect.

One evening in May, Kevin assembled the stable on the back lawn and invited everyone over to the garden shed. Marge's eyes lit up when Kevin plugged in the lights on the star, and Sam folded his arms across his chest with satisfaction. The priests and Mitch smiled as Maggie and Grandma Fran radiated joy at the sight.

They praised his work, but Kevin quickly advised, "I can't take much credit. I had a lot of help from Mr. Hartman, who designed it, and Sam, who helped pick out the wood and held things in place while I drilled and sawed. I also prayed to Saint Joseph and asked him to help me create this stable for his family."

One of Kevin's most attractive features was his inability to brag about his skills. He began to have confidence in Maggie's statement that believing is belonging. He even started to believe in himself. He wanted to use all of his God-given skills for the common good. It was as if the sky opened up, and a proclamation fell directly on him with the words from on high, "It's all grace." Surprisingly, the voice was that of Maggie.

Sam and Kevin disassembled the stable to store it in the shed until Christmas.

"Sam, do you have any secrets? You know, things you don't tell Mrs. Gallagher?"

"No, not really. Anything I tried to hide in the past, she discovered. Now, it seems more prudent to come clean. Better than her finding out on her own."

"Aren't you afraid she'll be mad or shocked?"

"Yeah, sometimes." Sam put his hand on Kevin's shoulder. "If someone is a true friend, they won't turn away. If they do, then that friendship wasn't worth much in the first place. Better to find out early."

CHAPTER 19

You have made us for yourself, O Lord,
and our heart is restless until it rests in You.

—*Saint Augustine of Hippo*

K evin swept the tiles of the prayer garden, turned to Maggie, and said, "I need to tell you something serious."

She had been watching him from the corner of her eye instead of studying. "What is it?"

He brushed the same tiles over and over as he chose his words. "This thing I have to tell you…it's sort of…I mean kind of…"

"Kevin, just tell me."

Oh man, now I've done it!

He kept sweeping. "I have a bit of a checkered past." His voice sounded nervous.

"I don't understand."

He wasn't sure how to begin, so he just went for it. "I used to hang out with a gang, and we did a lot of stupid stuff."

"A gang? What do you mean? Like Hell's Angels? What kind of stupid stuff?"

"No, nothing like Hell's Angels. You know, stuff like damaging mailboxes or wrapping houses in toilet paper. I feel bad and wish I had never done any of it. I realize now how wrong I was."

"Kevin, those are pranks, and it's crummy that you messed up mailboxes, but I wouldn't call that a checkered past."

"How about if I said I used to shoplift or break into homes and steal stuff?" He stopped sweeping, closed his eyes, and held his breath.

"Are you kidding? That's not funny."

"I wish I was, Maggie. It's the reason I work here." He lowered his head. "The sheriff sent me here for community service."

She was quiet for a moment. "Well, you're in the right place. Go to Confession. It's obvious you're sorry."

"No, I can't."

"What? Why not?"

"The priests will think less of me."

"Well, I know, and I don't. I think more of you. It's not easy to admit when you're wrong. Besides, you only go to one priest, and he's not allowed to share your confession with anyone, not even another priest."

"How can God ever forgive me for the things I've done?"

"Do you think your sins are so huge that they outdo the mercy of our good and gracious God? Don't flatter yourself. Even the devil doesn't have that much power."

Kevin started sweeping again. "You don't have to get snippy!"

"Yes, as a friend, I do! I care a lot about you, and…" She went on to tell him how Jesus's heart is moved when we humble ourselves and repent. She told him about the special graces bestowed during Confession to strengthen us against sin.

But most of it was lost on him because his head was buzzing. *She cares about me! No, she cares "a lot" about me!* He wanted to jump up and yell, "Yahoo!" but his thoughts were interrupted.

"Kevin, are you listening?" Maggie let out a huff.

"Uh, no, sorry. I mean, yes, I'm listening." He regained his composure. *She cares about me. A lot!* He breathed a little easier. His past was not an issue. *She likes me for who I am today.*

"I was telling you about Saint Augustine. Do you know about him?"

"Nope."

She continued, "He was an awful teen, and he hung out with a gang too. They got into all sorts of trouble. Augustine tells of a time they stole pears from a farmer, not because they were hungry, but for entertainment. They threw the pears at the farmer's pigs. His mother, Saint Monica, tirelessly prayed for his conversion."

"Throwing pears at pigs. That's not a big deal," Kevin opined.

"No, but the interesting thing is, as he grew older, that incident—stealing the pears for no good reason—stuck with him. He was also promiscuous and fathered an illegitimate child."

"Wow, and this guy is a saint?"

"Yes, and he felt sorrow for his sins, and God was working on him. Rather than wallow in his guilt, he started to look inward and realized his sinfulness was because of a restless nature. This restlessness drew him to God. Then, one day, he was sitting under a fig tree and heard a child say, 'Take and read.' So he opened a Bible, and his eyes fell on a passage in Paul's letter to the Romans that went something like, 'Put on the Lord Jesus Christ, and make no provisions for the desires of the flesh.' That one passage turned his life around."

"So you're saying that I'm restless?"

She smiled at him, and his heart started to pound. "I don't know, are you?"

Kevin leaned on the broom as she picked up her books. "Maggie, do you have to leave?"

"Yes. It's my turn to fix dinner tonight because I'm working tomorrow. Hey, do you want to meet me when I go on my dinner break tomorrow?"

His heart skipped a beat. *She still wants to hang out with me!* "Yes, I'll be there!"

It occurred to him that he had been trying to "fix" his restless spirit for a long time. Knocking over mailboxes and breaking into houses never seemed to fill the void in his heart. Being part of a gang didn't help much, but listening to Maggie's words soothed him.

***

Chuck became more and more annoyed with Kevin. He saw him in the cafeteria, yukking it up with the social outcasts. "So, Kev, why ya hanging out with these deadbeats?"

"Excuse me. Did I hear you correctly?" Kevin slowly rose from his seat as the kids at the table shuffled out of theirs in anticipation of a fight. The cafeteria became quiet. "I think you should apologize to my friends." Kevin clenched his fists.

Jimmy moved in behind Chuck, and Ben stood off to the side.

One of the boys Kevin was defending spoke up, "It's okay; we don't need an apology."

Chuck let out a nervous laugh. "C'mon, everyone, I was kidding around. You know, having a little fun." He turned to Jimmy and Ben. "Let's go."

"What the heck is going on with Kevin?" Jimmy asked Chuck as they left the cafeteria.

"If I had to guess, that Maggie Hartman is getting to him. He's become so soft since he's been working at the church. I need to pay her a little visit."

"Well, how are you gonna do that?"

"I'll figure something out."

***

Chuck entered Caplan's Department Store and spotted Maggie folding T-shirts as she hummed a melody. He sneaked behind a display of sweaters to spy on her, and his imagination took over. *Man, she is gorgeous. I'd love to take her out on a date. I'm sure I'd have a good time!* Maggie moved to a display of scarves and gloves, so he maneuvered his position closer but remained hidden from her until an abrasive voice interrupted his fantasy.

"Just what do you think you're doing?"

He turned to see Beverly glaring at him with her arms folded and tapping one foot on the floor. "Uh, I'm waiting for Maggie to finish so she can help me."

She eyed him suspiciously, and her curt manner continued. "What do you need? I can help you."

"Didn't you hear me? I said I'm waiting for Maggie." His voice increased in volume.

Maggie looked up and immediately stopped humming.

"Is everything all right over there?" Mrs. Gosling, the store manager, left the cash register and joined Beverly.

"Everything's fine!" Chuck's perturbed voice quickly turned serene. "I heard Maggie loves music, and I wanted her to help me pick a record album…uh…for my mom."

"I see," Mrs. Gosling answered with a bit of annoyance in her voice. "Maggie dear, can you help this young man, please? I'll be in my office if you need me."

Maggie started over and saw Beverly giving her hand signals. She was pointing two fingers at her own eyes and then two fingers at the back of Chuck's head. Maggie nodded.

"Hi, I'm Chuck. Remember me? I passed you one day on College Avenue when you were walking with your dog. We had a nice conversation."

Maggie looked down and repositioned a pair of gloves.

"Anyway, I heard you like music."

"Yes, I do, but what does your mom like?"

Chuck was staring into her eyes and not listening. "My mom?"

"Yes, I overheard you say you wanted an album for your mom."

"Oh yeah, that's right. Let me see." He put his finger to his chin. "She likes…I dunno…*The Sound of Music*."

Maggie walked to the music section, flipped through some albums, and pulled out the soundtrack from the movie. "Then she'll love this."

When she handed him the album, he grabbed her hand. "How would you like to go on a date with me? I could show you a much better time than that loser Kevin."

She tried to pull away, but he held on tight. "Let go of me!" she demanded in a loud, anxious voice. "You're hurting my hand!"

Beverly rushed over as he loosened his grip. She snatched the album and bumped Maggie out of the way. "I can ring this up for you." She turned to face Maggie. "Mrs. Gosling wants you in the office."

Maggie didn't move, but nervously rubbed her hand.

Beverly looked her in the eyes. "Now!"

She turned and hurried off.

Chuck sneered at Beverly. "You should mind your own business."

Beverly sharply retorted, "That's just what I did!" Then, in a sweet employee voice, she added, "That will be five dollars and forty-four cents with tax."

Chuck left the store with a purchase he didn't want and was baffled that nothing had gone as planned. He couldn't rely on Kevin anymore, and Maggie would never be interested in him as long as Kevin was around.

I gotta trick Kevin into another burglary and have my dad show up. When churchgoing Maggie finds out Kevin is a bad apple, she'll drop him like a hot potato. If I can't get Kevin back into the gang, I will destroy him. Then Maggie will be mine.

He smiled at his cunning strategy.

CHAPTER 20

I think, if God forgives us, we must forgive ourselves.
Otherwise, it is almost like setting ourselves
as a higher tribunal than Him.

—C. S. Lewis

K evin timidly opened the church's side door and spotted Maggie and Father James in deep conversation.

"Well, Maggie, Jesus tells us to go into our room, shut the door, and pray to the Father. Saint Paul tells us to pray unceasingly. So your question—'Does prayer change God's mind?'—is fair. I don't know that it changes God's mind exactly, but—"

She interrupted, "Then why pray?"

"Prayer is not magic, like rubbing a genie in a bottle and getting what you want. It's an encounter with the living God. It's a relationship that burns like a flame of love."

"Sooooo?"

"Think of prayer like a hurricane lamp. It surrounds the flame of love, your relationship with God, and protects it during the storms of life."

"I know everything happens in God's time, but I'm getting impatient. It's been so long, and God doesn't seem to be listening."

"We know God answers prayers in ways that we don't expect. Don't limit God by telling Him how to work. You continue doing what He asks of you right now. Pray your rosary. The grace you receive protects your flame, like a hurricane lamp. It's clear glass, so others can see how it lights up the room. The grace you receive in prayer is meant for others too. They see the way you live your life, the way you handle adversity, and the way you love. One form of prayer is to live your life so that others will see what it means to be in the right relationship with God. Believe me, when others see your flame, they'll desire it too. Saint Francis of Assisi said we should preach the Gospel at all times and use words when necessary."

"Hmm, I never thought of it that way."

"It's a process. You pray for others in need because you love them. It shows that you truly trust God and believe He's interested in your desire to help. Prayer mystically unites us with others. Jesus said to pray for your enemies. I don't know exactly how it works, but we develop a kind of compassion for those we hold in prayer. We become more like Jesus."

Kevin went to lean against the doorjamb, but missed and knocked into the prayer-card table.

Maggie turned in his direction, and her face lit up. "Kevin, how long have you been here? Long enough to hear my question?"

"Yes." He put his finger to his head. "The answer is that the sum of the square roots of any two sides of an isosceles triangle is equal to the square root of the…something, something, something."

Maggie and Father James laughed, and Kevin was happy he could amuse them since his stomach was churning inside, and he wasn't smiling.

"Kevin, what's wrong? Are you okay?" Maggie asked.

Father James went over and placed his hand on Kevin's shoulder. "What is it, Kevin?"

"Huh, um…" he said, closing his eyes. He couldn't think of how to say it. "Father James, I wonder if you might hear my confession."

Father James and Maggie looked like statues frozen in time. It took a few seconds for Father James to react. "Of course. Let me get my stole."

Maggie took his hand and said, "Kevin, I'll be here by the candles, praying for you." He could tell she was sincere. Father James entered the confessional, and she said, "I might even light one for you. Can I borrow a dime?" That made him smile.

Kevin looked at the confessional with trepidation. He separated the curtain, entered the tiny space, and knelt.

"May God, who has enlightened every heart, help you to know your sins and trust in His mercy. I remind you that our God is loving and merciful, so there is nothing that you could have done to turn Him away from you."

Kevin made the sign of the cross but could not raise his eyes. He looked down at his white-knuckled fist.

"Bless me, Father, for I have sinned. I can't remember how long it's been since my last confession."

"That's okay. I know it's been a while. Take your time. Jesus is here to forgive you."

"Father James, I've done so many…um…so many things that I don't…um…know where to begin…or how God…you know…um…how God will ever forgive me."

"Kevin, do you remember learning about the call of Saint Matthew in religion class?"

"No, Father."

"Matthew was a sinner. He would skim money off the taxes he collected from his people. He stole, lied, and cheated, and yet, Jesus called him to be an apostle. You're here because Jesus has called you. His grace is already pouring out for you. Do not be afraid."

Then it happened. It was as if the dam broke, and Kevin's words flowed freely. Sins buried deep in his soul welled to the surface and spewed as if they were coming from an uncapped fire hydrant, dousing the flames of shame. The tears fell, and he wiped his nose on his sleeve.

As he poured out his heart, long-forgotten transgressions that seemed harmless when committed now begged to be forgiven, and he acknowledged them all, the venial and the mortal. The crimes that had roared in his ears for so long—all the shameful acts—cried out to God for forgiveness. As the words left his lips, a feeling of lightness engulfed him, and a peaceful quiet descended upon the confessional.

Kevin finally lifted his eyes to see the priest's silhouette through the screen.

"Are these all the sins you have to confess?"

"I think so."

"You have made a good confession. The Lord rejoices over one who is humble and possesses true sorrow for his sins. Always remember that Jesus died on the cross for you. Did you get that, Kevin? For you."

Kevin raised his eyes and saw Jesus looking down on him from the small crucifix overhead. He felt something intimate in Christ's gaze that he had never experienced before.

"Our Lord's love is so great that He will not leave you an orphan. The Book of Isaiah tells us, 'Even if a mother forgets her child, I, the Lord, will never forget you.' Jesus formed the church so that you would never have to be alone. He has sent you great consolation in the love of your grandmother."

Kevin remembered when she had sat by his bed all night when he was sick with the flu.

"Your friendship with Maggie is also a gift to be treasured and respected. Never take these gifts for granted."

"I won't, Father James."

"For your penance, I want you to read Psalm 51. It may be Psalm 50 in your grandmother's Bible. It's the one that starts 'Have mercy on me, O God, in your goodness.' You read that tonight before you go to sleep."

"For all I've done, my penance is just reading a psalm?"

"Yes. Reading God's Word should become a new way to navigate life. It's the start of a new life with Christ and all He does for you with the help of His Blessed Mother and all the angels and saints. God offers you the great gift of mercy. He is a forgiving God. Now, you must forgive yourself and all who have harmed you in any way. You'll see how powerful this will be and how free your soul will become. You are a part of the Communion of Saints."

Father James paused, then continued, "A penance helps you change your life. It's not to punish you. It's a sign that you want to convert and avoid anything that hurts your relationship with God. Kevin, it would be good for you to make reparations for the things you've stolen or anyone you've hurt. If there is no practical way to do this, you can always put money into a poor box, help at a soup kitchen, or pray for those you have harmed. Does that seem fair?"

"Yes, it does."

"Saint John Vianney once said, 'The saints did not all begin well, but all ended well.' Now, make a good Act of Contrition."

He started with, "O my God, I am heartily sorry for having offended thee, and I detest..." and trailed off.

"Kevin, are you sorry for your sins?"

"Yes, very much. It's just that I don't remember the Act of Contrition prayer."

"You can say any prayer that tells God you're sorry. How about I teach you a simple prayer called the Jesus Prayer. You can repeat it after me. Lord, Jesus Christ, Son of the Living God, have mercy on me, a sinner."

Kevin repeated the prayer and barely held back another wave of tears as Father James said the words of absolution.

"God, the Father of mercies, through the death and resurrection of His Son, has reconciled the world to Himself and sent the Holy Ghost among us for the forgiveness of sins; through the ministry of the Church, may God give you pardon and peace, and absolve you from all your sins in the name of the Father and of the Son and of the Holy Ghost."

Kevin absorbed the words spoken over him and responded, "Amen."

"The Lord has freed you from your sins. Go in peace."

"Thanks, Father James."

Kevin pulled back the curtain to the confessional and stepped into a new life. Maggie was still kneeling with her rosary beads, and he marveled at her ability to pray. He couldn't explain it, but as much as he would have loved to share this moment with her, he knew this was between Jesus and him. He left the church and took the back roads home to enjoy the peaceful feeling. For the first time in a long time, he felt elated. No, he felt filled. The familiar empty feeling deep down felt not so deep, and he dared to believe it was gone.

Father James softly closed the confessional door and called Maggie's name, but she did not stir from her meditation. He knew her prayers for Kevin helped reconcile him to Jesus and the Church. God had heard her prayers. He looked at this child with tenderness. She had become his spiritual daughter.

"Maggie, it's time to close the church now."

She turned to face him. "You can tell when someone loves you by how they say your name."

"How's that?" He wondered if he had heard her correctly. He cocked his head to one side and waited for her to repeat her comment.

156

Instead, she reflected, "You remember when Jesus rose from the dead and met Mary Magdalene in the garden?"

"Yes."

"There was something special in the way Jesus said her name. That's when she recognized Him. He must have said Mary with such love." Maggie rose and genuflected to the tabernacle. "I think that Jesus calls each of us the same way. We only need to listen."

Once outside, Blaise roused from his usual spot and followed behind her.

Father James stood at the door and watched them walk up the hill. Under his breath, he repeated her name, "Maggie." He had to admit that she was right.

***

Kevin enjoyed a pleasant dinner with his grandmother and said, "Granny, put your feet up. I'll do the dishes."

She smiled and asked, "Kevin, are you all right?"

"Never better."

He finished the dishes and kissed his grandmother on the head. He went over to the shelves, removed the Bible, and said, "I'll put it back in the morning."

"Keep it as long as you like."

After he had left the room, she picked up the phone and dialed a familiar number. "Marge, you're never going to believe what just happened."

Chapter 21

The Eucharist bathes the tortured
soul in light and love.

—Saint Bernadette

The school bus's brakes squeaked as it slowed and stopped at the entrance of Saint Paul's parking lot. The driver was used to making a stop where the big dog sat every day, waiting for Maggie's arrival. She stepped off and waved goodbye.

Kevin saw her walking toward the garden and thought of how much his life had changed since he met her. "Hey, Maggie."

She said nothing but ran up to him, dropped her books, and wrapped her arms around his neck. She almost knocked him over with enthusiasm.

"Whoa!" He quickly looked around to see if any eyes were on them. "What was that for?"

She backed away and looked at him. "Kevin, I'm so excited for you! When you come to Mass on Sunday, you can receive Communion."

Kevin bent down to pick up the broom he'd dropped, but did not meet her eyes.

"What's wrong?"

"I dunno, Maggie. I'm not sure I believe in Communion."

"Huh? What do you mean?"

Father James came out of the church. "Hello, kids."

"Hi, Father James."

Phew, lucky for me, he didn't come out a minute earlier!

Father James could tell something was up. "Okay, what is going on?"

Kevin leaned on the wall of the garden.

"It's okay, Kevin. Tell him what you just told me."

She took the broom from him, and he felt her give his hand a comforting squeeze.

Father James leaned on the wall, and Maggie did the same.

Kevin cleared his throat. "Maggie said, once a person is free of mortal sin, it's okay to go to Communion."

"Yes, she's correct. Once one restores their relationship with the Lord through the sacrament of Confession, they can participate in Holy Communion. The Eucharist is the gift of Jesus's Body and Blood. It provides grace to stay spiritually strong and healthy for anything life throws at you."

"But what if I don't believe it?"

"What if you don't believe what?"

"What if I don't believe it's Jesus's Body? I'm sorry, Father James, but that seems a little far-fetched to me."

"Yes, it is a mystery. Have you ever read the Gospel of John, chapter 6?"

"I'm pretty sure I haven't."

"This is the chapter where Jesus tells the people that He is the Living Bread that came down from heaven. Anyone who eats this bread will live forever, and the bread that He gives for the life of the world is His flesh."

Kevin looked skeptical. "I don't believe that's what Jesus meant. Isn't the bread just a symbol? I don't see how we can eat his flesh."

"Well, there are many who think the same as you."

Kevin felt relieved. *Good, I'm not alone!*

"We see in the Gospel of John chapter 6, verse sixty-six that many of Jesus's followers turned away from Him because it was too difficult to believe. Jesus didn't stop them and say, 'Hey, wait, don't go. I was speaking symbolically.' No. Jesus said what He meant and meant what He said."

"Well, how do you know for sure?"

"The Greek translation of the verb Jesus used for the word *eat* means to gnaw upon or chew. Jesus was deliberate and graphic with the words He chose. He said you must gnaw upon or chew His flesh. He demands we express our faith that when we consume the host, the Eucharist, we believe that it has truly become His life-giving flesh."

Kevin scratched his head, and Father James smiled.

"Why don't you read John, chapter 6, this week? Ask the Lord to help your unbelief."

With a smile, Maggie handed Kevin the broom and said, "Sweep the dust bunnies from your mind and expect the unexpected!"

***

A few days later, Kevin was cleaning the gooey dust from the sills of the stained-glass windows. Father James entered and said, "Hi, Kevin. That looks like a tedious job, but it sure brightens up the window."

"I hope so." He kept scrubbing. "I've been reading John 6. What is the manna Jesus talks about?"

Father James sat down in the pew next to the ladder. "In the Old Testament, in the Book of Exodus, the Israelites were in the desert after they fled Egypt. They complained to Moses because they had no food. God sent manna every day so that the Israelites had something to eat. In the Psalms, it was called 'bread from heaven.'"

Kevin interjected, "So the manna kept them alive."

"Yes, and think about this. Jesus feeds five thousand by multiplying five loaves and two fish so the people would not collapse on their way home. This miracle in the New Testament keeps them alive, like the manna in the Old Testament, and both foreshadow the Eucharist. These miracles kept the people physically alive, while the Eucharist, the true bread from heaven, keeps us spiritually alive."

Father James got up to leave. "I see the last stained-glass window for you to clean shows Jesus at the Last Supper, when He instituted the Eucharist. Did you know that, long ago, uneducated people learned Bible stories by studying stained-glass windows?"

"No, I didn't."

"Food for thought as you scrub the last window."

***

On Sunday, Kevin and his grandmother sat up front. Sitting so close to Maggie preoccupied his mind, making it hard for him to focus. The first words that caught his attention were from Father Brendan's sermon.

> Today's readings are all about conversion. Saint Paul's conversion shows how God set him apart to preach the faith he once tried to destroy. His transformation happened because he opened his heart to the Lord. The Gospel story of Martha and Mary tells us that Mary sat at the feet of Jesus. Martha complained about her sister's unwillingness to help her serve. What did Jesus say? "Mary has chosen the better part, and it will not be taken from her." Mary had opened her heart to the Lord.

Father Brendan leaned over the podium to emphasize his point. "Have you chosen the better part? Have you opened your heart to the Lord?"

The congregation squirmed.

"If so, some will be happy about the change in you, but sometimes you will meet resistance from family or friends. They liked you better when you were not so good, generous, or prayerful."

Kevin immediately thought about Chuck and the gang. *You got that right!*

"Your spiritual awakening makes them uncomfortable because they see where they are lacking. But this is how we achieve sainthood, by allowing the Lord into our hearts."

During the Consecration, Kevin realized that Jesus had been calling him for a long time. His restlessness was similar to that of Saint Augustine until the saint chose the better path. Jesus was inviting Kevin to do the same.

The congregation recited, "Lamb of God, You take away the sins of the world, have mercy on us."

Everyone knelt, and Father Brendan held up the host and said, "Behold the Lamb of God. Behold Him, who takes away the sins of the world. Blessed are those called to the supper of the Lamb."

Then everyone replied, "Lord, I am not worthy that You should enter under my roof, but only say the word and my soul shall be healed."

Kevin went forward for Communion.

Father Brendan held up the host and proclaimed, "The Body of Christ."

Kevin answered, "Amen." It meant he believed, and deep down he suddenly knew this was where he belonged.

When Mass was over, Father Brendan announced, "The Mass has ended. Go in peace to love and serve the Lord."

As people left, Kevin approached Mitch. "Mr. Hartman, could I walk Maggie home?"

"Sure." Mitch put his arm around Kevin's grandmother. "How about you and your grandmother join us for lunch?"

Fran replied, "That sounds wonderful. I'll help you prepare the meal."

As they drove up the hill, she shared her excitement with Mitch. "Father's sermon was perfect for Kevin. I've seen such a change in him since he started working at the church, but I believe Maggie has had a role in his conversion."

Mitch smiled. "Yep, that sounds like Maggie."

***

Maggie and Kevin took their time walking home. He picked up a stick and threw it for Blaise. Maggie bent down to pick a wildflower, and when she stood up, their eyes met, and Kevin moved in closer. Maggie's lip quivered, and he thought his heart might burst. He placed his hand under her chin and leaned in for a kiss just as Blaise moved between them with a stick in his mouth. It disrupted the moment, but Kevin didn't take his eyes off Maggie.

"I have something for you." He reached into his pocket and pulled out a stone.

She looked at it with a wrinkled brow.

Kevin looked down. "Oops!" He turned the stone over. It had a ladybug painted on it. "I saw it at the church bazaar. A little girl had a table next to her mom's crafts, and no one noticed her or her painted rocks. I saw she had painted this ladybug, and I thought of you."

"That's so sweet. I love it. I guess the little girl was happy to make a sale."

"Yes, she was so excited, and I felt so bad for her that I bought five more rocks. Do you know anyone who'd like a rock with a pumpkin, or spider, or dog, or..." He couldn't finish his litany of painted rocks because they were laughing so hard.

***

Kevin found himself reading other psalms as well. He was drawn to Psalm 25, as it was a prayer for guidance and help. It lifted his spirits. He joined a Bible study on Saturday mornings, led by Father Brendan, and it gave him a whole new perspective on life. The fact that Maggie was there was all the incentive he needed.

Kevin performed reparations for crimes committed by putting money into the poor box for his transgressions against people. He humbled himself and apologized to the girls at school whose homes he had wrapped in toilet paper. He placed money in envelopes and left them in damaged mailboxes or inside screen doors of burgled homes, and he accompanied Maggie and Mitch to serve at a soup kitchen in Baltimore.

Mitch kept a close eye on Kevin by inviting him for weekend dinners and outings. He grew fond of the teen and found him to be a quick learner and an impressive apprentice at carpentry. He could tell Maggie and Kevin had become good friends and enjoyed seeing how they playfully teased each other. Their young love made him homesick for Len. He knew Kevin respected Maggie's promise about dating and could tell he was content to be with her under any circumstance. That was just how he had felt about Len.

CHAPTER 22

O my God, let me remember with gratitude,
and confess to Thee Thy mercies toward me.

—Saint Augustine of Hippo

K evin graduated from high school, and his grandmother threw a party. The guest list was small. The Gallaghers and Mitch presented him with tools and a carrying case.

Maggie gave him a sterling-silver monogrammed key chain attached to a Saint Christopher medal. She explained, "Saint Christopher will protect you when you travel home to see me." She giggled. "I mean us...all of us...that is." She blushed

He smiled, and Maggie added, "When I get my license this summer, I'll be able to come and see you at college."

Mitch quickly added, "Okay, let's not get ahead of ourselves."

Father Brendan said, "Kevin, I know you'll be busy with your studies, but we hope you'll come by and visit us whenever you are home for the holidays."

"I'm counting on it!" Sam gave Kevin a playful slap on the back.

Father Brendan continued, "Your paycheck was minimum wage, so here is a bonus to thank you for all the extra help you gave us." He handed him an envelope. "We will also offer a Mass for your intentions on the Feast of Saint Aloysius Gonzaga on June 21. He's the patron saint of youth."

"I don't know what to say." Kevin looked around at his friends, grateful for his blessings. They had taught him to look to the future and not dwell on the past.

Sam chanted, "Speech, speech," and others joined in.

Kevin's face reddened, but only for a few seconds. "I want to thank my grandmother for not giving up on me. Granny, I know you could have turned me out long ago."

Fran smiled from ear to ear.

"Sam, thanks for all that you've taught me. You and Mrs. Gallagher—"

She interrupted him. "Call me Marge."

"Okay, Marge. You and Sam are such a beautiful example of true love." He glanced at Maggie and said, "I hope to find a soulmate one day, like you two have." He lost his train of thought. "Um, Father Brendan and Father James, thanks for taking a chance on me. I wouldn't be on the right path today if you hadn't allowed me to work at the church. Mr. Hartman, you've been watching me closely because of my friendship with Maggie. I don't blame you." Kevin grinned, and everyone smiled. "Thanks for all your advice and the time you spent teaching me carpentry skills. Maggie, you are the brightest, most humble, and most spiritual person I've ever known. Thank you for being my friend. Thank you for teaching me what is truly important in life."

They clapped as Fran and Marge wiped tears from their eyes.

"Well," exclaimed Father Brendan, "are we going to slice this wonderful cake or just drool over it all evening?"

CHAPTER 23

Be engaged so that whenever the devil calls,
he may find you occupied.

—*Saint Jerome*

M aggie placed a sleeveless tie-died sweatshirt on the counter for Mrs. Gosling to ring up.

"You know, Beverly purchased the same sweatshirt yesterday."

"Yes, I know."

Mrs. Gosling handed Maggie her change. " I suggest you both write your names on your sweatshirts."

She called across the store. "Beverly, you're doing a great job on the window display. Maggie, I need you to do something artsy here inside the jewelry counter. Ladies, I'll be in the office if you need me."

A few minutes later, Beverly ran over to where Maggie was busy with the necklaces. "Uh-oh," she said, "it's him again."

Maggie turned around to see Chuck Wilson come into the store.

"Quick!" Beverly advised. "You go to the office and get Mrs. Gosling."

Chuck arrogantly strolled around the store.

"May I help you, young man?" Mrs. Gosling asked Chuck.

"Uh, yeah. I was looking for Maggie Hartman."

"Are you here to purchase something?"

"Yeah, I was looking for Maggie to help me choose a shirt."

"I can help you do that. What size do you wear?"

"No thanks," Chuck condescendingly replied.

"No?" Mrs. Gosling responded menacingly.

"I just remembered I have to be somewhere. I'll come back another time."

Mrs. Gosling went to the store office. "Maggie dear, who is that boy? I take it you don't want to see him."

"He keeps coming here, and he creeps me out."

"Well, he's gone now. Take your dinner break. I'll help Beverly with customers."

***

Kevin was driving down Main Street and saw Chuck high-tailing it out of the store. "What the heck!" He parked the car and found Maggie on the bench at their usual meeting place.

"Was that Chuck Wilson I saw leaving the store? Is he bothering you? Do you like him?" He handed her a hamburger and soda he had picked up from the Dairy Ranch.

Her hands shook as she unwrapped the burger. "He makes me uncomfortable."

"Maggie, that's called intuition."

"Tell me why."

"It's a long story, but you should avoid him and his friends. He's the leader of the gang I told you about."

Kevin confirmed her feelings, but she was conflicted. She believed everyone deserved a chance to prove themselves. "Is he going away to college?" Maggie asked.

"Yes, but he'll be here all summer."

"Well, we should pray for him."

"Pray for him!" he said in disbelief. "Why on earth would I want to pray for him? If he were drowning, I'd throw him a glass of water."

"You changed, and he can too. Maybe you're the one who can help him." Maggie continued, "Jesus said if your enemies are hungry, feed them; thirsty, give them a drink. When you do this, you heap burning coals on their heads."

Kevin said, "I like the heaping coals part."

Maggie slapped his arm playfully. "Let's talk about something else. Did you hear about the big storm that's coming?"

"Hurricane Agnes? I heard it hit the Florida Panhandle today, and it could be here by Wednesday."

"I've never seen a hurricane before. I wonder what it will be like?"

"It's been pretty destructive already. Maggie, I have something to do now." Kevin took her hand. "Are you gonna be okay?"

"Yes."

"I'll see you tomorrow."

***

"Hello, Sheriff Wilson, is Chuck home?"

He eyed Kevin suspiciously. "Chuck, someone's here to see you," he said over his shoulder without taking his eyes off Kevin.

Chuck walked down the stairs and slipped off the bottom step when he saw Kevin.

His father put out a hand to steady him. "You okay, son?"

"Sure, Dad." Then he said to Kevin, "Can I help you?"

"You and I need to talk."

"Dad, I'll be back in a minute."

The sheriff shrugged and went back to watching a ball game on TV.

"What the hell are you doing coming to my house?"

"Stay away from Maggie."

"Or you'll do what?" he asked sarcastically.

"Listen, Chuck, she's a good girl, and I don't want you hanging around her."

"Afraid I'll steal your girlfriend?"

"She's not my girlfriend; she's my friend."

Chuck stepped back to take a good look at Kevin. "You know what, Kev? I believe you. I'll leave her alone if you do something for me."

"Chuck, I'm done. No more break-ins. I've found something much better, and I would advise you and the guys to do the same."

"I just need help with one more thing, and then I'll leave Maggie and you alone."

"Forget it."

"No, listen. It's not stealing. I need help recovering something."

Kevin folded his arms across his chest. "Like what?"

"I borrowed my dad's autographed Brooks Robinson baseball. We were playing baseball in Ben's yard, and that pain in the ass, Jimmy, hit it over the fence and broke a neighbor's basement window. The old biddy that lives there said she wouldn't return the ball until we fix it."

"So fix it."

"I don't have the money, and you're so good at fixing things. I need you to do it."

"If I do, then you'll leave Maggie alone?"

"I promise."

"Okay, I'll leave work early tomorrow and fix it for her. What's the address?"

170

Chuck went into his house and wrote down the address and his phone number.

Kevin said, "Let her know I'm coming."

"I will. Call me when you go over so we can meet you there. Thanks, man, I appreciate your help."

"Yeah, whatever. You just better keep your end of the bargain."

As soon as Kevin left, Chuck went in to call Ben.

The sheriff asked, "Why did Kevin Jackson need to speak to you?"

"It's nothing, Dad. We aren't friends or anything. He overheard me talking to the guys about car detailing and wanted to know a good place to take his car, so I wrote down the address."

The sheriff returned to the den to watch the Yankees smear the Orioles.

Chuck dialed Ben's number. "We've got him."

"We've got who?"

"Kevin, you idiot. He's going to your neighbor's house on Tuesday afternoon to fix the window. All we have to do is get *her* out of the house and *Kevin* in. Think of some way to lure her out of the house."

"Like how?"

"I don't know. Think of something like 'Old biddy, can you tell me what kind of flower this is in your garden?'" Chuck offered sarcastically. "Then, when she returns to her house and finds Kevin, we'll run in to help her. You steal something of value and then plant it on Kevin. I'll get my dad to show up, and BAM! We've got him!"

"I dunno, Chuck, that seems complicated. How will we know when he goes over?"

"He's supposed to call me first."

Chuck was quite pleased with his scheme and rubbed his hands together with satisfaction. *Soon, Kevin will be out of the picture.*

***

Kevin drove straight to the "old biddy's" house and parked down the street so there was no chance that Ben would see his car. He walked around back and found the broken window. He measured it and went the first thing Tuesday morning to the hardware store and had a piece of glass cut to his measurements.

When he returned to fix the window, he approached the home, pulled a letter from her mailbox, and read the name on the envelope. He knocked on the door.

"Mrs. Hooper, I am here to repair the broken window."

"Oh, I thought Ben was going to have that done."

"Yes, he asked me to fix it for you."

"Well, wonderful, please come in."

"Oh no, ma'am, I can do it all from outside. I just wanted you to know I'm here."

Kevin removed the cardboard cover she had placed on the window, pulled the rest of the broken glass out, and scraped the old putty off. He fit the new glass into the window casement, resealed it with fresh putty, and then stood back and admired his work. He knocked on the door to tell Mrs. Hooper he had finished the job.

She went around the side of her house to look at the window. "Well, thank you so much, son. You did an excellent job. I'm so happy you came today. That big storm is coming. I would have a lot of water in my basement."

"You are welcome, Mrs. Hooper. Ben said he would be over to paint the putty to match the other window when it dries in a day or two. He asked if I could pick up the baseball for him."

"Yes, of course. Let me get it for you."

She handed Kevin the autographed baseball and a bottle of soda. "You look thirsty."

"Thank you, ma'am."

He smiled to himself as he got in his car and drove away. He had done everything Chuck asked of him, but on his own terms. He had fixed the window and retrieved the baseball. He didn't know what Chuck had in mind, but he was sure it wasn't good. He headed home for lunch and to make the phone call.

"Hey, Chuck, it's me, Kevin."

"Hi, Kevin, you ready to go fix the window?"

"Nope."

"What do you mean? I thought we had a deal."

"We did. I fixed the window, and I have your dad's baseball."

"You what? How?"

"It doesn't matter how. Keep your end of the bargain and leave Maggie alone. My granny took a picture of me holding the baseball. I held it close to the camera, so the autograph was in focus. I'll give you the ball, but if you bother Maggie again, I'll show your dad the photo. Got it?"

Chuck was furious, but he didn't want Kevin to know.

"Mrs. Hooper can corroborate my story. By the way, she's a sweet lady."

Chuck had to hold his anger in check. "Sure, Kev, I understand. It's okay. I meant it. I won't bother Maggie anymore. You didn't have to go to all that trouble."

"Well, maybe not. I just needed some insurance. I'll have the baseball with me at the church this afternoon, and you can pick it up there. I'll be inside if it is raining."

Chuck slammed the phone down, then picked it up to call Ben and relay the story.

"Now, what'll we do?" Ben asked.

"You go and get the baseball from Kevin."

"Why me? You should send Jimmy. He's the one who started this whole thing."

"Jimmy's a hothead, and I can't trust him to do anything without throwing a punch. I need you to go. End of discussion. I'll be at the Dairy Ranch at four o'clock. Bring the ball." Then he slammed the phone down.

Ben was stumped with this recent turn of events, but he had no choice. He'd rather grovel to Kevin than displease Chuck.

***

Ben showed up at Saint Paul's in the afternoon and climbed the steps to the church. The day was overcast, just like his mood. He was anxious and didn't know if his hands were moist from nerves or the intermittent rain. He entered the church and spotted Kevin and a priest fixing the hinge on the door to a confessional. Ben cleared his throat to make his presence known. When they looked up, Ben thought about leaving, but he froze.

Father James spoke up, "May I help you, son?"

"Father James, I think Ben's here to see me. Is that right, Ben?"

"Yes," he answered, but his voice broke, and he cleared his throat again.

"I have things to do in the sacristy. I'll leave you two alone."

"So Chuck sent you to pick up the baseball." It was a statement, not a question.

"Yeah, well, he had something to do."

"Save it, Ben. I know Chuck and how he uses people. I used to be in your shoes and would do anything he asked just for fun or fame, or what I thought was fame. But I've wised up because of the people God has placed in my life to show me there is a better way to live."

"You mean like the priest?" he said sarcastically.

"His name is Father James, and yes, like him and others. They helped me understand that my worth comes from God, who sent His Son into the world to die on the cross for me and you, Chuck and Jimmy. You should start living like you believe that instead of doing everything Chuck tells you."

Ben swallowed hard. He wanted to laugh or cry, but wasn't sure which. "I'm just here to pick up the baseball. I don't need a lecture from you. I know the things you've done, and you're no saint."

Kevin said, "Well, the saints didn't all start well, but they all ended well."

For a moment, he had Ben's attention, so he persisted, "I've changed, and you can too. All you need is to trust that God has a better plan for your life."

Ben wondered what to say next. He could see the change in Kevin and admired his conviction to be a better person. "I wouldn't know where to begin," he admitted.

Kevin's voice changed from adversarial to reassuring. "Well, you're in a church, and there's a priest in the next room. Why not go to Confession? That's when my conversion began. It started before that, but I knew I could turn my life around after I confessed my sins. I had a lot to confess." Kevin chuckled. "It felt great to let Jesus into my life." Kevin put his hand on Ben's shoulder. "Why not give it a try?"

The two stood under the crucifix. There was an uncomfortable silence for Ben, who finally said, "Are you gonna give me the baseball or not?"

Kevin dropped his head and shoulders with a sigh, walked over to his duffel bag, retrieved the baseball, and held it until Ben looked him in the eyes.

"Think about what I said. It took me a while before I came, but don't wait too long." Kevin let go of the baseball. "If you keep letting Chuck rule your life, I guarantee it will not end well."

Kevin had no idea how prophetic those words would become.

CHAPTER 24

*Act as if every day were the last of your life, and
each action the last you perform.*

—Saint Alphonsus Liguori

B en strolled into the Dairy Ranch with a smile and tossed
the ball to Chuck, who was sitting alone at a table.

"So how'd it go? Did he give you any trouble?"

"Nope, just handed it over like he said he would." Ben
attempted to sound gutsy.

"He didn't say anything? That's hard to believe."

Ben started to sweat. He hated it when Chuck could see
through him.

"What really happened?"

"Okay, so he tried to talk me out of hanging out with you
and Jimmy." Then Ben told him the whole conversation.

"So Kevin has confessed all his crimes?"

"Yep."

"Let me get this straight. Kevin told this priest—"

"Father James," Ben interrupted.

"I don't care what the priest's name is, you baboon. Do you
know what this means?"

Ben shook his head.

"The priest knows everything and can rat us out."

"I don't think that will happen."

"Oh, you don't!" Chuck sneered. "And why not?"

"A priest isn't allowed to tell anything from a confession. I saw a movie where the priest went to jail rather than tell."

"That's just in the movies, you dumb jerk!" Chuck pounded his fist on the table. When the waitress came over, Chuck said, "I'm outta here!" He nearly knocked her over as he brushed past her.

She called after him, "Who will pay the bill?"

Ben apologized and nervously pulled a dollar from his pocket for the half-finished milkshake. He caught up with Chuck in the parking lot.

"You get Jimmy and meet me here at five o'clock tomorrow. You better not be late! I'm tired of your pansy-pants excuses. I can't take a chance on Kevin keeping his mouth shut. The way he's acting, he might tell the whole world. We're gonna scare him into silence!"

***

The next day was June 21, the Feast of Saint Aloysius Gonzaga, and the day the Mass was offered for Kevin as part of the graduation gift from the priests. Kevin and Maggie left the church that morning, and he said, "You know, having a Mass said for me would've been the last thing I'd have cared about a year ago. It's just one of the blessings that have come into my life since I met you."

Maggie smiled, and Kevin took her hand.

"Sam will not be in today, and Father Brendan asked me to prepare the church for the storm. I'm going home first to help Granny with our house."

"What will you have to do at church?"

"I'm not sure about everything, but I know we'll have to fill sandbags and place them in front of all the basement doors on the grounds."

"I'll come by after work and help."

Kevin pulled her hand, swung her around, and kissed her lips. It was a quick, smooth gesture that took them both by surprise.

"Great!" he said, then ran to his car with the biggest grin.

Wait! Did he just kiss me? Yes, that was definitely a kiss!

A smile erupted on her face as she opened her umbrella and practically danced down Main Street.

Kevin turned the car radio way up and sang at the top of his lungs. He thought his heart might burst with joy. When he got home, he put the trash cans, grill, and lawn furniture in the basement and moved all the potted plants against the wall of the screened-in porch.

Granny's hand shook when she touched his arm. "Don't stay late at church. The news is saying this hurricane is going to be just awful."

"Don't worry." He hugged her. "I'll be home early."

***

The rain grew intense, and the awning over Caplan's Department Store offered little protection. Mrs. Gosling called to the girls, "Please bring the sidewalk display inside and close the awning."

They unlocked the wheels and pulled the display into the store. Maggie's blouse got caught on a hook, and two buttons popped off.

"Oh darn! That wasn't smart."

She pulled her tie-died sleeveless sweatshirt from her backpack, pulled it over her blouse, and checked that her ladybug pin was still attached to her shirt collar.

The store closed early. "You girls, get home now. The storm is coming."

Maggie ran to the church and found Father James and Kevin filling the last bag with sand. "I got here just in time," she joked.

"We've been discussing chapter 18 in the Gospel of Matthew as we worked," Father James explained. "Kevin was asking about forgiveness of enemies."

"Is this the chapter where Peter asks Jesus if he had to forgive someone seven times?"

"How did you know that?" Kevin sounded impressed.

Father James said, "Yes, Peter is asking at what point he can say, 'Hey, enough is enough!' We feel that way sometimes. When Jesus answers, 'Seventy-seven times,' He's not giving Peter a definitive number of times he has to forgive. His answer signifies something endless. We never stop forgiving, and I know that can be hard. It feels impossible in some situations. Jesus says to forgive from your heart, but that does not mean the wound will magically heal. No, you may ache for a long time. It means that your forgiveness is an honest act of the will, knowing that Jesus is there to back you up."

Maggie added, "I remember reading a story about Corrie ten Boom, who was a prisoner in a Nazi concentration camp during World War II. After her release, she met a Nazi soldier who had mistreated her. He asked her for forgiveness. She said, 'I cannot forgive you, but Christ who lives in me *can* forgive you.'"

Father James said, "That's a great example of forgiveness. Corrie was honest about her feelings but made an act of the will to forgive."

Kevin said, "I dunno. It seems like you're saying what a person did is okay if you forgive."

"It might seem that way, but it helps your relationship with God."

"How do you figure?" he asked.

"Think of it this way. Every time you say the Our Father, you repeat, 'Forgive us our trespasses as we forgive those who trespass against us.' You need to think about how you want God to forgive you for your sins, and then you need to apply that same mercy to those who have hurt you."

"But, Father, some things people do are bad, and you gotta get back at the person to make sure they never do it again."

Father James advised, "Saint Paul tells us, 'Never avenge ourselves, but leave it to the wrath of God.' In another Scripture passage, we hear, 'Vengeance is mine, says the Lord.' It's okay, and prudent, to avoid contact with someone who has hurt you. Be smart about protecting yourself from danger, and ask God to help you forgive."

Kevin shook his head.

Father James continued, "It is often our pride that causes us to cling to anger. The person who suffers most is the one who won't forgive. You can expend a lot of passion being angry and resentful, instead of using that energy for something good. It's better to let go of your pride and let God heal your wounds."

Just then, the wind howled, and they heard a loud crash. Kevin opened the door and looked outside. "Hey, a huge limb from the oak tree just crashed in the garden. I better move it."

"Kevin, leave it for now. Can you drive Maggie home? The rain is starting to pick up. I'll finish up in here."

***

Ben and Jimmy met Chuck at the Dairy Ranch, then they drove together to the church. Chuck parked his car in the corner of the lot and gave Ben instructions, "You stay here, but follow in my car when we leave."

"Why can't we stay together?"

"Jimmy and I'll go with Kevin, and you can follow us so we'll have a ride home."

"But where are we going?"

"We're just gonna have a little fun with Kevin, and I'll need you to bring the rope from the back seat when we reach our destination."

"Why do we need a rope?"

"Ben, shut up with your questions, and just do what I say."

***

Maggie and Kevin emerged from the church, huddled under an umbrella. His arm was around her waist, so he lifted her to avoid a puddle. She giggled, and his heart fluttered as she put her arm around him and squeezed him closer. In tandem, they ran to his car and didn't notice they had company until they bumped into Chuck and Jimmy leaning against Kevin's car.

Kevin's smile faded. "Why are you guys standing out in the rain?"

"Waiting for you," replied Jimmy in one of his petulant tones. "We're taking you for a little ride."

"No, you're not." Kevin's tone was abrasive, and he pushed Jimmy out of the way. "I've got to get Maggie home. Her uncle's expecting her."

"This won't take long."

Chuck grabbed the umbrella, and Kevin let go of Maggie to go after Chuck. He had him by the collar when he heard Maggie scream.

Jimmy had pulled Maggie into the back seat and slammed and locked the door. The thunder and rain added to the confusion as Kevin let go of Chuck to help Maggie. He got into the driver's seat and reached into the back to grab Jimmy.

Chuck jumped into the passenger seat and commanded through gritted teeth, "Turn around and drive."

A blunt object jabbed Kevin's rib cage. Chuck had pulled a small revolver out of his rain jacket. "What on earth are you thinking, Chuck? You're crazy. Someone's gonna get hurt!"

"Yeah, and it'll be you if you don't drive," Jimmy smugly offered.

"All right, but only when you let Maggie out of the car." Kevin gripped the steering wheel as his voice grew more angry.

Chuck considered the bargain. He hadn't expected Maggie to be part of the plan, but she gave him more leverage. "She stays with us." He cocked the gun and aimed it at Kevin's head.

"I'm not afraid of you guys, and I'll only drive when Maggie gets out."

"Okay, I have an idea." Chuck pointed the gun at Maggie. She screamed and covered her face.

"If you don't want Maggie hurt, you'd better drive."

"Chuck, you're insane! I'll see you behind bars for this!"

Chuck scoffed. "You threatening me?" He laughed and twirled the gun in front of Maggie.

With a smug smile, Jimmy said, "No one's gonna arrest the sheriff's son, you dope. His father lets him get away with everything."

"Okay, okay, I'll drive. Just put the gun down." Kevin's hands shook as he turned the key. The engine engaged, and he drove to the parking lot's exit.

Chuck said, "Turn left." He saw that Ben was following in his car and smiled to himself. *My plan to intimidate Kevin with the gun is working.* The sight of Maggie shivering in the back seat somehow excited him.

Father James emerged from the church and locked the door. He saw Kevin's car make a left out of the parking lot. He thought it odd that another car followed them out the exit since Father Brendan had canceled all church activities. He noticed the small black sheriff's star on the bumper and the local high school's sticker on the back window. Right then, a flash of lightning streaked across the sky, so James turned his attention to the storm, decided not to open his umbrella, and hurried to the rectory.

Kevin drove slowly. "Where are we going?" He tried to catch Maggie's eye in the mirror, but she had moved too far to the right.

They passed her house, but her uncle's car was not in the driveway. As they traveled College Avenue, also called Seven Hills because of the repeated hills and valleys, the lower sections began to fill with water. Kevin slowed down and stopped.

"We'd better turn around. The water could be deep and stall the car."

My past is back to haunt me, and now Maggie is in danger. He looked in the rearview mirror again, but only saw Jimmy leering at her.

Chuck said, "Keep driving." At the end of the road, Chuck delivered the next instruction, "Turn left and take it to the end."

Bonnie Branch Road ended, and Chuck instructed Kevin to turn right and pull off the road. This area was familiar to Kevin since they had spent many nights speeding up and down these roads, smashing mailboxes. An activity he had confessed and sorely regretted.

Chuck said, "Pull off the road and park by those trees."

184

"The car could get stuck in the mud. Look at the river; it's rising!"

"Not my problem."

Ben pulled in but parked close to the road.

Jimmy pulled Maggie from the back seat. Kevin got out with his fists clenched. Chuck came around behind Maggie, flashed his gun, and eyed Kevin.

"Turn around and walk toward the trees."

Ben joined them with the rope in his hand. "Tie his hands behind his back," Chuck ordered, and Ben nervously obeyed.

Kevin had his eyes on Maggie as he protested, "C'mon, guys, what's going on?"

"Shut up, Kevin; you'll know soon enough," advised Jimmy as his fist delivered a blow to Kevin's jaw.

Kevin's balance was off since Ben had tied his hands, and he fell over.

Maggie ran to help Kevin, but Chuck dragged her away.

Jimmy taunted and shouted at Kevin as wind and rain raged around them. "What did you tell the priest?"

"What do you mean, what did I tell the priest?" Kevin groaned as he lay on the ground. "What are you talking about?"

"In confession, Ben said you told the priest your sins."

"Yeah, that's right." He spit out blood as he spoke.

"Now we'll all go down!" Jimmy was seething.

"My confession is for me. It has nothing to do with you guys!"

"How can we believe you?" Jimmy shrieked, and the vein on his forehead bulged. "Ever since you hooked up with Maggie, we can't count on you anymore." He ran to Chuck's car and got the baseball bat.

"You, you son of a—" Kevin didn't finish as he looked over at Maggie. "Leave Maggie alone." *Lord God, please help me get up from the ground to help her.*

Maggie's tears mingled with the rain as she recited a prayer, "Saint Michael the Archangel, defend us in battle. Be our protection against the wickedness and snares of the devil—"

Ben lifted Kevin by his arms and said, "Oh gosh! Kevin, I'm so sorry. Get up. Quick." Ben nervously attempted to untie the rope.

Jimmy used this opportunity to thrust the bat hard into Kevin's stomach, which made Kevin drop back to the ground in agony.

Ben yelled, "Hey, you're being way too rough. You could hurt someone with that bat."

"Shut up, Ben. Chuck and I will handle this."

"This is a real-fair fight, you coward." Kevin could barely choke the words out. "You have a bat, and my hands are tied. You'd better not lay a finger on Maggie."

Chuck smiled and said, "Don't worry. I'm gonna take good care of her."

Jimmy menacingly swung the bat over his head, repeating, "Why did you confess to the priest? Go ahead, Ben, untie him. I am not afraid to fight him."

As Ben unloosed the binding, Maggie freed her arm from Chuck and ran toward Jimmy. "Don't you know anything about your Catholic faith? A priest can never reveal anything told to him in the confessional."

Jimmy took his eyes off Kevin, who sprang to his feet and lunged toward him, knocking him to the ground.

Ben threw up his arms and yelled, "Hey, this is getting way out of hand!"

Chuck yelled, "Ben, help Jimmy!"

But Ben stood there, frozen.

"Ben, did you hear me?"

But Ben covered his ears and closed his eyes as Kevin pummeled Jimmy's face with his fists. Then, his adrenaline

186

pulsing, Kevin bolted toward Chuck and tackled him. He punched him repeatedly while yelling, "Maggie, run! Get out of here!"

Maggie turned in a circle with a confused look on her face. The wind and rain from the hurricane made it difficult to see anything. The roar of the river was deafening.

Then Jimmy surged through the torrential downpour as he rushed toward them, his bloodied face violent and his eyes fixed on Maggie. He wielded the bat in a circular motion over his head with a wild, hysterical look.

Kevin jumped up just in time to push her out of the way. "Maggie, run to the road."

Jimmy swung the bat.

Kevin ducked to avoid the blow and yelled again, "Maggie, go!"

She started to run as Chuck shook off the attack from Kevin and chased after her.

Kevin ran after Chuck just as Jimmy raised the bat and swung, this time connecting with the side of Kevin's head. His body went limp, and he slumped to the ground.

Jimmy hovered over him, then let go of the bat as if to deny his part in the assault, his rant stifled by the sight of blood that oozed from Kevin's head. The wooden bat splashed in the puddle of rainwater surrounding Kevin's body as it slowly turned red.

The thunderous storm competed with the sounds of Maggie's screams that echoed through the woods.

CHAPTER 25

*The greatest grace God can give someone is to send him a trial
he cannot bear with his own powers and then sustain him
with his grace so he may endure to the end and be saved.*

—*Saint Justin Martyr*

Mitch covered his head with his briefcase and made a dash for the front porch. He unlocked the door, and Baise ran out. He called for Maggie and was surprised she wasn't home. He went to the window and witnessed rain and wind pelting the house, bending trees, and breaking branches. He called the rectory. "Father James, this is Mitch. Maggie isn't home yet. She called me from work and said she was stopping by church on her way home. Is she still there?"

Father James looked at his watch. "She left over an hour ago."

Mitch's stomach churned as he heard a branch hit the roof. He saw Blaise stand up with his chest puffed out and cock his head to one side. He then leaped off the porch, raced into the woods, and was gone.

Oh great! Blaise has jumped into the storm, probably to chase a deer!

"I'm going to walk up College Avenue toward the church and see if somehow she is—"

"She wasn't on foot. She was with Kevin in his car. They left together."

Now Mitch panicked. "I'll look for them in my car." Even though he felt Kevin was honorable and had grown fond of him, his fatherlike instincts kicked in. He called for Blaise, but the dog did not return. "Great, now both are missing."

Father James's car pulled into the driveway. "C'mon, get in. We'll search together."

They drove through Seven Hills, to the end, but stopped at Bonnie Branch Road since the small stream that flowed under the road had swelled, spilled over, and flooded the intersection. The police had set up flares, and a patrol car blocked the road.

Father James called out, "George, how bad is it?"

"It's bad. All the streams are full and flooding the river. Why are you out here anyway?"

Mitch leaned over to yell above the storm, "My daughter's missing. We know she was on College Avenue over an hour ago. I have to find her. You have to help me!"

"You'd better head to higher ground. When you get home, call the station, and they can put out an APB. That's all we can do right now."

"No, you don't understand. She's out here somewhere!"

Father James put his hand on Mitch's shoulder. "Mitch, we'll do what the officer suggests. Thanks, George."

When they reached home, Mitch called the county police and asked if they could be on the lookout for Kevin's car. "It's a…" Then he faltered. He was so distraught that he couldn't remember what make and model Kevin drove.

Father James took the phone, answered the officer's questions, and called the sheriff's office with the same information.

Mitch looked up Frances Jackson's number. "Hi, Fran, this is Mitch. Is Kevin home? No? Has he called to tell you where he is? When you see him, can you have him call me right away?" Mitch repeated his number. "Thanks so much." He placed the phone back on the hook and looked at James. "She's upset. She expected him home hours ago."

Father James looked around the room. "Blaise not back yet?"

"No. He always returns within a few minutes, but not this time."

The lights flickered and went out. Mitch lit some candles, and the two sat on the couch and watched helplessly as the storm enveloped the house, beating against the scenic picture windows.

CHAPTER 26

I know well that the greater and more beautiful the work is,
the more terrible will be the storms that rage against it.

—*Saint Faustina*

C huck attempted to cover Maggie's mouth as her shrill, agonizing screams competed with the roaring storm. She bit his hand, and he released her. She ran to Kevin.

The three boys stood still and held their breath in painful recognition of what had just occurred.

"I didn't mean to hit anyone. I was trying to scare them; that's all."

"You're a fool, Jimmy," Ben shouted above the sound of wind and pouring rain. "Look what you've done! We have to get Maggie outta here. It's not safe!"

"I'll take care of Maggie," Chuck yelled.

Maggie slumped into the blood-drenched puddle next to Kevin's body. She sobbed as she lifted his head onto her lap and rocked back and forth as a low, guttural moan emanated from deep within her throat, her eyes turned upward to heaven.

"Jimmy, get me the rope—"

Chuck was interrupted by a hollow, screeching noise. He looked up to see a gigantic tree, whose roots had loosened from the rain-swollen earth, hurtling toward the crime scene. Jimmy and Ben ran away as Chuck yanked Maggie from Kevin's body. She stared vacantly at the tree, then started screaming and flailing her arms and legs. Chuck dragged her away from Kevin, whose body suffered another blow when the tree plummeted to the ground.

Chuck lifted her to a standing position and loosened his grip. She kicked him in the shin, frantically pushed him aside, and started to run but slipped on the mud-soaked leaves. Chuck grabbed her arm, and they both fell to the ground as Maggie began her prayer again.

"Saint Michael the Archangel, defend us in battle," she cried as the wind and rain whipped around them. She tried to push Chuck off as she finished her prayer, "And do thou, O prince of the Heavenly Host, by the power of God, cast into hell Satan and all the evil spirits who prowl about the world seeking the ruin of souls."

Chuck yelled in her face, "Shut up, wouldja! I'm trying to think!"

He pinned her arms to the muddy ground and wasn't sure what to do next. He had allowed the demons to tighten their grip on his soul, and the splashing rain danced around him as if it were the devil's relentless, torturous applause.

I know she'll never want me now.

He was obsessed with her and realized this was the closest he'd ever get to the beautiful Maggie Hartman. Her frightened eyes were on him, and a part of him wanted to take her into his arms and carry her to safety. But she had witnessed everything, and he could not let her go.

A slow-moving hush came upon them as the wind diminished. An eerie stillness swallowed the storm. The eye of the hurricane hovered over them, giving the impression that an all-knowing God was watching.

Then, three solemn words escaped Maggie's lips in a prayer-like whisper, "I forgive you."

Her utterance was so unexpected that it felt like a slap in the face. Chuck's anger swelled and seethed with regret, not for the situation, but because he could not dominate someone so willing to forgive.

Maggie closed her eyes, and her sudden calmness bewildered him. He was captivated by the beauty of her soul, yet he resented the fact that he had no power over her. The eye of the storm passed, and the howling wind and pelting rain resumed. He let go of her arms, placed his hands around her neck, and tightened his grip.

At that moment, a powerful force jolted his body. A dark creature had come bursting through the dank, rain-ravaged woods, knocking him off Maggie and landing squarely on his chest.

Stunned, Chuck let out a frantic shriek as the animal's snarling mouth exposed teeth that glistened in the rain. The beast's snout was close to his face, and he felt its low, bellicose growl vibrating throughout his body. The animal was oppressive, and its hot, ominous breath was suffocating.

Jimmy found the baseball bat and headed toward Chuck, who was trembling under the weight of Blaise.

Ben pleaded, "Jimmy, put the bat down before someone else gets hurt!"

Maggie scrambled to her feet, disoriented. *How can this be? Blaise?* She saw Jimmy heading in their direction with the murderous bat as Ben followed. She screamed, "Blaise, come here!"

A lightning flash tore across the sky, so close it appeared to touch their heads, and Jimmy and Ben fell to their knees.

"Blaise, please hurry!"

But he wouldn't budge, and the rain slid down the fur, over his snarling muzzle, and dripped onto Chuck's face.

He squealed like a frightened child. "Get this monster off me!"

Jimmy got up, ran toward Blaise, and raised the bat to deliver a fatal blow.

"Blaise! Blaise, come here!" Maggie pleaded, but the wind and rain drowned out her voice.

She looked down and realized she stood on the brink of the Patapsco River. She was frantic. The river was close to overflowing, and even if Blaise were to obey her, there was no place for them to run.

Jimmy brought the bat to his shoulder, as if he were a baseball player ready to hit a home run.

Another flash of lightning struck so close to Maggie that the hairs on her arms stood at attention. The firebolt took the form of a sword, and it split the riverbank, plunging her into the river.

The air was thick with blinding rain as Jimmy swung the bat with all his might. Blaise gave his hostage one last fierce snarl, then sprang into the air after Maggie and disappeared over the embankment. Jimmy just missed Blaise, and the centrifugal force of the bat spun him around so that he delivered the destructive blow to Ben's knee, who crumbled to the ground, cursing and writhing in agony.

Chuck rose to his feet and screamed, "You fool! Now look at what you've done! We gotta get Ben to my car."

"What will we do with Kevin?" asked Jimmy above Ben's agonizing moans and the whipping rain.

"We leave him here. The rising water will wash him away. If not, it will be obvious that the fallen tree killed him. As for us, we were never here."

194

"How will we explain Ben's knee? It's a mess, maybe dislocated or something."

"How do I know, Jimmy?" Chuck shook his head. "We'll make something up, like he was injured when we helped someone in trouble in the storm. That'll be a good excuse for our faces being bloody."

"And Maggie?" asked Jimmy.

"She's toast!" Chuck said with an unfamiliar feeling of remorse in the pit of his stomach. "I don't see how she or her dog can survive…" His thoughts trailed off as he looked at Kevin's lifeless limbs protruding from under the massive tree and then stared for a moment at the place where Maggie had fallen into the river, which swelled more by the minute. "We need to get Ben home. I think he's passed out from the pain."

They picked Ben up and put him in the car.

Chuck felt in his pocket. "Oh no! My father's gun is missing!"

They searched the area, and Chuck found it near the river's edge. He bent down to pick it up and inadvertently pointed it at Jimmy.

"Watch where you point that thing!"

"Don't worry; it's not loaded."

CHAPTER 27

Pray as though everything depended on God.
Work as though everything depended on you.

—*Saint Augustine*

The jagged rocks and boulders scraped and bruised her legs as the river swept Maggie away. Everything happened so fast that all she could do was keep her head up and try not to swallow muddy water.

A buoyant tree trunk came barreling down the river within inches of her head, and she latched on to the protruding branches. It jerked her forward like a skier behind a speedboat. She called for God to help, but her plea was a water-choked gurgle.

The twilight and rain made it difficult to see anything other than shapes, but she couldn't mistake the figure, with ears pinned back and bulging eyes, who was entangled in the branches of the tree to which she clung. The ferocious current had delivered Blaise into her arms.

"Good boy, Blaise, good boy," she desperately gasped. "We'll be all right."

The rapids propelled them along with the debris collected by the turbulent storm. She held on to Blaise's collar as his strong legs paddled helplessly against the foamy water. They bounced and rocked downstream until the branch she was gripping got wedged between two enormous rocks.

She cried, "Thank You, Jesus!"

Maggie used the branch as a foothold, pulled herself onto one of the rocks, and held tight to Blaise's collar. "C'mon, boy." But his paws kept slipping off the wet stone, causing Maggie to lose her footing. They slid back into the water, dislodging the branch, which quickly disappeared downstream as the river devoured them again.

Blaise was a strong swimmer, but the rapids created by this deluge proved too forceful even for his muscular breed. An eddy created by the water swirling around enormous rock formations pulled her under. Her head bounced off the boulders, and she was pulled into the vortex. Blaise was immediately submerged in the watery undertow as well. Somehow, the odd combination of their bodies spit them out of the roaring whirlpool and sent them downstream like rag dolls.

Their next obstacle was Bloede's Dam. The two were whooshed over the precipice and pulled down into furious water. Fortunately, the sheer force of their descent bounced them loose from the undercurrent and back into the brutal waters.

The hurricane loomed above and continued to pump water into the river. The bloated waters overflowed the riverbank and entangled Maggie in cables and ropes. It took a few seconds before she realized the ropes belonged to the swinging bridge, and the weight of the wooden walkway was dragging her down. She desperately clawed at what felt like tentacles pulling her underwater. Pleading for strength, she prayed, "Jesus, please help me! My guardian angel, rescue me."

She thought her lungs would burst as the water rushed over her face, and she descended deeper into the rapids. Then, a feeling of peacefulness enveloped her, and she loosened her grip on the ropes. The chaos dissolved around her, and she gazed upon the most beautiful lady she had ever seen; she was holding a small child in her arms. The child lifted a cross that burst into a blossoming tree. Maggie raised her arms to touch the vision and felt her body rise above the water.

A large tree had sailed down the river, and its trunk slid under the dilapidated bridge. When the branches met the disintegrating wood and ropes, it forced the structure up and lifted Maggie above the rapids. She drew a breath, sputtered, coughed, and inhaled the precious air.

The tree continued to lift her several feet as the bottom of the tree lodged itself against a boulder. Rushing water pushed the top of the tree to a standing position. The ropes suddenly loosened from her body, except for one that tightened around her arm and cut deep into her skin. She dangled like a tattered flag on the battlefield and called out to God for help, but the only name that erupted from her lips was "Mommy!"

She swung around to reach a branch with her free arm and pulled herself up, which released the tension of the rope from her bloodied, injured arm. Her peripheral vision caught sight of Blaise slipping and sliding across what was left of the bridge's wooden walkway as he made it to safety.

"Blaise, go get help," she yelled as the ropes squeaked then snapped, breaking the tension on the tree and catapulting Maggie back into the water that had risen high over the rocky riverbed. The tree that saved her from the bridge fell over and became a life raft as she clung to its branches. Her faithful companion ran through the woods, barking and keeping pace with her.

The river and cold rain were rapidly depleting her strength. She shivered in response as she stretched her arms and legs across the tree to keep from falling through. She raised her head to call out for Blaise, but her voice dissolved into uncontrollable sobs.

Suddenly, the tree jerked to an abrupt halt when its limbs wedged into the riverbank, causing Maggie to lose her grip and fall deep into its branches. The muddy riverbank acted as a sludgy paste that held the limbs steady enough for her to climb out of the rapids and reach the point where the water was only about a foot deep. Blaise waited impatiently, running in circles and coaxing her forward with every woof and whimper.

Blaise, having four legs, could manage easier than Maggie, who trudged through the shallow water on shaky, bleeding legs as she headed for higher ground. She slipped and landed on her hands and knees, her energy spent.

Blaise rushed into the shallow current, grabbed the hood of her sleeveless jacket with his teeth, and pulled until she could crawl higher on the hill. When they reached safety, Maggie toppled over from exhaustion. Blaise crumpled to the ground next to her, as if he were a stuffed animal that had lost its filling, his warm body protecting her from hypothermia. They lay motionless for hours.

***

By morning, the hurricane had passed, and its blustery beating had dwindled to soft rain. Sheriff Wilson rubbed his eyes and got closer to the TV. "This is unbelievable."

"What did ya say, Sheriff?" a deputy asked from his desk.

"Come here and look. That can't possibly be Main Street. It's nothing but a river."

The deputy joined him, and they watched as the local news helicopter showed aerial views of the devastation in Ellicott City and surrounding areas.

The sheriff shook his head. "I've never seen anything like this. From here to Baltimore is a mangled mess of collapsed bridges, damaged buildings, and downed trees. You can't see the roads!"

The deputy turned up the volume to drown out the whirring sound of the generator as the newscast continued:

> *Fire crews and law enforcement are grateful for all those who offered their small boats and played a part in the rescues as they worked through the night. There have been several reported deaths. Police will notify families before they release the names.*

The sheriff walked over to his desk, but did not sit down. He realized that Chuck had been lucky to have made it home safely. He was still angry that his son had been out in the storm.

"Tommy, I'm heading out to see where I can be useful. I'll have my walkie-talkie if you need me."

"Okay, Sheriff."

He got in his cruiser and headed out to the Elkridge Truck Stop to see if they were open, and he hoped they were serving coffee. He made several stops to clear the roads of tree branches, one mangled tricycle, and a USPS mailbox that the storm had dislodged. He called Tommy and instructed him to inform the post office.

The cup of coffee revived him as he sat at the truck stop's bar. He fielded calls coming in on his walkie-talkie and overheard a conversation between two patrons having breakfast.

"Pardon me, but I couldn't help but overhear your conversation. Are you headed to West Virginia? This is not a good time to travel."

"Yes, I know. I'm Dr. McGuire, and this is my nephew, Josh. We're headed there to help the underprivileged. The destruction from Hurricane Agnes means we're needed now more than ever."

"I see." He took a napkin and drew a map. "The storm destroyed several roads, so your trip will have some detours. These are the ones I know, so be careful." He handed them the napkin.

The doctor noticed his hand was shaking. "Sheriff, are you feeling all right?"

"Yes, I'm fine. I think I've had too much caffeine on an empty stomach."

"You better eat something. Try the pancakes; they're delicious. Doctor's orders."

The sheriff answered some more calls, took the doctor's advice, and then left the truck stop to see where he could be helpful.

***

Blaise raised his head at the sound of a siren in the distance and nudged Maggie several times before she showed any signs of life. She sat up slowly and felt sharp pains in her arms and legs. She was cold, her chest and head ached, her mind was fuzzy, and her clothing, caked with wet leaves and mud, clung to her body.

They had slept through the night, and the day drearily arrived through the haze in the sky. Water was rapidly flowing a few feet away, carrying all sorts of debris. She shuddered at the sight.

She saw lights in the distance and slowly rose, carefully placing one foot in front of the other, trudging along with Blaise through the soggy, wooded landscape. She felt dizzy and stumbled from one tree to the next for support. The Baltimore and Ohio railroad overpass at Route 1 was just ahead.

"How on earth did we get here?"

She heard the hum of a generator and realized the lights were radiating from the Elkridge Truck Stop. She cleared the woods and had to lean on damaged cars and fence posts to reach the back parking lot. She was about to walk up onto the deck but noticed the sheriff's car parked in front and quickly dove behind an unattended pickup truck.

The sheriff emerged with a cup of coffee and a walkie-talkie. He faced in the opposite direction of the truck that hid Maggie and Blaise from his view. Blaise let out a low, aggressive growl, and an alarm went off in her head.

She panicked. *What should I do?*

The bed of the truck held a tent. Peeking in, Maggie saw boxes, sheets, pillows, blankets, and bags of clothing. She quietly lowered the tailgate and painfully climbed up. Blaise jumped in after her. It was an agonizing reach, but she lifted the tailgate to the closed position. She crawled to the front, wrapped herself in a blanket, and heard a woman say, "Thanks for the travel advice, Sheriff."

The truck doors opened and closed, the motor started to rumble, and the truck rolled off the gravel parking lot onto the road. Once they were underway, Maggie peeled back the flap on the tent to let in some air. Blaise rested his head next to hers on the soft pillow. Nothing made sense, and she felt exhausted, achy, and chilled.

The engine purred, the truck vibrated, and she and Blaise fell fast asleep.

CHAPTER 28

Let nothing disturb you, nothing frighten you;
all things are passing; God is unchanging.
Patience gains all; nothing is lacking to those who have God:
God alone is sufficient.

—Saint Teresa of Ávila

T he sheriff parked his cruiser next to a rescue crew as they dismantled a fallen tree. He yawned as he stood with some county officers and watched the men work with chain saws to cut the tree into sections. "What's going on, Mike?" he asked one of the officers. "This tree isn't blocking the road. Why all the fuss?"

"Someone is pinned under the tree."

The sheriff looked closer. "Is he alive?"

"I don't think so. I felt for a pulse but couldn't find one. The medical examiner is here, and he'll make it official."

"Who does that car belong to?" the sheriff asked and yawned again.

The officer flipped out his notepad. "It's registered to Frances Jackson. We've already sent an officer to her home."

The sheriff gasped.

"Are you okay, Sheriff?"

"I'm fine. It's been a difficult night."

"Yeah, tell me about it." The officer went back to watching the buzzing chain saw.

The crew hauled the branches away so that the forensic investigator had room to stoop, crawl, and closely inspect the body from all angles. He pulled a magnifying glass from his bag and examined the victim's head. The sheriff could hear him speak into his handheld recorder.

"There is an indentation on the right temporal lobe of the head, resulting in trauma to the brain." After noting other aspects of the body's condition, he concluded, "The probable cause of death occurred from a tree limb that struck the victim's head as it made its descent." He replaced the recorder and magnifying glass in his bag and went to his car for a blanket to cover the body.

The sheriff approached and recognized Kevin immediately. He drew in his breath and placed his hand on his head. He suddenly felt ill, walked into the woods, and threw up his pancake breakfast. While bending over and wiping his mouth with a handkerchief, he noticed the condition of the ground. The deep gouges in the mud and the disturbance of leaves caught his attention. *What happened here? Perhaps a struggle?*

Following the clawed earth, he spotted a baseball bat near the riverbank. He stooped down, picked it up, saw "CW" carved in the knob, and dropped it like a hot potato. *Holy cow, Chuck! Why is your bat here?*

He looked toward the downed tree and was relieved no one noticed him. He used his foot to cover the bat with leaves, then joined the group again, his heart pounding with apprehension. He would have to wait until everyone was gone to retrieve the bat.

While the coroner placed the body in the ambulance, the sheriff looked into Kevin's car and noticed a flowered backpack on the floor of the back seat. He heard another distress call over the county police radio and said, "I can wait for the tow truck, so you can answer that call if you like."

"Thanks, Bill, that would be helpful."

Before the tow truck arrived, the sheriff removed the backpack, dunked it a few times in a muddy puddle, and placed it and the bat in his cruiser.

***

Mitch fell asleep on the couch just after dawn. Father James quietly slipped out and returned to the rectory to let Father Brendan know he was back from keeping watch with Mitch. Father Brendan sat at his desk with tears in his eyes.

"Brendan, what is it?"

"Fran is in the kitchen with Marge and Sam. We just got back from the morgue. Some rescue workers found a body crushed under a tree this morning. It was Kevin."

"Oh dear God, no!" Father James's knees went limp, and he flopped into a chair with his head in his hands. He looked up with tears in his eyes. "Maggie was with him."

***

When Mitch awoke and looked out the window, the events from last night crashed in on him. "Maggie!" he called out in desperation, and his voice echoed through the empty house. "Father James?"

The only response was the ticking of the windup alarm clock.

He sat up and rubbed his eyes to erase the last twelve hours, but reality set in. Maggie was still missing. There was a note on the table.

I've gone to the rectory to check in with Father Brendan.

Mitch tested the phone to see if the power had returned. "Darn it!" He slammed the receiver down. "What if Maggie is trying to call me? Or the police are trying to reach me?" he fretted. "I guess they would come in person."

There was a knock at the door.

"Maggie?" *No, she wouldn't knock.* Mitch froze, and he felt his chest cave.

The door slowly opened, and Father James stood at the threshold. Mitch could tell by the look on his face that he had bad news.

"What is it? Is Maggie okay? Oh God, please, no!"

Father James grabbed Mitch as he crumpled. "It's not Maggie," he said emphatically. Then he repeated in a more subdued tone, "It's *not* Maggie."

It took a moment for the message to sink in. "Oh, thank God!" Mitch exclaimed.

Father James released his hold on Mitch's shoulders and slumped onto the couch.

Mitch asked, "Then why do you look so—"

"It's Kevin. Fran is over at the church right now with Father Brendan. I wanted to come and tell you what happened. The police found Kevin's car near the spot we turned around last night."

Mitch sat down next to James. "Well, what happened?"

"For some reason, he got out of his car. A tree fell and crushed him."

Mitch had been fighting back tears, but the news of Kevin opened the floodgates. He pulled out his handkerchief. "Are they sure that it's Kevin?" He wiped his eyes and blew his nose.

"Yes. Marge and Father Brendan took Fran to the hospital morgue to identify his body."

"He had just turned his life around. I can't believe this!" There was a short silence before Mitch could ask, "And Maggie?"

Father James sighed. "No sign of her."

"Do the police have any ideas?"

"No, but they will investigate." Then he looked around the room. "Mitch, did Blaise return?"

Mitch had forgotten about Blaise. He shook his head.

Father James was hopeful. "Perhaps they're together. You know he's devoted to Maggie. Blaise will protect her." His words of comfort limped into the silence that hung in the air.

Mitch's voice was soft when he asked, "Do you know how Blaise got his name?"

He shook his head.

"Maggie's best friend, Annie, had a Chesapeake Bay retriever named Glory. Beautiful animal. Powerful swimmer. She was in heat and, unfortunately, got out one night. It wasn't long before they realized she would have a litter. The pups arrived on the evening of February 2. Glory delivered five little pups before the clock struck twelve. Ten minutes after midnight, the final pup was born. Maggie said they should name him Blaise after Saint Blaise, whose feast day is February 3."

Father James smiled.

"Annie and Maggie played with the pups every day after school. Annie's parents were amazed at how Blaise would gravitate to Maggie, no matter who else was in the room. They found a home for all the pups except for Blaise. They had saved him for Maggie." Mitch stared out the window, took a deep breath, and his voice quavered as he said, "When I adopted Maggie, she asked if I would adopt Blaise too."

"Don't lose heart, Mitch. God's in control." Father James's words did not supply much comfort, but Mitch understood the sentiment.

There was a knock on the door. Mitch looked like a deer caught in the headlights, so Father James opened the door to find the sheriff on the front porch. For the second time that morning, Mitch's heart stopped.

"Mr. Hartman?"

He could barely answer yes.

"I found this backpack out on Route 1," he lied. "The book inside has your address on it. It belongs to someone named Maggie."

Mitch stared at the slightly waterlogged ladybug on the cover. "Yes, that's her journal." Mitch's hand shook as he reached for the items.

"I know you called our office last evening. Has Maggie returned?"

He choked as he said no.

Father James said, "We know Maggie was with her friend, Kevin Jackson, yesterday afternoon. I last saw them together about six o'clock."

"I see." The sheriff was visibly downcast. "I have some news about Kevin."

"Yes, we know of Kevin's accident." Mitch had trouble maintaining his composure.

Father James put his hand on Mitch's shoulder to steady him.

"Mr. Hartman, I suggest you stay put in case we need to reach you or if Maggie returns. We'll continue our search for her."

Mitch fought the anxious feeling that was playing havoc with his stomach. "Thank you."

***

Sheriff Wilson walked back to his cruiser with an uneasy feeling. He had more questions than answers and didn't know where to begin. His lie about the backpack was in vain since

Mitch and the priest knew that Maggie had been with Kevin. He was relieved that he was the one to find the baseball bat. He had given Chuck that bat for his birthday. Why it was at the accident scene was a mystery, and where was Maggie?

He opened the door to his cruiser and sat down. He leaned over, pulled the wooden bat from the back seat, and examined it closely. He observed deep grooves in the wood and knew the indentations came from hitting objects other than a baseball. He also noted the faint discoloration, a reddish-brown patch, with a few hairs stuck in the splintered wood. He'd witnessed enough accident scenes to know this color meant blood. The storm had cleansed it a little, but the telltale remnants, deeply embedded in the dents of the bat, remained. He couldn't shake the forensic investigator's comment about the trauma to the victim's head and knew a baseball bat could inflict such a wound.

***

The Ellicott City cleanup was immense, and it overwhelmed the residents of this little town. Mangled cars and bicycles, uprooted trees, telephone poles, and wires clogged Main Street under the Baltimore and Ohio Railroad bridge. The muck consisted of muddy oil, charcoal grills, lawn furniture, shattered glass, and countless other items the storm had dislodged. A child's mud-caked jacket lay close to a splintered crib, and the upper part of a mannequin, stuck in the quagmire, reached out for help. It was a horrific sight.

Sadly, there were bodies mixed in with the raw sewage and toxins. Phone lines were still down, but the grapevine took over, and Mitch's chest tightened whenever he heard the rescue workers had pulled another body from the wreckage.

With every fiber of his being, Mitch prayed that Maggie was alive and safe, even though each day that passed unraveled his thread of optimism. He knelt before the monstrance every Wednesday and prayed, "Please bring Maggie home." The only consolation he received was the enduring call to trust. He felt rather than heard a gentle coaxing. *Stay close to the Blessed Mother.* She would lead him to a place of peace in this valley of tears. His heart went out to families each time he heard that workers discovered another body along the Patapsco River. Still, he was grateful Maggie was not yet among the victims identified.

***

The police department was overwhelmed with calls, and their APB for Maggie remained in effect. They put in extra hours protecting businesses, directing cars at intersections where traffic lights were out of service, and calming citizens who were distraught over losing their homes and livelihoods.

The sheriff's office stepped in to help, and Sheriff Wilson took an active role in the search for Maggie. Kevin's death and Maggie's disappearance tormented him. *Was it a coincidence that Kevin showed up on my doorstep, a day before the storm, looking for Chuck?*

But when he had questioned his son about the bat, Chuck appeared calm and collected, almost as if he had rehearsed his answer. "What! I wondered what had happened to that bat. I bet Kevin stole it from me. You know how he was always getting into trouble. He was such a thief!"

"Chuck," the sheriff had cautioned, "we do not speak ill of the dead." Then he turned and walked out of the room.

The sheriff had kept abreast of Kevin's behavior at church. He felt responsible for the community-service arrangement, even though it was Frances and Father Brendan's idea. The reports had been positive. Kevin had turned over a new leaf. Again, the sheriff wondered why Chuck would think Kevin had taken his bat. According to Chuck, he and Kevin did not hang out together.

**

Hurricane Agnes took the lives of eight people in this little town and left 704 people homeless. Roughly 103 homes and fifty businesses suffered significant damage. Only one person remained missing, a fifteen-year-old named Mary Magdalene Hartman, who went by the name of Maggie.

CHAPTER 29

Feed the hungry
Give drink to the thirsty
Clothe the naked
Shelter the homeless
Visit the sick
Visit the imprisoned
Bury the dead.

—The Corporal Works of Mercy

D r. Clare McGuire and sixteen-year-old Joshua McGuire headed out on a church mission to help the under-privileged in and around Shepherdstown, West Virginia. The doctor's brother, Frank, had invited her to participate in this humanitarian mission. He belonged to the Christian church that sponsored the outreach program. It was more accurate to say her brother had coerced her since the doctor they had originally enlisted was injured and unable to work. They desper-ately needed someone to fill the Doctors on Wheels position.

Clare asked her nephew, "So how did your dad rope you into coming on this mission trip? You in the doghouse for some reason?"

"It's the only way I could earn a car this year. He said I needed to be more serious and not joke around so much." Josh turned on the radio.

"Look at the devastation from the hurricane," Clare remarked as they drove through the countryside.

"How'd he get you to come, Aunt Clare?"

"It's complicated. Let's say my life took an unexpected turn." Clare cleared her throat, fighting the panic and pain in her chest. "This will be a good way to step back and reevaluate my future."

Josh teased her, "Well, your future can only go up. This mission pays practically nothing!"

"I know. But the church will cover my expenses and bolster my resume." She chuckled lightheartedly to cover her anxiety. "And I get to spend time with you."

The hit song "Lean on Me" came on, and they sang the words together. Their conversation was light, and the journey was slow due to the hurricane's damage to bridges and roadways. They ate the sandwiches Clare had packed and decided to stop at Cooper's Mini Mart to get some drinks and use the bathroom.

The sudden absence of engine noise and movement woke the two stowaways. Maggie looked around. *Where am I?*

After about ten minutes, Clare returned to the truck to survey the map.

The sound of the door slamming prompted Maggie to move the flap on the tent to look through the back window. The passenger door opened, and a boy about her age got in and handed the woman a soda. Maggie ducked.

The woman checked her watch. "We're almost there and should arrive by three o'clock." She started the engine and pulled away.

Maggie's mind was blank. *Why am I in this truck, covered in mud, with bruises and cuts all over my body? Gosh, my body aches! Maybe they're kidnapping me!*

The truck eventually pulled onto a gravel driveway, jostling them before coming to a stop. Maggie heard a woman's voice.

"I'll go introduce myself to Pastor Jeremy. Can you get my kit from the back?"

Maggie panicked. *What should I do?*

Suddenly, the tailgate opened.

Blaise scrambled through the bags of clothing and greeted the intruder with a fierce growl.

"Holy cow!" The boy backed up and stumbled over a tree stump. He landed on his back. "Help!" he screamed as the dog stood boldly on the tailgate, glaring at him.

When they heard the commotion, Clare and the pastor rushed from the church to check out the situation. By this time, Maggie had moved painfully through the piles of sheets and clothing to get to the tailgate.

"Oh my goodness! What's going on out here?" Clare exclaimed as a crowd of volunteers surrounded her truck. She saw a mangy dog beside a young girl as she attempted to stand on the tailgate. Clare yelled, "Everyone, back up!"

She and the pastor arrived just as the girl stood up, immediately turned pale, and fainted. As her limp body fell forward, Clare and the pastor caught her.

"Let's get her inside the medical tent," the pastor ordered.

The church grounds acted as the hub for the humanitarian mission. The medical tent functioned as a small hospital for those who needed treatment. Smaller volunteer tents spotted the church grounds and provided shelter for volunteers and patrons. Each tent boasted fans and lights powered by a church generator, containers of water, plastic cups, and fruit bowls.

The dog jumped down and worked his way into the hubbub surrounding Maggie, and no one dared challenge him. He followed them into the tent, sat down next to the cot that held Maggie, and rested his snout on her pillow.

Clare's cursory exam revealed bruising and cuts all over her body and one deep, oozing laceration on her left leg. Rope burns had singed her arm and led the doctor to believe she had escaped from bondage. She had no broken bones, but dried blood clung to her skin.

Maggie woke up and looked around at all the faces that hovered over her. Clare saw the fear in her eyes as she struggled to get up.

The doctor held her down. "Don't be afraid. No one will harm you. You're safe."

Maggie's stiffness relaxed, and the dog whimpered.

"I'm Dr. Clare. What's your name?"

Maggie looked puzzled.

"Do you understand? Can you tell me your name?"

Maggie looked frightened again. She turned pale and said, "I feel sick."

"Her blood pressure must be dropping!" Clare said and quickly turned the patient onto her side.

Maggie's color returned.

"Josh, get my medical kit from the truck."

By now, quite a crowd of volunteers had gathered. "Please. Everyone clear the tent." Clare added, "Except for you," as she put her hand on a young girl's shoulder. "May I ask your name?"

"It's Paula."

"I would like to examine her, and I think she might feel more comfortable with a girl her age present."

Clare knelt next to the dog. He smelled of grimy hair and mud mixed with mildew. She carefully moved his collar to look at his identification. A bone-shaped metal tag bore the name Blaise. "Is this your dog? I like his name, Blaise."

Maggie repeated, "Blaise."

Clare shone her penlight in Maggie's eyes to measure her pupil dilation and observed the most beautiful crystal-blue color she had ever seen. Her hair was matted and muddy, but Clare suspected it was a lovely blonde color when clean.

Clare asked again, "Sweetheart, can you tell me your name?"

Maggie looked puzzled and burst into tears. "I don't know my name or why I'm here."

Blaise nestled his nose closer to Maggie with another whimper.

"I'd like to examine you. Would that be all right?"

Maggie nodded.

"First, are you thirsty?"

"Yes."

"Paula, would you pour a cup of water?" As Clare helped Maggie sit up, she asked, "Are you hungry?"

"A little."

Paula got a banana from the bowl, and Clare advised, "Take your time. Drink and eat slowly."

Maggie drank the water and finished the banana.

"Are you feeling better?"

"Yes, can I have another cup of water?"

"Of course." Paula refilled the glass.

Maggie lowered the cup so Blaise could drink. He slurped it down gratefully even though his tongue had trouble fitting inside the cup.

Clare smiled. "I'm sure we can find a bowl for him later."

Josh handed Paula the medical bag through the tent opening.

Clare and Paula helped Maggie remove her clothing, down to her bra and panties. Clare noticed a little ladybug pinned to her blouse and remarked, "This is very special."

Maggie rubbed the pin between her fingers and smiled.

Clare calculated her age at around fourteen. Her examination revealed a healthy heart, strong pulse, and clear lungs, and her blood pressure was reasonable, considering her condition. She looked in the girl's ears, throat, and nose, felt her glands, and checked her reflexes. She pressed her abdomen to see if she had any pressure sensitivity. She was dehydrated. Clare cleaned her cuts and dressed the wounds on her leg and arm.

"Do you know how you got these marks on your arm? It looks like they might be from a rope tied very tight."

Maggie shook her head.

Clare was impressed with the young girl's composure; she had calmed down quickly while in a stressful situation. "Paula, would you go to the truck and find some clothing that might fit? You can ask the boy who handed me the medical kit to help. His name is Josh."

"Sure." Paula picked up the discarded clothing and saw a name inside the tie-dyed sweatshirt. She showed Clare and left the tent.

Clare read the name Maggie, which was printed in impeccable lettering, and found a beautiful crystal rosary in the zippered pocket. She asked, "Do you remember anything at all? Like where you live? Did you get in my truck when we stopped at Cooper's Mini Mart?"Maggie just stared into space.

"There is a name in your jacket. It's Maggie." Clare showed her the jacket, and Maggie stared at the label.

Paula returned with some clothing.

"Paula, where do we bathe around here?"

Paula opened the tent flap and pointed to a small house by the church. "That house is where the doctor lives during the mission."

Clare helped Maggie to her feet, wrapped her in a sheet, and walked her to the truck as the pastor dispersed the crowd that had gathered outside the tent. Clare grabbed her shampoo, soap, and towel from her suitcase and headed for the house. Blaise followed.

Clare called to Josh, "Take the dog over to the hose and use some of your shampoo to wash him."

Josh called back, "You're kidding, right? Did I hear you correctly?"

"Yes, his name is Blaise." She winked at Maggie. "He doesn't bite too hard if you're gentle."

Blaise got to the threshold, and Clare said, "Stay."

Blaise obediently sat down.

Josh gingerly headed over to him. As Blaise turned and eyed him ominously, Josh called to him, "Come here, Blaise. Good boy."

Blaise didn't budge.

Paula came over with a thick slice of ham from one of the heating trays left over from lunch and handed it to Josh.

Now, he had Blaise's attention. He took a deep breath. " I just hope I get out of this with all ten fingers!"

CHAPTER 30

Great occasions for serving God come seldom,
but little ones surround us daily.

—*Saint Francis de Sales*

"Dr. Clare, could I have a word with you? It's about Maggie."

"Sure, Pastor, is there a problem?"

"I cannot be responsible for her any longer. I don't have a signed release from a parent or guardian." He was very agitated. "She's lovely but doesn't fit our parameters for a youth volunteer."

"What do you mean by volunteer? She is a patient and supposed to be resting."

"Didn't Maggie tell you she's been helping at the camp?"

"I leave before she wakes up, and she is already asleep by the time I return. I had hoped she would rest during the day. You know how sick she was from the infection her leg wound caused that first week."

"Yes, I know, but she's very persuasive. After a few days of rest, she wouldn't sit still. She said she would do anything

I needed, like clean soup pots or wash and fold laundry. I was amazed when she offered to weed the church garden."

Clare handed Josh some medical supplies to take inside. "I'll sign a volunteer release form for her, but I don't want her overworked. She's still recovering."

"It's not just that."

"There's more?"

"Yes, I don't want my young people exposed to some of the things she's been sharing. Parents send their teens to this mission because many of our activities reinforce their faith."

"What sort of things?"

"She speaks about the Blessed Mother and prays with a rosary. I don't want parents to think we are indoctrinating their children."

Clare responded, "I'll talk to her so she understands she's a patient here and must abide by your rules."

"Don't get me wrong; she's a pleasant worker. She antici-pates what people need, never complains, and is always cheerful. When I asked her how she could be so joyful with so much misery around her, you know what she said?"

Clare was becoming annoyed. "I haven't a clue."

"She said it was her 'little way.'"

"Listen, Jeremy, it's only been three weeks since we arrived, and I'm doing everything possible to locate her family. Josh and I are up early, we sometimes see fifty patients in a day and drive to places so remote they aren't even on the map, then plop into bed exhausted at night. While doing all that, I've visited the sheriff's office, community centers, and churches, and there's no report of a missing girl that fits her description. What else do you expect me to do?"

Jeremy timidly responded, "Perhaps she could accompany you and Josh on your rounds. She's helpful and works hard, but I can't risk having her here. She's a liability to the program."

220

"A liability?" Clare rolled her eyes. "Really?"

"She prays over people, and I have no idea what she's saying."

Clare rubbed her forehead as Pastor Jeremy continued, "Your only other option is to take her to the authorities, and Social Services will assume the responsibility for her placement. Let them locate her family."

"I'd rather find her family myself. I want to make sure she's safe."

Josh returned to pick up more supplies. "Aunt Clare, let Maggie come with us. Maybe someone will recognize her while we're out. We could go by Cooper's Mini Mart. I bet that's where she got in the truck. Maybe that would jog her memory."

Clare sighed. "Okay, I guess that makes the most sense."

Josh said, "Yes!" under his breath.

**

The following morning, Maggie climbed into the truck. Blaise positioned himself in front of the vehicle. Clare beeped the horn, but he wouldn't move.

Maggie advised, "I think he wants to come."

"Oh, for goodness's sake!"

"I'll open the tailgate so he can jump in the tent." Josh was out the door before Clare could object.

Clare closed her eyes, counted to ten, and put the truck in gear.

Their first stop was for a man in a wheelchair who lived in a trailer with his daughter. Maggie couldn't be any help, so she sat in the sun and pulled out her rosary.

Josh looked out the trailer's window and saw her playing with crystal beads and moving her lips as if she were talking with someone.

"Hi, Christie, how's your dad doing?" Clare asked.

"He has good days and bad."

Josh stretched his neck out the window to get a closer look at Maggie and asked under his breath, "What's she doing?"

"She's praying the rosary," Clare said as she pulled a thermometer out of her bag.

"The what?"

"The rosary. My grandmother, your great-grandmother, used to pray the rosary."

"How do you pray with it?" he asked.

Clare let out a huff of air. "Never mind. Leave Maggie alone, and don't question her about it. If the rosary comforts her, we need not show our distaste for it."

Josh wondered why it was displeasing to his aunt, but he knew she was not much for any religion.

"Just pay attention to Mr. Goode here. I need you to lift him from the wheelchair onto the bed so I can examine him."

Clare turned to her patient and asked, "How are you feeling, Mr. Goode?"

He took Clare's hand and said, "The rosary is a beautiful meditative prayer."

"Dad, let the doctor do her work."

Clare changed the bandage on the patient's leg. "Christie, you're doing a good job. Here are more bandages and antibiotics. Keep doing what I told you, and call if there is any redness or inflammation around the wound. I'll be back in a week."

Outside, Clare surveyed a map as Josh loaded the equipment. "Tell me about my great-grandmother."

Clare lowered the map. "Well, there isn't much to tell. She was my maternal grandmother, and she was Catholic. As a child, I was fascinated by her devotion to the rosary. My father told me that it was a silly superstition. He said, 'They think if they recite a bunch of prayers over and over, it will gain them heaven.' You remember your grandfather was a Protestant minister, and he encouraged me to learn passages from the Bible."

Clare rolled up the map and held it like a microphone. "'And when you pray, do not keep babbling like pagans, for they think they will be heard because of their many words.' That was one of the verses I had to learn."

She unrolled the map and circled their next stop. "Maggie, come on, we're leaving for the next appointment."

***

Chuck slammed the phone down in the upstairs hallway. "Jimmy, we gotta get over to Ben's house. He's been out of the hospital for over two weeks, but his mom keeps putting me off when I say we wanna visit."

"That sucks! How are we gonna coordinate our story?"

Chuck answered, "Maybe we show up on his porch. I'll convince her to let us in."

They headed for the front door and stopped halfway down the stairs when the sheriff said, "Where's the fire?"

"Oh hey, Dad, I didn't know you were home."

The sheriff had been dozing on the living room couch, exhausted from the overtime. "You two sound like a herd of elephants."

"Sorry, Dad. We were heading over to see how Ben is doing."

"Well, that is mighty kind of you to visit a friend as he recovers from surgery. But I think you need to stay here and clean up the mess in your room. I look around the city and see all the destruction, and your room doesn't look much better. The difference is that the townspeople take pride in their community and have already begun the cleanup. You should do the same and take better care of your possessions."

The sheriff was still angry about the condition of Chuck's baseball bat, and he was trying to ignore any thought that it played a role in Kevin's death. He was not convinced Chuck was telling the truth. "I'll check on Ben for you."

"But, Dad—"

"I'll tell you how Ben is doing."

Chuck and Jimmy swallowed hard, looked at each other, and Jimmy said, "I'll see you later, Chuck."

As soon as the sheriff drove off, Chuck called Ben's home. "Hi, Mrs. Murphy. May I speak with Ben? Please?"

"I'm not sure I can get the phone to reach the couch, but let me try." She stretched the accordion cord but had to put the phone down to move the lamp.

Chuck tapped his fingers impatiently. "C'mon!" he said into the phone.

Ben's mother finally got the phone close to Ben, who had to lean in to hold the receiver against his ear. Just as he said hello, the doorbell rang.

Chuck only had time to say, "Don't tell my dad anything about what happened. Remember, Ben, you're just as guilty as we are!" Then Chuck slammed the phone down, and Ben was left staring at the receiver.

Ben's mom answered the door, and he heard, "Hello, Mrs. Murphy, how's Ben doing? I wanted to check on him."

"Sheriff Wilson, how kind of you to come by. He's doing a little better. Thank you." She stood in the doorway, and there was an awkward silence between them. She didn't invite him in.

"Would it be all right if I came in for a moment?"

"Well, Ben is quite tired."

The sheriff assured her, "I'll only stay a moment," and brushed past her.

Ben was on the couch with his leg propped on the coffee table. He loosened his grip on the receiver, which was yanked from his hand as the cord retracted.

Mrs. Murphy nervously grabbed the wayward phone as it slid across the table and onto the floor. She placed it on the base and said, "Ben, say hello to the sheriff."

"Sorry if I don't get up, Sheriff," Ben said, slurring his words.

"No problem, Ben. How ya feeling?"

"Not so good. The doctor had to put my kneecap back or something. I'll have to do physical therapy—"

Mrs. Murphy interrupted, "Sheriff, I would offer you a cup of coffee, but I only have instant."

The sheriff felt she had purposely intruded on the conversation to tell him about the coffee. She made no offer for him to sit down, and he wondered why she was so nervous. "Are you okay, Mrs. Murphy?"

"Why yes, of course. I'm just worried about Ben. He's been saying weird things in his sleep. I'm sure it's the medicine."

This piqued the sheriff's interest. "What kind of weird things?"

"Oh, they don't make much sense. I better check the oven." She abruptly left the room.

The sheriff called over his shoulder, "Thank you, I'd love a cup of instant coffee." He looked down at Ben. "It's been another difficult week. So tell me, how'd you injure your knee?"

"Didn't Chuck tell you?"

"Yes, but I'd like to hear it from you." The sheriff saw him squirm a little.

"Well, it's hard to remember."

"Just try, Ben."

"Well, it was raining hard, and…um…"

"Go on, Ben."

Just then, Mrs. Murphy returned with a cup of coffee. "Here you are, Sheriff. I brought cream and sugar too."

"Thanks, I drink it black."

"I overheard you ask Ben about the accident. He doesn't remember anything."

The sheriff looked at Ben. "Is that true, Ben?"

"Yes, sir."

The sheriff sat on the chair next to the couch and looked at Ben. "Do you remember the baseball bat?"

Ben broke out in a sweat, his eyes widened, and he blinked a few times, then wiped his forehead with his sleeve.

Mrs. Murphy said, "Sheriff, I think this is too much for Ben."

The sheriff's stern eyes stayed focused on Ben.

"Mom, I think I need another pain pill."

She looked at her watch and took the medicine bottle from the table. Her hand shook as she tried to open the container of pills.

The sheriff calmly reached up, took the plastic bottle from her, flipped off the cap, and handed it back to her.

"Sheriff, I think it best if you leave and allow Ben to rest."

The sheriff sat a few seconds more with his eyes fixed on Ben, who had closed his. He picked up the coffee, took a sip, and stood. "Thanks for the coffee, Mrs. Murphy. I'll show myself out."

He sat in his cruiser and tried to remember, in detail, the night of the storm when Chuck and Jimmy showed up soaking wet, scratched, bruised, and bloodstained.

***

Chuck had spoken very nervously. "Man, what a horrible night! We saw this guy drive off the road. He ran over a mailbox and got stuck in some bushes. We ran to help him,

226

and our faces got pretty scratched up from the branches. Ben slipped on a rock and cut his knee. Blood was everywhere, but he said it didn't hurt too much. So we drove him home."

"So where did this happen, son?"

Chuck was talking faster than usual. "It was raining hard. I don't remember where."

"I see. Well, I'll get the details from the accident report."

Chuck looked surprised. "There will be a report?"

"Sure," the sheriff responded, "any time property damage occurs, there's a report. Was the driver okay?"

"What driver? Oh yeah, he was fine." Chuck quickly changed the subject. "Dad, I'm sorry I didn't call from Ben's house. Time got away from us, and we were worried about Ben. His mom was upset, so we thought it best to leave. It all happened so fast that I didn't think to call."

Jimmy never looked up during Chuck's explanation, but he nodded in agreement. The sheriff remembered that the phone rang in the middle of Chuck's explanation, and he was grateful for the interruption. He had neither the desire nor the energy to deal with his son, and being called into the office was his escape. Chuck was eighteen now, and, sad as it sounded, the sheriff looked forward to him leaving for college.

Later, he discovered that Ben's injury was serious. It happened that, the night of the storm, his deputy sustained a deep wound while rescuing a dog. He took the deputy to the emergency room, then went to get a cup of coffee from a vending machine, and met a doctor doing the same.

"Rough night, huh, Bill?" the doctor asked.

"One for the books," the sheriff answered.

"I just operated on a kid from the high school. Maybe your son knows him, Ben Murphy."

"Was it his knee?"

"Yes, how did you know?"

"My son told me he slipped on a rock, but it wasn't that bad."

The doctor was surprised. "Slipped on a rock? That kind of injury would only occur if he fell ten feet after he slipped. He fractured his patella, and fissures were evident in the tibial plateau."

"Could I have that in plain English?"

"Oh yeah, sorry. His kneecap and shinbone suffered significant trauma. It looked like someone had taken a sledgehammer to it. It will be a long, painful recovery."

***

As the sheriff backed out of Ben's driveway, the gut feeling he had had the night of the storm returned. *My son is not telling the truth. What kind of father am I when my son cannot trust me?*

As he drove to his office, the sheriff attempted to solve the puzzle. He felt Kevin's death, Chuck's bat, and Ben's knee were connected, but how? Ben had broken out in a sweat when he mentioned the baseball bat, and Mrs. Murphy seemed to be protecting Ben from disclosing anything. The fact that Maggie Hartman's backpack had been in Kevin's car haunted him. A sobering thought surfaced.

I tampered with the bat and backpack. Now I'm entangled in Chuck's web of lies.

CHAPTER 31

Lord, help me to make time today
to serve you in those who are
most in need of encouragement or assistance.

— *Saint Vincent de Paul*

W ithin a week of joining Clare and Josh, Maggie had become proficient in taking blood pressures, temperatures, and pulse rates, which freed Clare up for the complicated medical issues. Josh was the brawn of the group and vital to Clare's daily rounds. He could pick up furniture or patients and easily carry boxes filled with medical supplies. There was no time to relax during the first few weeks. Clare faced situations she had never encountered before, even in her simulated disasters or triage training during medical school.

The most suspenseful challenge came at the end of the fourth week. Clare had spent seven days treating families with dysentery. She, Josh, and Maggie returned on a Sunday evening when the camp was quiet since the volunteers were not due back until Monday. The three were looking forward to a bite to eat, a cool shower, and a restful night.

They were about to unload the medical supplies when a car rumbled up the gravel driveway and slid to a stop by the truck. A man got out of the car and waved his arms. "Please help my wife. She's in labor. Please."

"Where is she?"

"In the back seat. She's crying. The baby is coming early. Please help her."

Josh and Clare got the pregnant woman out of the car and into the medical tent.

"Josh, see if you can get the generator going. I need light." Clare turned to the patient. "What's your name?"

"Janet."

"And I'm Pete," the nervous husband interjected.

"Maggie, I need you to get the birthing kit from the truck and the flashlight."

Clare examined Janet and listened to the baby's heartbeat.

"The baby's heart is strong, and you're dilated ten centimeters. This is all good except... Josh, where is that generator? I need light!"

"I'm trying, but I can't get it started!"

Pete was standing over Clare, nervously twisting his baseball cap.

"Maybe you could help Josh with the generator."

"What? Oh sure."

"OW!" Janet groaned.

Clare directed Maggie, "Figure out a way to set up the flashlight so I can see."

Maggie used the bananas in a fruit bowl to hold the light steady.

"Perfect. Now get the towels from the shelf."

She placed the towels under Janet. "Get behind Janet and hold her up. Janet, I know you want to push, but not yet."

Maggie raised Janet and held her hand.

"Okay. Now push! Good, good."

Janet pushed and groaned.

"Relax a moment. I see the baby's head."

Janet leaned back on Maggie.

"Okay, push again. You're doing great. Beautiful!" Clare held a towel in position as she eased the baby into her hands. "A beautiful baby girl!" Clare rubbed the infant on her back.

A tiny cry greeted the world.

"Ah yes, a good set of lungs." Clare laughed.

Maggie placed pillows under the head of the new mother.

"Maggie, hand me two clamps and get the scissors."

After Maggie handed her the clamps, Clare clamped the umbilical cord. "Now, cut in between the clamps."

"What? You want me to cut it? Are you sure?"

"Yes, I'm sure." Clare looked at her and smiled.

Maggie's hands were shaking as she cut through the rubbery cord.

Clare cleaned the newborn up and wrapped her in a towel. "The baby is small, maybe five pounds." She looked at Janet. "Open your blouse." Clair laid the baby on Janet's chest so the newborn could hear her heartbeat.

"Hello, little one." Janet smiled.

The generator sputtered and rumbled, and the lights came on. Josh yelled, "Yahoo!"

The new dad ran in and knelt beside his wife and brand-new daughter.

Just then, Janet cried out.

Pete was panic-stricken. "Why is she in pain?"

"It's just the afterbirth." Clare placed the stethoscope on Janet's abdomen. "Oh my."

"What is it?" The husband was frantic.

"I hear a heartbeat! You're having twins!"

"Twins!" Pete stood up and turned pale. "I feel dizzy."

Clare tried to grab him as she called out, "Josh, I need you!"

Josh rushed over, but was a few seconds too late. He found Pete slumped on the floor; he appeared to have hit his head on the side of the cot on his way down. The sharp edge had cut his forehead, and blood was spurting from the wound.

Maggie froze as she stared at the bloody patient on the floor.

Clare looked at Maggie. "I need you to get behind Janet again. Hold her up like before."

Maggie's eyes glazed over.

Janet emitted another agonized moan and said, "For God's sake, Pete, you're not being helpful! OW!"

Maggie stared vacantly into space.

Clare got up, put her hands on her shoulders, and looked her in the eyes. "Maggie, I need your help."

Her eyes were blank, but she said, "Please help Kevin."

Clare blinked a few times. "What?" Then she shook Maggie hard enough to get her attention and said in a soft, deliberate voice, "I need you to get behind Janet and help her deliver this second baby, just like you did the first time. Can you do that?"

Maggie's eyes refocused on Clare. "Yes."

"Josh, run up to the house and call the operator for an ambulance."

The second baby, a boy, was delivered, and Clare and Maggie performed the same clamping-and-cutting ritual.

Janet now held two infants next to her heart. "How's Pete?" she asked as the two bundles rested on her chest.

Clare bent down to attend to the gash on Pete's head. "It's not deep, thank goodness." She lifted his head and placed a folded towel under it. "Maggie, bring me the suture kit, shine the flashlight down here, and hand me the instruments when I ask."

As Clare stitched the patient's head, Maggie delivered everything requested while holding the light steady.

Josh returned. "The ambulance should be here in ten minutes."

Clare squeezed Maggie's hand and remarked, "We make a good team."

***

A bond between them formed that night when Clare, Josh, and Maggie learned they could depend on one another. Clare appreciated this stabilizing force, as her future hung in the balance. She kept a close eye on Maggie and noted that she had uttered a name from her past.

That night, Maggie woke up screaming and crying a bunch of incoherent words about the water, broken trees, and bridges. Then, with agony in her voice, she cried, "Kevin," and held out her arms.

Clare came into her room and grabbed her outstretched hands. She held on to Maggie until she settled down. Blaise laid his head on her pillow.

Once she had calmed down, Clare asked, "Maggie, who is Kevin?" and watched her closely for a reaction.

Maggie sniffled. "I don't know. Why?"

"Are you sure?"

Maggie's eyes teared up. "I can't remember," and she started to cry again.

"It's okay. It was just a bad dream. You're safe here with me and Blaise. Shhh." Clare held Maggie in her arms and rocked her for a few minutes until she felt Maggie's body relax. "Shhh, that's it. Go back to sleep now. I'm right next door if you need me." Clare left the room.

Maggie rolled over, so that she and Blaise were nose to nose, and said, "Kevin," as she drifted back to sleep.

***

The next day, Clare shared Maggie's nightmare with Josh.

"Wow, Aunt Clare, what do you think it means?"

"I'm not sure, but this could be her memory slowly returning. I don't know if Kevin is friend or foe. See if you can tactfully get some answers. Here she comes."

Maggie approached, and Clare said, "You two, make yourselves useful by reorganizing the supplies in the truck. Let me know what provisions we need for the supply run in a few days." Clare left to make some calls.

Josh handed Maggie a clipboard and pen. "If I call out the items, would you check them off?"

"Sure."

When they had completed the job, Josh took the list to Clare.

"I'll be out in a few minutes. I'm on hold with the hospital supplier now. This part of the Doctors on Wheels is a pain in my— Yes, I'm still here," she said into the phone and rolled her eyes at Josh.

He left and found Maggie sitting under a tree with her rosary. Josh knew his aunt had advised him not to talk about the rosary, but curiosity was his middle name. *I'll start with a question about the rosary, and work my way around to the nightmare.* He sat down. "Maggie, what are you doing with those beads? Can I see them?"

Maggie handed him her rosary, and he examined the crucifix and beads. "What does it mean?"

"I don't remember much about it, except to say the Hail Mary and Our Father. Somehow, that calms me down when I'm scared."

He gave the rosary back. "Are you scared now?"

"Yes, sometimes. I'd like to know what happened to me and why I can't remember. The Blessed Mother helps me meditate on the life of Jesus when I pray the rosary. She is always there to comfort me and lead me to Jesus."

"Like how?"

"The other day, I meditated on the Third Joyful Mystery, the Nativity, and my mind drifted to Bethlehem. I could smell the hay in the stable and hear Mary singing to Baby Jesus."

Josh wrinkled his brow. "Really? Then what?"

Maggie smiled. "Saint Joseph put a shawl around me because I was cold and gave me a piece of bread because I was hungry. He didn't use words, but somehow I knew it was the Bread of Life and it would be enough. I don't need anything else except this moment in time when Jesus came to earth and then promised never to leave."

"Right, because He lives in our hearts."

"Yes, but it's more than that. He promised to be with us always, until the end of time. The bread that Saint Joseph handed me is somehow connected to Jesus's real presence."

"Maggie, this seems a little far-fetched."

"I know. I've been in the Garden of Gethsemane too. You know, when the soldiers come for Jesus?"

"Yes, I'm familiar with His arrest."

"He takes my hand and hides me behind a huge boulder so that I'm safe."

"Safe from what?"

"I don't know. Just safe. I don't have to worry because He's in control."

"In control of what?"

Maggie looked at the crucifix. "He's in control of everything I hand over to Him."

Clare came out and called, "Josh, Maggie, come on. I'm ready to leave now."

They all climbed into the truck.

"You two had your heads together out there."

"Dr. Clare, why can't I remember things? I have these thoughts, but they seem incomplete and dreamlike. Like something's missing."

"Maggie, amnesia is a complicated medical condition. Sometimes there's something so horrific that one's mind obstructs the memory."

"So that would mean I'm trying to block something out. Am I crazy?"

"No, you were pretty battered when we found you. A knock on the head can injure your brain so that it's incapable of remembering until that area heals. Sometimes things come back slowly, bit by bit, and sometimes all at once. Give yourself time. Don't be anxious; it will happen as your body allows it."

Clare drove slowly through a new neighborhood, hoping Maggie would recognize something. "So what were you two discussing?"

"I was just telling Josh how I get messages when I pray the rosary."

Clare was concerned. "What do you mean by messages?"

"It's hard to explain, but God speaks to me when I pray with it."

"What do you mean God speaks to you?" *Is she hearing voices now?*

Just then, Maggie noticed a ladybug on the dashboard. She placed her hand next to the little creature; it climbed onto her pinkie. "Well, the other day when I prayed, I remembered when Mary and Joseph took Baby Jesus to the temple, and Mary received some pretty awful news."

"That doesn't sound very calming," Josh opined.

Clare responded, "That was when Simeon told Mary a sword would pierce her heart."

"Yes," Maggie replied as the ladybug crawled up her arm.

Josh asked, "So how does this make you feel better? I don't get it."

"Well, I feel the Lord telling me to trust that things will work out. I mean, God has already blessed me with the two of you, and maybe some greater good will come from all this, even though I don't know how."

Clare considered Maggie's response. *I need to borrow her rose-colored glasses.*

"I'm sure it was difficult for Mary to hear those words from Simeon, but she never lost faith in God. It was awful to watch her son be crucified, but she trusted God anyway. All that was replaced with joy when Jesus rose from the dead. I believe the Lord is telling me to trust Him, so I do."

Clare was intrigued. "You get all this from reciting Hail Marys over and over?"

"Uh-huh." Maggie yawned as the ladybug ventured back down her arm and wandered on the back of her hand. She rested her hand on the dashboard, and the ladybug climbed off and leisurely made its way to the windshield, as if surveying the road ahead.

It started to rain, and Clare switched on the windshield wipers. The rhythmic sound they produced had a soothing effect. Maggie yawned again, closed her eyes, leaned against Clare, and fell fast asleep.

Clare looked down and observed the ladybug pinned to Maggie's blouse. Then she looked at the ladybug on the dashboard. It reminded her of a little beacon of joy on a gloomy Saturday afternoon, a bright-colored guide in a storm-threatening sky.

CHAPTER 32

Count it all joy, my brethren, when you meet
various trials, for you know that the testing
of your faith produces steadfastness.

—James 1:2–3

On their hour-long drive from Shepherdstown to Berkeley Springs, Maggie peacefully slept on Clare's shoulder and had no idea of the significance of this Saturday in July. It just happened to be her sixteenth birthday.

***

Back home in Maryland, Mitch rose early even though, on Saturdays, he usually slept in. He wanted to be with the people who loved Maggie as much as he did, so he headed to morning Mass.

As he passed Maggie's room, her ladybug journal caught his eye as it lay on her desk. He took a moment to sit inside the castle where she studied, prayed, and slept. He picked up her pillow, smelled the sweet honeysuckle fragrance, and could not hold back the tears.

***

The two priests closed their breviaries as they sat on the garden bench. Father Brendan sighed. "It has been a month now, James. I keep expecting to see Kevin spreading mulch or planting something. And Maggie, where could she be? She just disappeared off the face of the earth, like Enoch in the Old Testament."

"I know," Father James quietly replied. "This will be a difficult day for all of us. Mitch is coming. We have to remain hopeful for his sake." Father James stood up. "I'm going in to get ready for Mass."

"I'll stay here in case Mitch wants to talk."

Mitch entered Mary's Garden. "Blessed Mother, I've come to Maggie's favorite place to ask a favor of you and Jesus. Can you give me a sign that she's safe? I need your help." He sighed. "Mary Magdalene, she shares your feast day. There must be something you can do."

Father Brendan overheard Mitch's prayer, so he walked around the wall to find Mitch on the bench with his eyes cast down. He had no idea what to say but knew not to leave him alone. He came closer and tried to sit.

But Mitch held up his hand. "Stop," he shouted.

Father Brendan jumped back.

"I'm sorry, Father Brendan. I didn't mean to scare you. But look...here on the bench."

Father Brendan had to squint and finally retrieved his reading glasses to see what had caught Mitch's eye. "Ah," he said, "a ladybug."

"Yes. I had asked the Blessed Mother for a sign that Maggie was safe, and this ladybug appeared. You know how attached Maggie is to ladybugs."

"Yes, I know." Father Brendan chuckled. "Mitch, do you know the legend of the ladybug?"

He shook his head.

"In the Middle Ages, swarms of insects were destroying the crops across Europe. The people decided to call on the Virgin Mary for help, so they all prayed the rosary. Soon, little bugs appeared…feeding on the plant-destroying pests, saving the crops! The farmers called these little insects the beetles of Our Lady. Eventually, they became known as lady beetles or ladybugs."

"So you think it's a sign that God answered my prayer?"

"Mitch, the most difficult and perfect prayer we can make to God is 'Thy will be done.' Faith consists not so much in receiving a sign, but rather in being the sign of God's love."

Mitch was silent.

Father Brendan rested his hand on his shoulder. "Mass will begin in a few minutes." Father Brendan turned and entered the church.

Marge and Sam came from the parking lot and found Mitch on the bench with the ladybug on his finger. Marge sat next to him and hugged him. "Can Sam and I sit with you and the ladybug at Mass this morning?"

"Yes, but I'll leave the lady here." He placed the tiny ladybug on a flower and noticed the spot where Blaise usually stationed himself in the shade. The deserted space embodied the loneliness in his heart.

Sam took Marge's hand and placed his other hand on Mitch's shoulder as they entered the church.

After Mass, the church emptied, but Mitch stayed behind to pray. He felt close to Maggie and Len there and found comfort in the smell of melted candle wax and incense. He had brought Maggie's ladybug journal with him and brushed his finger lightly across the image. He'd never opened it, but today, on her sixteenth birthday, there was a strong desire to connect with her.

He turned to the first page, which had swelled from its submersion in the muddy water. Maggie's name and address were printed neatly across the top of the page, a Scripture verse just below them.

> *Rejoice in your hope,*
> *be patient in tribulation,*
> *be constant in prayer.*
> *—Romans 12:12*

He thought how appropriate that quote was for Maggie and him. At the very bottom of the page, she had printed:

> *This book was given to me by*
> *Beverly Baker on July 22, 1966.*

It was hard to believe that was six years ago. He turned the page. The heading read:

> *The Day We Buried Mommy and Daddy*

His heart caught in his throat, and Mitch didn't think he could read on, but he was captivated by the first few lines, and then he had to finish.

> *Uncle Mitch held my hand, but there was still a big hole in my heart. I wanted to cry, but I held back my tears. I was scared about what would happen to me. He poked my arm when it was time for Communion because I wasn't paying atten-tion. I told Jesus I didn't want Uncle Mitch to leave me. I started to cry but could hide my face behind my folded hands. When I knelt, I heard a little voice inside my head say, "My Mother*

will watch over you. Uncle Mitch will care for you. I will send you a sign." When I opened my eyes, there was a little ladybug! I knew this was the sign Jesus had sent. He told me not to be sad, that Mommy and Daddy were with Him. They needed me to be strong, and I had a lot of work to do. Many people need to know Jesus the way I know Him, and I need to help them find their way.

To keep from crying, Mitch placed his fist in his mouth and bit it. He knew it was because of Maggie that he was closer to Jesus. *If the ladybug was a sign for Maggie, it could be a sign for me!*

Father James emerged from the sacristy, saw Mitch bent over in the pew, and rushed over, fearing he was in physical pain. Mitch handed him the journal, which was open to the page he had just read. Father James sat down next to Mitch and read the entry. Tears appeared in the priest's eyes as well. They exchanged no words but remained in the presence of Jesus in the tabernacle for a long time.

Father James's thoughts were of Maggie. *Six years ago, your acceptance of a new life helped me surrender to God. If a ten-year-old could do it, I knew I could too. Maggie, you helped me realize my worth as a priest. I am still here, but where are you?*

***

Father James left Mitch in the church and walked to Saint Mary Cemetery. He remembered the Mass of Christian burial he had celebrated for Kevin one month ago. He shivered slightly at the mystery surrounding the youth's death and Maggie's disappearance. He recalled the words he had spoken to the congregation.

Our faith reminds us to pray for the souls of the faithful departed. It is one of our spiritual works of mercy. Human life can sometimes seem too short to be worth much in our eyes, but God's love is eternal. Many here today know that Kevin had recently returned to the Church and the Sacraments. He had done so because he discovered that prayer is the fulcrum of a relationship with God. He embraced this compelling truth and found that God does not love us because we are worthy, but that we are worthy because God loves us. Many saw a beautiful transformation in him this past year. He became a source of joy, especially to his grandmother, Frances.

Look at the hills that surround our church. God clothes them with the beauty of wildflowers and the fragrance of honeysuckles, which are here today yet gone tomorrow. This reminds us of the fleeting nature of life on earth and the importance of preparing for eternity with God. He made us from clay, the dust of the earth, and we are beloved dust.

On that day, Father James and Father Brendan had led the congregation up the hill to Saint Mary Cemetery, where the gaping hole waited to receive Kevin's body. He blessed the coffin before the pallbearers lowered it into the sacred ground. The mourners filed by and dropped handfuls of sand onto the top of the plain pine box. That was when he saw it, moving across the top of the coffin, disturbing the sand ever so slightly…a tiny red-and-black ladybug.

The clouds drifted onto the clear-blue sky as Father James stood over Kevin's month-old grave and finished his prayer, "I believe in the communion of saints, the forgiveness of sins, the resurrection of the body, and life everlasting. Amen."

CHAPTER 33

Never try to evade the cross that God sends you,
for you will only find a heavier one.

—*Saint Philip Neri*

The truck grew quiet as Josh leaned against the passenger window and dozed off. Clare couldn't reach the radio with Maggie asleep on her shoulder, and she could use a song, even a sad song—anything to fill the silence. She hated the quiet because her thoughts always wandered to the one thing she desperately tried to avoid.

Here I am, driving on a muddy road in West Virginia with two teens in my truck, a beast of a dog in my tent, and only a few dollars in my pocket. Why? Because of him! She accelerated as her bitterness surfaced. *Good work, Clare! You had to fall in love with the infamous Dr. Gregory Simpson.*

Clare had not realized how popular he was until she had poured all her emotional energy into their relationship. She had helped build the medical practice, working next to Greg all day, and had even spent the nights in his arms. It was a dream come true. Her heart had ignored the clues, but her head finally figured it out. *He never intended to marry me.*

In hindsight, she realized he had set up the practice to cater to him. Of course, she had her patients, but they always deferred to the older, more experienced Dr. Gregory for advice. *No wonder he didn't want me to contribute money or place my name on the legal documents. He said it was for my protection, but now I realize I was nothing more than an afterthought, not a partner or future wife.*

Then, finding him in the arms of one of her patients had crushed her. She wished it didn't still hurt so much. *Is it just my pride, or do I really miss Greg?* She had to admit it was a little of both.

He didn't even say he was sorry. My departure should have been more dramatic. I should have hurled a dish at him, like in the movies, or slammed the door. Instead, I feebly packed some clothes and drove away. I walked out on my job and what I thought was the love of my life. Can anyone be more pathetic?

She had crashed on a friend's couch for a couple of days, soaking the throw pillows with her tears, before calling her brother, Frank.

After a few minutes of sympathizing, Frank said, "Clare, you can't just sit around having a pity party. You're better than that. I, your older and wiser brother, have the perfect solution." He told her about his church and the D-O-W program. "They need a doctor right away to visit underprivileged areas in West Virginia."

"What! Wait. How are you involved with this D-O... What did you call it? And why do you need me?"

"D-O-W, the DOW, stands for Doctors on Wheels, and I'm on the board of directors. The DOW family doctor, Dr. Andrew, was injured and will be out for a few months. You would be perfect to fill in."

"I don't know, Frank; this is so sudden."

"Look, I know you're in a fragile state, sis, but helping others is a great way to forget your troubles. You can use this time to keep practicing medicine while figuring out your next move." Frank was very convincing, just as he'd been when they were kids.

"I'm not even licensed in West Virginia. I'll have to think about it. Give me a week or so."

"Clare, we need you now! The lawyer on the board will expedite a provisional license. I'll send Josh to help you pack up your stuff from Dr. S-O-B's home office, so you don't have to face him alone. It's a win-win."

Some win-win! Here I am…on some godforsaken road and—

Clare hit a pothole, and it jarred the truck. "Ouch! This broken road feels like my life!" she grunted under her breath, causing Maggie to stir a little. She looked over and noticed Maggie's arm; the rope-burn scars were still visible.

What happened to you, Maggie? Are you running from someone? Maybe we're not so different, except that you have faith in God, and I've lost mine. Are you faking amnesia? I wish I had more time to investigate, but I'm overwhelmed. How did I get into this predicament? Oh yeah, the charming Dr. Greg!

Two days after Clare had called Frank, he showed up with his son, Josh. He handed her a map and gas money and unfolded a waterproof tent that fit inside the back of her 1964 Studebaker Champ pickup. Clare had borrowed the truck from Frank as a temporary means of transportation, but she was still driving it two years later.

"How on earth did you get a tent made so quickly and to fit so perfectly?"

"Let's just say being an engineer in a large firm has some perks."

The truck was a forest-green, three-speed, manual-transmission, six-cylinder vehicle that needed a paint job. The tent was to protect the boxed supplies and linens that local churches had dropped off the same day Frank and Josh arrived.

"You don't waste any time! Guess I'm not the only one my big brother looks after."

As it turned out, they never had the opportunity to put any of Clare's things into storage. News about the destruction caused by Hurricane Agnes prompted them to leave the morning after the storm, hoping the highways were passable.

Clare wanted to let go of the past. *I better keep my eyes on the future.* So she buried her heartache in work. Her days were filled with stitching cuts, dispensing medications, and follow-up treatments, not to mention keeping records, all while trying to unravel the Maggie mystery. She barely had time to eat or sleep. Many country roads needed repair, and most homes were still without power. All these elements added to her increasing number of patient injuries and illnesses.

Maggie and Josh distributed water and canned goods and gave out clean linens and clothing since the town laundromat was not in service. They followed Clare as she went from trailer to trailer, ministering to the needs of the people. Maggie kept a record of Clare's diagnoses and medication disbursement. Josh performed the heavy lifting.

Time passed quickly, and it was hard for Clare to believe she had left Maryland a month ago. She slowed down as she drove through the town of Berkeley Springs and turned on a small wooded road that led to the trailer park she had visited her first week at the mission. She had encountered pitiful conditions then, and life did not look any better for the residents now.

Clare and Maggie entered a trailer. A woman with gray streaks in her black hair was bent over a small stove. She wore an apron, and when Maggie saw her, she blurted out, "Aunt Marge!" Then, she covered her mouth and looked around the trailer very slowly.

Clare said, "Maggie, her name is Helen." Clare saw Maggie's eyes glaze over as she felt for the door handle behind her.

Maggie turned, swung the door open, rushed down the small steps, past Josh, and started to slip and slide across the muddy landscape.

"Maggie, where are you going?" Josh yelled and looked up at Clare standing in the doorway. She motioned for him to follow her.

Maggie was running haphazardly; she picked up speed when she hit the street.

Blaise jumped off the truck and was in hot pursuit.

"Maggie, stop running," Josh yelled. But she didn't look back.

He finally caught up to her, grabbed her arm, and pulled her close. She was crying so hard that she couldn't catch her breath. He thought she would have a heart attack.

"Maggie, it's okay; don't cry."

But she wouldn't stop. He circled her arm around his neck, placed his arm around her waist, and half lifted, half dragged her back to the trailer. She kept stumbling, and Josh did his best to hold her steady. As they reached the truck, her knees buckled.

"Aunt Clare!" he called. "Come quick."

Clare helped hoist Maggie onto the bed of the truck.

Blaise jumped up next to her and whimpered.

"What happened?" Josh asked.

"I'm not sure, but something clicked in her memory."

"When I caught up to her, she wouldn't—no, it seemed like she couldn't—stop crying. I didn't know what to do. I got her back as best I could. I hope I didn't hurt her."

Clare was examining Maggie's eyes with her penlight. "Did she say anything?"

Josh was still shaking. "She said, 'God, please help me remember.'"

CHAPTER 34

If, then, you are looking for
the way by which you should go,
take Christ, because He is the way.

—*Saint Thomas Aquinas*

Josh knocked on the kitchen door.

"The door's open," Clare called.

He found Clare sitting at the kitchen table, staring at a telephone book, a cup of coffee in her hand. "Aunt Clare, are we going on rounds this morning?"

"Yes, but I thought I'd let Maggie sleep in after yesterday's incident. She said another name from her past—Aunt Marge. I don't believe she's making any of this up, and I'm trying to find a doctor nearby to help."

"You mean like a psychiatrist?"

"Well, maybe a professional can help her piece together Kevin and Aunt Marge. I need to do something before I return to Maryland." She sipped her coffee. "Would you like a cup?"

"Sure. The coffee at the volunteer tent stinks."

"I'm surprised you stayed here so much. You could have gone home with your dad on weekends. You know that's the reason he visited every Friday."

"I know, but I like hanging out here. There's always a pickup football game in the afternoon, and the Friday-night bonfires have been fun."

Clare poured him a cup of coffee. "Well, you've been a great help."

"Oh yeah, that too." He smiled.

She closed the book. "I'll go see if she is up. I've worked her hard, and I hope the extra sleep is what she needed."

Josh sat sipping the hot liquid and almost spilled it when he heard Clare come barreling down the stairs.

"Maggie and Blaise are gone!" Clare frantically paced the small kitchen. She shoved a note into his hand. "Here, read this."

> *Dr. Clare,*
>
> *Thanks for all your help. I need to find my way home now. Things are starting to come back to me, and I've imposed on you long enough. I know I'm a child of God and that Jesus is with me wherever I go. Tell Josh thanks for being such a good friend.*
>
> *Love, Maggie (if that really is my name)*

"Oh God, Josh, this is awful! It's possible Maggie escaped from a bad situation and doesn't know who or what she is running from. She could remember just enough to put her back in danger."

"I'll search around here, then head towards town," he said.

"Good. I'll tell Pastor Jeremy what's happening, then drive to the bus station. Maybe she's there."

Josh's heart was racing. He hadn't been honest with his aunt about why he stayed on the weekends. It was fun to be around Maggie. He had never met anyone like her and was fascinated by a girl who was silly enough to talk to ladybugs and humble enough to listen for an answer.

Maggie, where could you have gone? I don't know why you would think you are in the way. You've been great.

He told other volunteers to check all the tents. "If you find Maggie, let the pastor know."

He ran past the fire pit and thought of how her face glowed when she sat around the bonfire. She sang along with everybody as the pastor played his guitar. Josh was sure the glow on her face reflected the flame that burned in her heart more than the heat from the fire. If she saw someone who looked lonely, she plopped down next to them, gave them a shoulder bump, and smiled. She had a way of making everyone feel welcome.

After thoroughly searching the surrounding area, he headed to town, looking in store windows and restaurants. His chest was tight from fear that he might never see her again. *What will I do if she disappears forever?*

After checking the bus station, Clare drove slowly through the streets, watching for any sign of the teen. *Maggie, where are you?* Tapping her fingers on the steering wheel, she impatiently waited for the red light to turn green. Clare closed her eyes. *Dear God, if Maggie is right about You, please guide me to her. And maybe get Your Mother involved?*

A horn beeped. Clare opened her eyes and stepped on the gas. Maggie had become a part of her. She loved her faithful heart. Maggie, thinking she was a burden, forced Clare to examine her attitude. *Perhaps I dismissed her beliefs too quickly.*

Clare remembered an incident from a couple of weeks earlier; this was not the first time she could not find Maggie.

***

Clare went into Maggie's room to say good night, but her bed was empty.

252

After checking the house, she called, "Maggie, where are you?"

"I'm down here."

Clare leaned out the window and saw Maggie lying on a blanket in the backyard, Blaise resting by her side. "What are you doing?"

"Come down."

"Maggie, why are you lying out here?" Clare asked as she stood next to the blanket.

"Lay down and look up at the stars."

Clare sighed deeply but did as instructed. It was peaceful, but Clare refused to let the peacefulness in. "Maggie, for goodness's sake. We have a full schedule tomorrow. I don't have time for this. You need your sleep too." Clare sighed. "Maggie, I will be leaving soon. I am concerned about you."

"I know, but I believe it'll work out."

"You have to face reality." Clare reached for Maggie's hand. "I don't want you to end up in foster care."

Maggie continued to stare at the stars.

"Can't you remember anything?"

Maggie whispered, "I am trying to remember. I believe I will when God allows it. He's waiting for the right time. Laying here and looking up at the stars, I hear God's voice."

Again with the voice. Clare asked patronizingly, "And what does God say?"

Maggie calmly responded, "Be still and know that I am God."

Clare huffed. "Well, that isn't very helpful." She immediately regretted her harshness. Maggie's faith never wavered. Her trust in God was unfathomable to Clare; it was certainly strong enough for two people.

***

Perhaps the Lord wants me to follow Maggie's example and just trust in Him.

Oh, Clare, stop it! That's absurd.

How can I entertain such thoughts after all that life has dealt me? I've worked hard to get to where I am, and God never lifted a mighty hand to help me.

She continued to drive aimlessly, feeling resentful and defeated.

And just where are you, Clare?

She parked on Washington Street, stepped out of the truck, and slammed the door. "I'll tell you where I am." She stomped into the park. "In the middle of nowhere"—she threw her arms up in the air—"trying to keep my head on straight and care for hundreds of people, and search for a runaway"—she dropped her arms, plopped down on a bench, lowered her head, and took a deep breath—"who has somehow managed to get under my skin and make me view my world differently." She looked up and saw Josh running in her direction.

"No luck," he hollered.

They met on the corner of Washington and Church Streets. Clare felt helpless.

"Aunt Clare, where can she be?" Josh hung his head.

Clare let out a sigh of defeat.

Woof!

Josh lifted his head and looked over Clare's shoulder. "Look!" He pointed behind her.

She turned and saw the most beautiful sight. It was Blaise, sitting on the front steps of Saint Agnes Catholic Church. They ran up the stone steps and greeted Blaise in front of wooden doors slightly ajar.

"Good boy, Blaise!"

They squeezed through the doors and waited for their eyes to adjust to the dim light. Josh spotted Maggie up by the altar and started toward her.

Clare grabbed his arm and whispered, "Let's hang back here and let her have this time alone."

The church was empty, so they sat in a back pew to watch Maggie as she stood before the statue of Mary and Joseph holding the Baby Jesus. Maggie reached into her pocket and pulled something out. A clunking noise reverberated throughout the church when she placed a coin through a metal slot, then lit a candle and knelt to pray. A few moments passed, and she got up, walked over to the railing surrounding the altar, and looked up at the crucifix hanging above the tabernacle. She slowly knelt, rested her head on the communion rail, and started to cry.

"Now…I think we should go be with her," Josh anxiously whispered.

Without saying a word, they walked up and knelt on either side of her. Clare put her arm around Maggie and drew her close.

Maggie looked up at the tabernacle, then threw her arms around Clare's neck.

Thank You.

CHAPTER 35

Cast all your anxieties on Him,
for He cares about you.

—*1 Peter 5:7*

The remaining weeks of Clare's position with DOW sped by. The power and water supplies had been restored to most of West Virginia, reducing the number of illnesses due to unsanitary conditions. There were fewer patients to visit; and the number of patients seeking medical attention on the grounds had slowed to a manageable number. Clare wanted a smooth handoff to Dr. Andrew, so she and Maggie organized records, inventory, and patient-status charts, but Clare's main concern was finding a safe solution for Maggie.

Questions plagued her. Could Maggie keep Blaise once foster care stepped in? Could Frank and Teresa stay in contact with her? Would she be allowed to visit her once she sorted everything out with Greg? She had no idea how long that would take. Just the thought of Greg set her teeth on edge.

I'm not like Maggie, who believes God works behind the scenes. That's great when you're a kid, but the real world demands more.

Clare anticipated Dr. Andrew's return with pleasure and apprehension. *I've got to get home and figure out the rest of my life. If Greg has filled my position, I'll have to find a new practice. A regular paycheck would be helpful. I can't live in limbo forever. But what will happen to Maggie?*

***

Frank and Pastor Jeremy were waiting for Clare and the teens when they returned from their rounds. When Maggie saw Frank, her heart sank. She knew Josh's father was coming for him since school was only a week away. She had been dreading this moment.

It both surprised and comforted her when Josh took her hand. He opened the car door and said, "Maggie, can you help me get my stuff from the tent?"

They slowly walked to the volunteer tent, where Josh had slept all summer. Maggie looked at Josh and noticed his hair curled around his ears. It had gotten pretty long, and it seemed natural for her to reach up and brush it out of his eyes.

"Maggie, I knew this day would come. I wish I didn't have to leave."

God, I know you're in control, but I'm scared.

She watched Josh stuff his clothes, shoes, and toiletries into his duffel bag, and then he turned to look at her.

"I've never met anyone like you, Maggie. I want to stay in touch if you want to. Here's my address and phone number." He slipped a piece of paper into her hand. "And I thought you might like to have this. It's a photo of us at the bonfire."

Maggie looked at the photo and then pressed the gifts against her chest. She could barely find her voice to say thank you.

"I only live about twenty miles away. I hope to get a car this year, and I'll come to visit you."

She slipped the photo and address into her pocket and burst into tears. "But, Josh, I won't be here." She covered her face and said, "What if I end up even farther away? What if I never remember?" *What happens when you get busy with sports? Or if you have a girlfriend?*

Josh reached out and drew her close.

She put her arms around his shoulders, and something tugged at her heart. He felt so solid beneath her fingers. He reminded her of someone, but who? She felt safe when she was with Josh. He had been the parachute that kept her floating above the storm, up in the clouds. *But it is not time, or safe, for me to land yet.*

She looked into his eyes and wondered if she'd ever kissed a boy. *No, we should* not *kiss! That would make it even harder to say goodbye.*

Maggie tried to push away, but Josh pulled her back, lowered his head, and rested his chin on her forehead. "Don't cry, Maggie. I'll pray for you and visit you wherever you are. I promise."

Maggie looked up, and her lips gently brushed his. It was all by accident, yet she felt an electric sensation in her body.

He hugged her again, let go of her arms, turned, and walked out of the tent.

***

Meanwhile, Frank nervously hugged Clare and whispered, "Hey, sis, we have a slight problem."

Clare pulled away. "What's wrong?"

He cleared his throat and continued, "Dr. Andrew had a bit of a setback." Frank played with the gravel in the driveway with the toe of his shoe. "Would you consider staying on until December?"

Clare took a step back, as if to dodge the question. "What? NO!" She turned and walked around for a moment, talking to herself. "I cannot believe this!"

Okay, okay, stay calm. She looked up at Frank and Jeremy, who looked quite tense. "Give me a minute to think."

She walked away and tapped her foot. This whole experience had been rewarding. The people she served appreciated her and highly regarded her medical advice. Her breakup with Greg had shaken her, but the mission work had restored her confidence. *But I'm ready to move forward to the next chapter in my life, whatever it might be.*

She walked back to face Frank and Jeremy. "I...I-I don't think I can," she stammered and put her face in her hands as she leaned on Frank's shoulder. "I can't keep my life on hold forever."

"Clare, I'm sorry to ask this, but you've done so much good here." He lifted her chin to look at her. He smiled and said, "I love you, sis, and I'll respect any decision you make."

Clare thought about Maggie and what would become of her. Her mind flashed to the premature twins she and Maggie had delivered and Mr. Goode, whose leg wound hadn't completely healed.

Jeremy added, "If you stay, I'll continue to provide meals and someone to do your laundry and anything else you may need."

Frank added, "I spoke to the principal at Josh's school."

"Our old high school? Is Rickety Richards still the principal?"

"No, now it is Phil, a friend of mine. I told him about my niece, who is visiting, and he said she was welcome to attend classes until December."

"Your niece, huh? Now, *that's* interesting."

"Well, she's kinda like a niece since you're her guardian."

"How will I get her there and keep my appointments here?"

Jeremy spoke up, "A private bus for the school picks the students up, and one of the stops is here at the church."

"Well, you two have it all figured out." Clare frowned.

"Come on, Clare, your adventure continues." Frank was clever.

She had prepared her head to return to Maryland in a week, but perhaps her heart was not quite ready. She was still pretty raw from her breakup and had to confess that her work here filled a hollow in her heart.

I had hoped that Greg would call me after I gave Gladys, our office receptionist, my number. He might not want me back in his practice after I took off without a word. A few more months away might give me a fresh perspective. Maybe Maggie is right. Perhaps it's best to let God take control of my life.

Josh walked over. "Aunt Clare, thank you for taking me under your wing." He hugged her and cleared his throat. "I had the best summer ever."

Clare hugged him back. "I couldn't have done it without you."

He swung his duffel bag over his shoulder and walked to his father's car.

"Dr. Clare, will you stay? Please?" Jeremy's eyes begged her to say yes.

Clare took a deep breath. "Yes, I'll stay until Dr. Andrew arrives."

Jeremy hugged her tight. " Thank you!" He released his hold on her. "I have to get over to church for a meeting. Frank, I'll see you next week when the board meets."

Clare sighed and looked at Frank, who said, "By the way, Teresa, your sister-in-law, has invited you and Maggie to join us for Sunday dinners whenever you can. She's sad that you only managed two family dinners all summer." He hugged her and walked to the car. "See ya, sis!"

***

Maggie stood in the tent and tried to pull herself together. She didn't want Clare to know how upset she was that she and

Josh were leaving. She found the tissue box, wiped her eyes, blew her nose, and left the tent in time to wave goodbye as Frank and Josh drove down the gravel driveway.

Clare walked over to Maggie and put her arm around her shoulders. "Maggie"—Clare smiled—"I've decided to stay on here a few more months."

"Really!" She hugged Clare. "That's awesome! But why? I thought you had to get home, and Dr. Andrew was taking over."

"Yes, funny how things turn out sometimes. Also, my brother worked it out so you can attend Josh's school for a few months. Would you like that?"

"This gets better and better!"

***

Maggie knelt by her bed and thanked the Lord for answering her prayer not to be separated from Dr. Clare. When she got under the covers, she was too excited to sleep. Clare came in to say goodnight, and Maggie asked, "Dr. Clare, why did you decide to stay? I know you wanted to get home. Is it all because of me?"

Clare sat on the edge of her bed. "No, it's not all because of you, sweetheart, but I want to find your family. Dr. Andrew will return mid-December, and Frank and Jeremy made me realize how much the people here depend on me." Clare became silent as a thought entered her mind. "I guess everything happens for a reason."

"Dr. Clare, did I hear you correctly?"

Oh gosh. Did I say that out loud? Clare quickly remarked, "I'll stay 'til the Advent season."

CHAPTER 36

The endurance of darkness is
the preparation for great light.

—*Saint John of the Cross*

The governor of Maryland stood on the corner of Maryland Avenue and Main Street and congratulated the residents of Ellicott City for being so resilient. "It's hard to believe that just four months ago, this street was fourteen feet underwater," he said, pointing to the B&O Railway overpass towering eighteen feet above him. "The floodwater rose from the Patapsco River, almost completely covering these railroad tracks and devastating every store and business on this street. But today, as we celebrate this city's bicentennial, I want to congratulate everyone on your hard work and dedication to restoring Main Street to its historic appearance."

The crowd cheered.

"Now, I would like to take a moment of silence for those who lost their lives in the wake of Hurricane Agnes."

***

Beverly had organized a prayer vigil at school when it reopened. Every day, a group of students gathered to pray a rosary for Maggie's safe return.

The sheriff was tireless as he worked the case. He had communicated with local and surrounding jurisdictions and circulated a description of Maggie, and hoping for a clue to her disappearance. He contacted local newspapers with her photo and description, asking anyone with information to contact the sheriff's office.

His motives were not entirely pure. If Maggie was alive, he needed to find her before anyone else. She was the missing piece of the puzzle. He didn't like thinking his son was in any way responsible for Kevin Jackson's death or Maggie's disappearance, but there were too many coincidences. The sheriff began to wonder to what lengths he would go to mitigate the consequences of Chuck's involvement.

***

There was a knock on the door. Mitch was expecting Father James for their weekly Saturday hike on the trails that hugged the Patapsco River. They had an unspoken motive. The two looked for any lead—a morsel, a clue—anything that might lead them to Maggie.

He opened the door and found the sheriff on his porch. Even though he was not in uniform, Mitch had a sudden flashback, a vivid memory of the sheriff standing on his doorstep four months earlier. His heart began to race, and his face grew hot and clammy.

"You okay, Mitch?"

No, I'm not okay. My niece vanished without a trace four months ago! "Sheriff, I wasn't expecting you."

"I was driving past your home and thought I'd check in."

Father James was walking up to Mitch's house when he came upon the car in the driveway. He noticed the black sheriff's star on the bumper and the local high school decal on the back window. His memory returned to the night Maggie and Kevin left the church parking lot. The car in the driveway was the car that followed them. He was sure of it. He knocked on the door.

"Hello, James. Come in." At Father James's request, Mitch had dropped the formality of calling the priest Father. Mitch was ten years his junior, but they had formed a close friendship while spending many hours together since Maggie's disappearance.

James asked, "Is that your car in the driveway, Sheriff?"

"Yes, but my son Chuck is the one who usually drives it. The state police had it on the chopping block, so I got it for a song. I had to paint over the police emblems and black portions in the drab tan color to match the rest of the vehicle. I even left the bullet hole in the fender by the license plate. I'm not one to waste money."

"Well, I can understand that," Father James said as he rubbed his chin.

"Thanks for stopping by, Sheriff." Mitch shook his hand. "I appreciate all your efforts."

"Not a problem. I'll be in touch."

After the sheriff departed, Father James stood staring out the window as if seeing something in the distance.

"James, you okay?"

No reply.

Mitch's voice grew louder as he almost shouted, "James! Whatcha looking at?"

"I'm not sure." He continued to stare. "That car, I saw it follow Kevin out of the church parking lot the night of the storm. I recognize the black sheriff's star on the bumper."

"You never mentioned that before."

"I'm only remembering it now."

"So a car followed them…" Mitch pulled out his journal to enter this new information. He kept notes of anything associated with the night of the storm. He even made the sheriff show him where he found Maggie's backpack. (Mitch had no idea that the sheriff had fabricated the location). He also interviewed Maggie's friends, Sam and Marge, the priests and teachers, but so far, his note-taking had been an exercise in futility.

He put the pen behind his ear. "Many people have that sticker if they contribute to the Sheriff's Fund."

"I know, but the car also had that lion decal on the back window and that ugly tan color." Father James plopped down on the couch. "I knew that seemed odd that night. I had a bad feeling. I wish I had…"

"James, stop and think about it. Why would the sheriff be following Kevin?"

"The sheriff just said that his son drives the car. A while back, Brendan told me that Chuck was a bit of a bad apple, but the sheriff had no idea. Either that or he covers for him. Brendan wasn't sure which."

"Maybe we should tell the sheriff what you saw."

"I'm not sure that would do any good. What would we say? Father James thinks you or your son are involved in Kevin's death."

"Yeah, that wouldn't go over well."

"What information did he have for you today?"

Mitch looked at the journal with his notes in it. "Just checking in with me." Mitch flipped through the pages. "The usual stuff, like have I received any mysterious phone calls or letters." He stopped riffling, held the book open, and snapped his head up to look at Father James. "When I talked with Beverly, she told me about a guy named Chuck who came by the store and harassed Maggie."

"Hmm."

Now Mitch plopped down on the couch next to the priest. "Do you think it's the same Chuck? Maybe I should confront him myself."

"Hold on, Mitch, I'm not sure that's going to do any good, especially if his father is covering for him."

"Do you think the sheriff knows something?"

"I like to assume people have good intentions until proven otherwise. I suggest you go back to the police department. See if they have anything new to offer."

"They don't have any leads either." Mitch threw his notebook across the room. "Why am I keeping these notes? They are a waste of time. This information on Chuck might be promising, but I can't follow it up without looking unhinged, which I am!" Mitch blew air out of his cheeks. "I don't think I feel up to hiking along the river today."

"It'll do us both good. Let's get out and clear our heads. Perhaps we'll discover a new lead."

Mitch rose and went to the mudroom to get his hiking shoes, which were lined up next to a smaller pair of lonely boots.

CHAPTER 37

For I know the plans I have for you,
says the Lord, plans for welfare and not
for evil, to give you a future and a hope.

—*Jeremiah 29:11*

C lare called up the stairs, "Maggie, the bus will be here any minute. It's cold this morning, so don't forget your scarf!"

Maggie bustled down the stairs, balancing her books and backpack.

Clare was about to take a bite of toast when Maggie brushed by her, grabbed the toast, and headed for the door. "Hey, I was about to eat that."

Maggie giggled. "Oh, sorry, I thought you were handing it to me." She opened the door, and Clare ran up behind her to playfully grab the toast, which caused them both to laugh. Maggie and Blaise ran down the gravel driveway as the bus doors opened. She patted Blaise before boarding and turned around to wave to Clare.

Blaise lazily lumbered back to the house. Clare put his food in a bowl. "Blaise, I don't understand Maggie. She's acting like she hasn't a care in the world."

Clare put another piece of bread in the toaster, and a Scripture passage that her father made her memorize came to mind:

Jesus instructed His disciples to take nothing with them — no food, no sack, no money in their belts…

That is Maggie, totally trusting God. I wish I could be like that.

The toast popped up and snapped Clare back to her reality. "No, staying here with Maggie would be impossible. It's mid-December, and my time here is almost up. I've got to get back home and figure out my next move. I'll have to face Greg someday, so I may as well rip the Band-Aid off. That's what the DOW has been, one giant Band-Aid."

Blaise finished his meal and sat down next to Clare.

"You're a good listener, boy." She ruffled his ears. "What hurts the most is that Greg has not tried to contact me. Instead, he had Gladys call me to say they needed me back at the office." Clare furiously scrubbed the dishes in the sink. "Really! That's all I get? I'm needed at the office. The nerve of him!" She slammed the dish into the rack, and it cracked. "Oops! Okay, Clare, calm down."

She continued her soliloquy, "In a way, the Maggie mystery has taken up any extra time I might have had to dwell on my failed romance. That's been good for me, but my concern is for Maggie. The therapist she's been seeing hasn't had any breakthroughs either." She picked up a dish, dried it carefully, and thought of something Maggie had said a few days earlier when she worked with the stage crew to get the stable scene ready for the school Christmas show.

***

"As I put the hay in the manger, I remembered something."

"What was it?" Clare asked with enthusiasm.

"I remember being told that the Holy Family is my family too. That as long as I stay close to Bethlehem, I'll never be alone."

"Maggie, that's wonderful. Who told you this?"

"I don't remember who said it, but it made me realize I'm not lost. I'm exactly where God needs me to be."

Clare was used to Maggie's belief that God would work everything out. "And how do you know this?"

"When I prayed the rosary, I thought of Joseph and Mary and how they would've preferred being around their family when the baby was born. But, centuries before, God had told the prophet Micah that the Messiah would be born in Bethlehem. So it was all part of God's plan that Jesus be born there."

Clare responded, "So let me see if I have this right. You're saying that you are here in an unfamiliar town, with no memory or money, no real place to call home, and it's all part of God's plan?"

"I guess I am."

***

Oddly, I'm in the same situation, except I have my memory, an unhappy one, but a memory just the same.

Clare sat at the table, reached for the kitchen phone, and dialed Social Services.

***

The meeting with Nancy Carr from Social Services went better than expected, so Clare called Frank. "I'll be in your neighborhood. Can you meet me for coffee?"

They sat at a small table by the window. Frank handed her a coffee. "Just the way you like it, cream with two sugars. So what's up?"

"These past six months I've tried everything I know to find Maggie's family. I've shown her picture to area churches and schools, brought her with me on rounds, checked the police missing persons—"

"Clare, settle down. I know you've tried everything. You've gone above and beyond, which has always been your style. It's okay to let go now and—"

Clare took a deep breath. "I've decided to take Maggie back to Maryland with me."

"You what?"

"Yes, I've thought it through and cleared it with Social Services. I have a case agent, Nancy Carr, and as long as I report to her every week, she's good with the arrangement."

"Clare, listen, I know you have a compassionate heart, but this is a little over-the-top. It's hard enough to raise a teen, and you have so much to work out when you return."

"I know. It seems like a lot, but Maggie has brought joy into my life. Looking back at the year I spent with Greg, I never felt joyful. Oh, I had some happy days and nights"—she grinned—"but, mostly, I spent my time fixated on winning his approval, trying to be flawless, and perfecting my medical skills to impress him. Maggie has changed all that for me. She believes everything happens for a reason. At first, her faith annoyed me, but now it calms me."

"Clare, you don't know anything about her."

"I know she trusts that God has her best interest in mind. That's a hard pill for me to swallow, no pun intended, but now I want to believe it too. Her intense love for Jesus and Mary is so deep that she trusts that the Lord will work everything out."

"I can see you've given this a lot of thought."

"Yes, I have, and I wish I had that kind of faith. Dr. Andrew will return to the DOW next week, and my time here is up. Gladys, the receptionist I hired for our practice in Maryland, called me yesterday. Greg wants me to come home."

"Well, Dr. S-O-B misses you. It only took him six months. I hope you've come to your senses."

"I'll see what he has to say when I return. I'm a little miffed that he didn't call me himself. He's either too embarrassed by what he did or upset with me for leaving. I guess I'll find out when I return."

"You know I never approved of that arrangement. God knows you deserve better."

Clare sipped her coffee. "Maybe…somehow…Maggie is the better."

Chapter 38

He who walks with wise men becomes wise,
but the companion of fools will suffer harm.

—*Proverbs 13:20*

"Is this all you want, Sheriff, a pack of cigarettes and a bag of frozen peas?"

"Yep, that'll do it," he said as he put the cigarettes in his coat pocket, grabbed the frozen vegetable bag, and headed for the exit.

The cashier looked up. "Sheriff Wilson, you forgot your change."

But the sheriff was already at the door and didn't turn around. He walked across the parking lot, leaned against his cruiser, and lifted his collar against the cold December air. He lit a cigarette, something he hadn't done in over ten years.

A few minutes later, he spotted Ben limping out of the physical therapy building. He puffed a smoke ring, then dropped and crushed the cigarette into the blacktop. He wished it would be as easy to squash his suspicion that Chuck and his friends were responsible for Kevin's death. He had learned his son was a master at evading questions. Jimmy was useless in a cross-examination, no matter how casual; he resorted to anger when a question frustrated him, which was an effective evasive technique.

It had been almost six months since Maggie's disappearance, and he figured Ben's defense mechanism would have eased up. He also believed Ben was the weakest link in the chain and the last hope for answers. So the sheriff called out, "Hey, Ben, how's your physical therapy going?"

Ben looked up. "What? Oh, not bad, but it's still kinda painful."

"Do you have a minute? I want to talk with you." The sheriff could see Ben tense up.

"I need to get home and ice my knee after the workout."

The sheriff held up the bag of frozen peas. "Already thought of that. Now, take a moment and get in the cruiser."

They both got in, and the sheriff handed Ben the bag. He shivered when he placed the frozen peas on his knee. They drove around as the sheriff talked about baseball and the Orioles and asked about his courses at the community college and if he planned to transfer next year. The sheriff drove toward College Avenue by Saint Paul Church and through Seven Hills.

The sheriff finally got to the point, "Ben, I want you to know that I don't hold you responsible for anything that happened."

"What do you mean?" Ben asked, his voice quavering.

"Chuck and Jimmy told me everything. They said none of it was your fault, so I want you to know that." The sheriff was bluffing and hoped Ben would take the bait.

"I...I don't understand." He nervously squeezed the bag of peas.

The sheriff made the left turn onto Bonnie Branch. "Ben, the baseball bat with blood was found at the scene. I know what happened," he said with certainty as he made a right turn and pulled into the spot where the rescue workers had found Kevin's car.

Ben held his breath, and his eyes grew wide. He trembled as his face turned red, and he burst into tears. "We were just trying to scare Kevin. I know I tied his hands, but Chuck and Jimmy are right. I didn't do anything else to him. I didn't know Jimmy was gonna beat him up or hit him in the head with the bat." Ben covered his face with the bag of peas and started to rock back and forth. "Jimmy said it was an accident, and the blood spurted out, and I can't get that image out of my head." He sobbed. "I'm so glad you know. It's been terrible holding it in. I'm so sorry it happened." He wiped his nose on his sleeve and continued to manhandle the bag of frozen vegetables.

The sheriff stared out the windshield. "So the tree falling on Kevin happened after Jimmy hit him with the bat." It was not a question.

"Yes, we all heard the tree start to fall, and Chuck pulled Maggie out of the way."

The sheriff's eyes opened wide. *So Maggie was with them.*

Ben continued, "Chuck saved her life, but I'm sure Chuck told you that."

The sheriff nodded. *Maggie would have never been in danger if they hadn't dragged her and Kevin out on that stormy night.* It was worse than he suspected. His mind wanted to scream, *Where is Maggie?* but he kept silent, hoping Ben would reveal everything.

"And that's when your knee was damaged."

"Maggie's huge dog jumped out of the woods and knocked Chuck off her."

My God, what was Chuck planning to do? It gets worse by the minute!

274

"Chuck called for help, so Jimmy ran over with the bat. I ran behind him and begged him to stop. I didn't want anyone else to get hurt. He swung the bat, but the dog jumped off, and Jimmy hit my knee instead," Ben admitted through his convulsive gasps.

The sheriff was quiet, then interjected, "And Maggie?"

"The river swept her away, and the dog jumped in after her. That's all I remember 'cause I passed out from the pain." He placed the bag of peas back on his knee and lowered his head. "I feel like this is my punishment for having any part in this. And what's worse is we've been hoping that Maggie is dead so she can't tell what happened." He sniffed. "Kevin told me that I should stop hanging around Chuck and Jimmy because it wouldn't end well." Ben lifted his head. "No offense, Sheriff."

"None taken." *That was actually good advice.*

"I should have listened to Kevin, but I didn't want to hear it. He told me I could turn my life around, like he did, and said I could start by going to Confession. I'm so stupid. I wish I had listened."

The sheriff was in a panic. He tried to think of the charges against the boys. Ben had been seventeen at the time of the incident, but Chuck and Jimmy were eighteen. They were adults. As for Maggie, now he knew they were to blame for her disappearance. He had personally combed the paths along the river for months, but hadn't found a trace of her or the dog. *She's an even bigger mystery. Why has no one found her body?*

"Sheriff, what should I do?"

The sheriff's mind returned to the conversation at hand. "Maybe you should go to Confession. Go see Father James over at Saint Paul Church. Tell him everything you just told me. Clear your conscience. Okay?"

"But he'll make me go to the police."

"I am the police, Ben. You've come to me."

"Okay."

"Now listen." The sheriff's voice was deliberate as he continued, "Do not tell anyone about our conversation. Do you understand? And as Chuck's father, I order you to stay away from him and Jimmy. You got that? They're not to know we talked. Understood?"

"Yes, understood."

The sheriff handed Ben a towel from the back seat so he could dry his eyes. He turned on the engine and pulled away from the scene of the crime. "I'll drive you back to your car. Don't talk anymore, and pull yourself together."

He was frantic as he drove. His advice for Ben to go to Confession was a way to keep Mitch and Father James apart. The sheriff had seen them walking the river's edge and deduced that they were looking for clues to Maggie's disappearance. The sheriff hoped that once the priest learned what happened from Ben's confession, he'd stay away from Mitch.

I have to buy myself some time to figure out how to handle this new information. Ben confirmed my suspicions, and I hate knowing the truth. It's worse than I imagined. He had tried desperately to ignore the clues that led to his son's involvement. *If Ben eases his conscience in Confession, and Father James can never share the information, who needs to know what happened? What good could it possibly do now? We'll get through this, and I'll work on being a better father.*

CHAPTER 39

You must believe in the truth that whatever
God gives you is for your salvation.

—*Saint Catherine of Sienna*

T he trip back to Maryland took less time than the one Clare had made six months earlier. If any signs of the hurricane still lingered, a beautiful dusting of fresh-fallen snow covered them. They stopped for lunch at the Double-T Diner in Catonsville, Maryland, a few miles from Clare's home office, and requested a window seat to watch the truck.

Clare reached into her purse and pulled out an envelope.

"What's that?"

"I'm not sure. Pastor Jeremy handed it to me on my way out the door this morning." Clare slowly broke the seal and found five crisp hundred-dollar bills. "Whoa! I was not expecting this!"

"What does the note say?"

"Thank you for all you did to keep the DOW running smoothly. You are in our prayers. The board members signed it."

Clare smiled. "I see you have an envelope as well."

Maggie's face lit up. "It's from Josh. I gave him one too. I miss him already."

Clare patted her hand with a smile. "You'll see him soon. Frank and Teresa invited us for Christmas."

A waitress interrupted. "What'll it be, hon?"

After they ordered their food, Maggie saw Clare's face cloud over. "What's wrong?"

"I don't know what to expect when we get to my office. I misjudged Greg. I thought of myself as Mrs. Greg Simpson for so long that I lost my identity."

"I guess being away from the situation was a good thing."

"Yes, that is true."

"What would have happened to me if you had never found me? Seems like the Lord took care of me when you broke up with Greg."

Clare grimaced. "So you believe that God's plan was for me to break up with Greg so I could find you?"

"Well, maybe. Is that so far-fetched?"

"Maggie, that's absurd. My finding you had nothing to do with my breaking up with Greg or God. If anything, it had to do with my mistakes, and I've made plenty."

"Mistakes are only mistakes if you don't learn a lesson from them. That's what I believe. Things aren't always what they seem."

Clare was slightly irritated with Maggie's theory. "Well"—she took a deep breath, looked at Maggie, and smiled—"whaddaya say we rediscover our identities together."

Maggie interjected, "I think your identity's intact. You're a giving person. You just spent six months helping the less fortunate in West Virginia and taking care of me. You followed Christ's command to love your neighbor as yourself. I should call you Saint Clare."

"A saint!" She laughed. "Now that's a stretch." *But that's you, isn't it, Maggie? You always find the good in people.* Clare knew her mission work was not done for the love of Christ, but simply as an escape.

They finished their meal just as Blaise poked his head out from under the canvas truck cover and barked at a woman getting into her car. The startled woman dropped her bag on the ground, and the contents rolled out.

"Uh-oh, Maggie, I'll pay the bill. You better go help that lady."

Maggie grabbed her coat and ran outside. She apologized to the lady as she gathered the contents of her bag and handed them to her.

"Oh my," she gasped, "I thought he was a bear!" She laughed. "My husband always says, 'Edith, you're way too jumpy.'"

Maggie reached up and put her arm around Blaise's neck. "He's more like a cuddly teddy bear. I think the smell of your carryout food got his attention. I'm so sorry. Did it get messed up?"

"No, it's stew. Luckily, the top didn't come off the container." The woman got in her car and drove away.

Clare came out, and she and Maggie got into the truck, but Clare hesitated to start the engine. *I've been dreading this moment for six months; I've gone over the scene in my head hundreds of times. Greg will tell me how sorry he is for being unfaithful. He'll beg me to come back.*

"Dr. Clare, how far is your home from here? It feels like home already, probably because I'm with you."

"It's not far."

I may not be welcome there. Greg might be angry that I left and won't forgive me. He could withhold a good reference, or, worse, he might blackball me. I sent a letter saying I would return on December 18, but he never acknowledged it. I have no idea what to expect.

She nervously turned the key in the ignition and drove to the house.

***

Edith hurried home to her husband. "I have a surprise for you. The diner was having a special on your favorite, Brunswick stew."

He set the Christmas edition of the *Baltimore Magazine* on the table and opened to page 7. She handed him the bowl and noticed the photo of Main Street. "It's hard to believe that Main Street was underwater six months ago, and today Christmas wreaths and lights decorate the store windows."

She bent over the magazine and looked closer at a little photo insert in the bottom right-hand corner. She picked it up to get closer to the photo and took her husband's reading glasses off his face.

"Hey, I need those glasses. I was reading that!"

"This is surely the dog I just saw…and this girl, Maggie."

"What dog? Who is Maggie?"

"The girl in this photo. It says she's been missing."

"Edith, what are you talking about?"

"There was a huge dog in a tent in the back of a truck. I nearly jumped out of my skin and dropped your stew when he barked in my ear. This teen with blue eyes and blonde hair ran out to apologize. I am certain this is the girl and her dog."

"Come on, that photo is pretty small. You can't be sure."

"No, I guess I can't," she said as she continued to read. "But, look, here's a number to call if you have any information. I will phone the authorities anyway."

***

Clare was shocked when she drove to her home office and saw a FOR SALE sign on the lawn.

Maggie asked, "Are you selling your home?"

"Maggie, it's true that I lived here, but it's not my home. I mean, I don't own it. It belongs to Dr. Simpson."

"Well, your name is on the sign out front."

"Yes, that's true," Clare said as anxiety swelled in the pit of her stomach. She was attempting to take it all in. Greg's car was not in the driveway, and snow covered the front walk.

She unlocked the front door, and Blaise charged in, slipping on the envelopes delivered through the mail slot. Clare and Maggie picked up the mail and placed it on the reception desk next to a handwritten note from Greg. She was surprised he was not in the office. And where was Gladys?

She reached for the note and then pulled her hand back. *Why a note? Where is everybody? This place should be bustling with patients.* A foreboding feeling came over her, but she didn't want to upset Maggie.

"Let's get you and Blaise settled." She showed Maggie where the bowls were in the kitchen cabinets so Blaise could have some water and food. "How about I show you around."

She tried to be calm but knew something was wrong. The house felt empty even though the furniture in the room was from her parents' home. She had inherited it since Frank and Teresa purchased everything new when they married.

Downstairs, they entered the examination rooms, and her uneasiness increased when she noticed Greg had removed all his medical instruments. They went upstairs, and Maggie went into the first bedroom to put her suitcase down. After that, she found Clare sitting on the bed in the second bedroom, her head in her hands.

Clare turned to Maggie. "Greg removed all his things." Maggie sat down and put her arm around Clare's shoulders; Clare leaned her head against Maggie's. "I figured we wouldn't be here long anyway. I just don't get it. Has Greg moved our office?"

She looked at Maggie. "Don't worry. I'll get back to work, and we can rent a place. You can decorate your room the way you would like."

These words of assurance were all for show. Clare didn't feel confident about anything, and the thought of Greg's note waiting for her on the desk did nothing to ease the ominous feeling.

They went downstairs so that Clare could sort through the mail, deliberately leaving the note from Greg for last. Clare looked through the office appointment book. There were no entries after December 15. *That was four days ago.*

Maggie plopped down next to Clare at the dining room table. "You guys sure get a lot of magazines," she said as she sifted through the pile.

She came across the *Baltimore Magazine* and would have passed it by, except something caught her eye. The front cover was split in two. One side showed a street decorated for Christmas. The other side of the page was the same street with a river running through it. She saw the Caplan's Department Store sign sticking out above the water. Something familiar about the sign made her turn to page 7 to read the story.

A smaller version of the magazine cover displayed the caption, "Ellicott City, Six Months Later." Then, her eyes fixated on the photo in the lower right-hand corner of the page. She looked at it closely. *It's me with my arm around Blaise!* A small heading over the photo read, "Maggie Hartman Still Missing." Her head started to swirl, and she suddenly felt very dizzy.

Clare finally got up the nerve to open Greg's envelope. She could hardly believe the words on the page:

I hope you had a good vacation.

"Vacation!"

> *You'll need to pay the electric bill, or BG&E will turn off the electricity on December 21st.*

"That's in two days!"

> *You're welcome to stay in the house until I find a buyer. I've been offered a position at Mount Sinai Hospital in New York City and couldn't turn it down. It's such a prestigious hospital. Oh, by the way, Gladys and I are getting married.*

"You're marrying Gladys!"

> *A baby is on the way.*

"A baby!!!"

> *Greg* (He had drawn a little happy face over his signature.)

Clare was furious. She crumpled the note, threw it across the table, and turned to Maggie. "Can you believe that son of a—"

Maggie's face had contorted into something Clare recognized from her time spent in the emergency room during her internship. Her expression was a mixture of pain and shock. "Maggie, I'm so sorry. I shouldn't have said that."

Maggie's expression became more stricken, and she started to shake.

"Oh dear." Clare put her arms around Maggie. "We're going to be all right. You don't have to worry."

Tears streamed down Maggie's face. She attempted to speak, but her mouth was a gaping hole, and no sound came out.

Clare looked down and saw the photo. She lifted the magazine to read, "Maggie Hartman is still missing. Contact the sheriff's office with any information." A hint of reverence tinged Clare's voice when she whispered, "Oh...my...God."

***

There was a knock on Edith's door. "Wow, I didn't expect the sheriff himself to show up."

"We follow up on every tip we receive and exhaust every lead. So you think you saw Maggie and her dog in a truck? Do you know what kind of truck?"

"It was green."

"Any make or model?" the sheriff asked, a little annoyed at her lack of information.

"No, but it had a tent in the back. I guess that was for the dog. Wait, let me check with my husband." She hollered into the next room, "Hey, Joe, what kind of truck does Hank love to show off? You know the one he drives around for fun?"

"It's an old 1960-something Studebaker. Why?"

"The truck the dog was in looked like Hank's."

"You said this happened outside the Double-T Diner on Route 40?" questioned the sheriff.

"Yes."

"Okay, Mrs. Clark, thanks for your observation."

"I hope you find her, poor thing...missing all this time."

The sheriff drove straight to the diner. After showing Maggie's photo and asking a few waitresses, he located the one who had served Maggie and Clare.

"Hi, hon, whatcha need?"

"Did you wait on the girl in this photo earlier today?"

"Hmm, let me see." She reached for the photo, squinted her eyes, and pursed her lips, which were so thick with red lipstick they looked like a bright maraschino cherry. She fumbled for her glasses, which dangled from a beaded chain, and placed them on her nose. "That's her, hon. Real sweet. She was with an attractive dark-haired woman."

"Did they pay by check?"

"Nope, cash and left me a nice tip."

"Can you tell me anything else? Did you notice if they had a dog with them?"

"We don't serve dogs here, hon."

The sheriff rolled his eyes.

She leaned over one of the booths, smacked her gum, and addressed a young couple. "Hey, you two about done kissing? We need this table." She brushed past the sheriff and got back to work.

The sheriff knew this wasn't much to go on, but it was something. Two people had now identified Maggie. It shouldn't be hard to find the truck. He radioed the office and asked a deputy to check the DMV.

Has Maggie been living here for six months, right under my nose? How is that possible?

The truth was bound to come out, and it was time to confront Chuck. He was tired of his son's charade anyway. He had indulged him for far too long and had looked the other way when he should have been more of a disciplinarian.

"*Spare the rod and spoil the child,*" his wife used to say, quoting the proverb. He needed her now, but it was her choice to leave. She didn't like what he and their son had become.

He sighed. "I don't like myself much either."

CHAPTER 40

Do not neglect to show hospitality to strangers,
for thereby some have entertained angels unawares.

—*Hebrews 13:2*

C lare quickly scanned the magazine. It was a story of the courage, fortitude, and gratefulness of those who had worked to restore the damaged buildings on Main Street to their original character. Two sentences described the teen who had disappeared the night of the storm.

Maggie grabbed Clare's arm and would not let go as dry heaves and sobs overwhelmed her body.

"It'll be okay, sweetheart. Don't try to talk just yet."

Blaise whimpered as Clare rocked back and forth with Maggie in her arms. "It's okay, boy," Clare whispered. "She'll be okay." But Clare wondered if that was true. *Have I put this child in danger by bringing her back to Maryland?* Clare moved Maggie to the couch.

Blaise nuzzled up to her, and Maggie put her arms around him. Memories flashed through her mind like fireworks exploding against a dark sky. She was playing on a beach with her parents, then remembered their caskets. She saw Mitch handing her a bouquet of roses, Father James holding a host, Marge standing at the stove, and Father Brendan dozing at his desk. Scenes from her life soared in and out of her mind, warping time and space.

Clare knelt, and Maggie buried her head in the doctor's shoulder and sobbed. "Maggie, take your time. It's okay. I can call the sheriff and find your family."

Maggie stiffened. "No! You can't call the sheriff!"

The night of the flood rushed in. She remembered Kevin trying to protect her and the bat hitting his head. The vision of him slumping to the ground in a puddle of blood forced its way in. Chuck's face flashed before her, and she wailed again.

"No, don't call the sheriff. It was his son who killed Kevin."

"Kevin?" Clare recalled Maggie shouting his name in a dream. "Maggie, what do you mean? Are you sure?"

Maggie buried her face in her hands.

"Okay, just try to relax and let the memories slowly come to mind."

Clare's tone was soothing, but Maggie's mind swelled with terror. "It was Chuck. He had a gun. Wait, it was Jimmy who hit Kevin with the bat, but Chuck was on top of me, and he tried to strangle me." She wailed.

"Stop thinking for a moment." *I have to get her to settle down enough to make sense.*

"Maggie, let's pray a "Hail Mary" together."

When they had finished, Clare said, "Okay, now, tell me about your parents."

Maggie leaned into Clare again. "They died in a car accident, and my Uncle Mitch brought me to Maryland to live with him— Oh no!" Maggie sat up straight. "Uncle Mitch must be beside himself with worry. I have to get to him. Can you take me?"

"Yes, of course, but tell me about the sheriff."

"His son, Chuck, is the one who kidnapped me and Kevin. The sheriff always covers up for Chuck." Maggie closed her eyes and told Clare what happened that night as well as she could remember. "Kevin was trying to shield me from Jimmy, who hit him in the head with the bat. Then Blaise"—she stopped speaking and hugged his neck again—"came out of nowhere and knocked Chuck off of me. Lightning flashed, and the rain kept pouring down, and, suddenly, I was in the water. When I woke up, I heard sirens. I walked toward some lights at the truck stop and saw the sheriff. That's the last thing I remember."

"The Elkridge Truck Stop on Route 1?"

"Yes, I remember now. I climbed in the truck to hide from the sheriff."

"I remember the sheriff. I told him he should eat some pancakes because his hands were shaking, and he gave us an alternate route since some roads had flooded."

"They were trying to hurt Kevin, all because of me!" She started shaking.

Clare took her in her arms again. "Maggie, what happened was not your fault."

Well, this explains the amnesia. I'm amazed she survived the river! God was watching over her.

Clare grabbed some tissues. "We should let your uncle know you are alive. You love your Uncle Mitch?"

"Oh yes, very much. My aunt Len, his wife, died, and he was lost and so lonely. I can't imagine how he's doing without me."

"Okay, we need to call him. Do you remember your phone number?"

Clare sat at the desk, picked up the receiver, and slammed it down. " Good grief! I can't believe Greg had the phone disconnected!"

She rested her elbows on the desk, put her head in her hands, and thought out loud, "Okay, here's what we do. You write your uncle a note. Will he recognize your handwriting?"

"Yes, he should."

"Okay, write the note, and I'll deliver it and bring your uncle back here. What's your address?"

Maggie recited her address then said, "Dr. Clare, I should come with you."

"I don't think that's a good idea. Call it intuition. Something I wish I had paid more attention to in the past." *I would also like to check this Uncle Mitch out myself. There might be more to this story than Maggie remembers. I'm not turning her over to anyone just yet.*

Clare got some notepaper from the desk and handed Maggie a pen.

"I'm not sure what to write."

"Oh, right, this will be a bit of a shock. How about, 'Dear Uncle Mitch, the lady who bears this note is a trusted friend. She'll explain why I am not with her, and she will bring you to me. Trust her. I love you and miss you. See you soon.'?"

"I signed it, 'Love, Maggie-doodle.' He sometimes calls me that."

"Nice touch."

Maggie had an idea. "Here, take my ladybug pin. He'll recognize it if he doesn't believe the note."

"Did your uncle give this to you?"

"Yes."

Clare smiled. "I knew it came from someone special." *But I am still checking him out!*

Clare pulled out her map and found the address on College Avenue. She knew the street, and it was only a few miles away. She had a bad feeling about the sheriff, and maybe it was spilling over to the uncle. It might just be silly paranoia, but her antenna was up. After Maggie's story, she wasn't ready to trust anyone anytime soon.

***

Clare found Mitch's home and pulled into the circular driveway. She stepped out of the vehicle and into soggy melted snow. " Shoot, I should have put my boots on." She shivered and wondered if it was her cold feet or the dire situation.

Will Mitch believe me?

With Maggie's note and pin in her hand, she took a deep, trembling breath and knocked on the front door. A tall man with tired eyes and tousled hair answered the door. "Mr. Hartman?"

"Yes."

"Mr. Mitch Hartman?"

"Yes again."

"I'm Dr. Clare McGuire. This sounds a bit forward, but may I come in?"

Mitch was not in the mood for another woman trying to weasel her way into his life to get his mind off Maggie. *However, this one has an unconventional approach—no makeup, no casserole or bottle of wine, and a poor choice of footwear.* "I'm sorry, but I am in the middle of my work here and—"

Clare extended her hand with the ladybug pin. Mitch almost fell over but held on to the door. He reached for it, but Clare pulled her hand back.

"That belongs to Maggie. Where did you get it?" His voice was frantic, almost pleading.

"Maggie gave it to me. She's okay. May I come in?"

Mitch opened the door all the way, and she entered. He tried to remain calm, but his head was spinning out of control.

"I have a note from her."

Mitch took the note and devoured the words as if he were a starving man. His eyes went up and down the paper several times.

Clare stepped into the living room to look around. There was a framed picture of Maggie, Mitch, and Blaise on the table that also held a Bible opened to the Psalms, a small statue of the Blessed Mother, and an Advent wreath with purple and pink candles.

"Advent, the season of waiting," Clare said under her breath.

"You can take me to Maggie?"

She turned around. "Yes."

Are you really who you say you are? Why are you looking around like you're casing my home? The excitement on his face quickly turned to suspicion, and he crossed his arms over his chest. "Well, why didn't you just bring her to me?" He waited for this so-called Dr. McGuire to have a good answer.

Instead, she headed out the door. "I'll explain on the way." Clare opened the truck door and looked at Mitch, who stood frozen in the doorway. "You coming?"

He stood a few seconds more, deciding what to do, then grabbed his coat and keys from the hook and followed. He tried to think clearly, but the note from Maggie had his heart pounding in his ears.

Once in the truck, Clare handed him the pin. He caressed it as if it were Maggie herself. He looked at Clare and wondered what kind of doctor she might be. She seemed assertive and self-confident.

"My family practice is in Catonsville. I know you have a million questions, but the story will be Maggie's to tell. I can fill in where needed. When I found her six months ago, she was badly cut and bruised, dehydrated, and suffering from amnesia. We've been living in West Virginia."

"West Virginia!"

"Today, her memory returned after she saw her photo in *Baltimore Magazine.*"

Clare drove past Saint Paul Church and made the turn onto Maryland Avenue. As she went around the corner, a siren and flashing lights went off behind her truck.

Mitch saw the panic on her face as she looked in her side mirror and blurted out, "Uh-oh! Somehow, he knows. But how?"

"Knows what?"

Suddenly, Mitch's body jerked back when she stepped on the gas; then it propelled forward when the tires screeched to a halt at the red light.

The sheriff got out of his cruiser and walked toward them.

She tapped the steering wheel. "C'mon, turn green!"

"What the hell is going on? Are you running from the police?"

"No, of course not!"

"You'd better come clean right now! Are you looking for money?"

"No!!!"

"A ransom?"

"That's ridiculous!" She lowered her voice and, from the corner of her mouth, said, "I don't trust the sheriff."

Something in that statement resonated with Mitch.

"Good afternoon, ma'am. I need your license and registration, please."

As Clare rifled through her purse, Mitch leaned over. "Is there a problem, Sheriff?"

"Is that you, Mitch? Why are you in this truck?"

"Why did you pull us over? We weren't speeding."

"No, um, I just…" Traffic started backing up behind his cruiser. "I…I…just…wanted to…see what's in the tent of the truck."

Mitch realized the sheriff was fumbling for a reason and became quite irritated. "Do you have a warrant, Sheriff?

The sheriff looked contrite. "No, but I…"

"Dr. McGuire and I have someplace to be right now. If you could—"

The sheriff interrupted Mitch, "My concern is that this tent is dangerous because it obscures the driver's vision."

"That's the reason you pulled us over?" Mitch's annoyance grew.

Clare stopped fumbling in her purse. She mumbled, "You had no concern with the tent six months ago." Then, louder, she said, "The tent isn't a problem. I use my side mirrors."

"Sheriff, you have your answer," Mitch answered angrily. "You're holding up traffic."

"Guess you're right," he said in agreement. Then he caustically added, "Drive carefully, Doctor."

He walked to his cruiser as Clare put her truck into gear and turned right onto Main Street. She saw in her side mirror that the sheriff had made a left and let out the breath she had been holding. "Phew!"

She looked at Mitch. "I'm surprised you did that for me."

"Yeah, I'm surprised too." But he had his misgivings about the sheriff as well. He had Maggie's pin in his hand and the letter written by her, so he decided to play along. He hoped this woman was not some psychopath who had kidnapped Maggie six months ago.

Clare drove over the bridge into the borough of Oella and headed up Old Frederick Road. She made some winding turns through a neighborhood and pulled into a driveway. She bolted from the truck and ran to the front door.

Mitch was careful to check out the surroundings before he got out. *She could have an accomplice or a gun.* He read the sign:

> *Gregory Simpson, MD*
> *Clare Anne McGuire, MD*
> *Family Practice*

So she truly is a doctor.

He slowly got out as Clare unlocked the door. Mitch caught sight of Maggie and hesitated only a second before he ran across the slushy pavement, slipping once before reaching her. He felt like a thirsty traveler who had found an oasis in the desert.

As the two embraced in the doorway, Clare stood back and delighted in the reunion. She thought her heart might burst as she watched Mitch and Maggie, overcome with joy, get down on their knees and hold on to each other.

So this is what authentic love looks like. Maybe Maggie is right. God is in control.

CHAPTER 41

Do not walk through time without
worthy evidence of your passage.

—*Pope John XXIII*

The sheriff pounded his fist on the steering wheel after he let Clare drive away. *Well, that settled it.*

The doctor fit the description from the waitress, and Edith Clark had described Maggie and her dog. With Mitch in the truck, there was no other answer. Maggie was alive. *But how did she survive, and where was she these last six months? Why did Mitch purposely keep this secret from me? I fear the answer to that question.* He pulled into his driveway. *I'll give my son one more chance to come clean.*

He found Chuck and Jimmy sitting in the living room, playing a new video game called Pong. The sheriff was ashamed. His son was eighteen years old, home from college for the Christmas break, and playing games rather than working for a few weeks to earn some money. He stood in the doorway and watched the skill Chuck possessed at such a mundane pastime.

"So where's Ben?" he asked.

Chuck didn't miss a beat and continued to play as he said, "Oh hey, Dad. I didn't hear you come in. We haven't seen him. I think he's working at his uncle's gas station over the break."

Jimmy's eyes never left the TV screen. "Man, you're an expert at this game!"

The sheriff waited then said, "They found Maggie."

Chuck froze, and the Pong started bouncing haphazardly from side to side on the screen. "Maggie who?" he said, his voice quavering as he tried to regain control of the Pong.

"Maggie Hartman. You know, the girl who's been missing since the night of Hurricane Agnes."

"Oh yeah, that Maggie. That was so long ago that I'd forgotten about her. Where'd they find her body?"

"What makes you think they found her body?"

"Oh, you just said they found her. I figured she must have drowned."

"I didn't say they found her body. I said they found *her*. Why would you assume she drowned?"

Chuck dropped the control stick but didn't answer his father.

Jimmy said, "Hey, I have to get home. I'll see you later, Chuck."

"Sit down, Jimmy," the sheriff commanded. He added, "I had your baseball bat analyzed," which was a lie. "Do you know what I discovered?"

Both boys were silent.

"Blood. They found the discoloration on the bat to be blood. Now, what I want to know is, what will Maggie's story be when she has the chance to tell it?"

Chuck's voice sounded desperate as he replied, "How would we know? We hardly knew her."

The sheriff spoke through gritted teeth, "One last chance, Chuck. Tell me the truth."

Chuck looked away, so the sheriff turned to Jimmy, who was cowering in the corner. "Jimmy?" the sheriff asked, pronouncing his name with a tone of disgust.

Jimmy shoved his hands into his pockets but said nothing.

"So I hear crickets," the sheriff said, his voice suddenly devoid of emotion. He looked at Chuck, then Jimmy, and back to Chuck. He looked at the pizza boxes and moldy dishes spread around the room. "Sorry to have interrupted your game."

The sheriff left the house, got into his cruiser, and drove the wooded hills of Ellicott City to try and make sense of it all. *Where did I go wrong? When did I stop being a good father?*

He heard the steeple bells of Saint Paul Church chime in the distance.

***

Clare stood inside the door and watched Maggie and Mitch's joyful reunion. Even Blaise joined in the celebration as he jumped all over Mitch. She had never witnessed such affection and warmth. Clare allowed herself to melt into the love that permeated the scene, then silently slipped upstairs. *I don't belong here right now.*

She thought of her father, who had demanded obedience and submission, but never displayed the tenderness Mitch showered on Maggie. Her breakup with Greg was another blow to her fragile state, and now she would lose Maggie, who had been a gentle companion on the broken roads of West Virginia. All the emotions of the last six months came crashing in, and her body succumbed to exhaustion.

She could not bear being in the room she had shared with Greg, so she went into the spare bedroom and collapsed on the bed.

***

"Dr. Clare." Maggie softly shook her shoulder.

"What? Huh? Oh, I must have fallen asleep." She looked at Maggie, and everything came rushing back. She panicked. "Is everything okay? Are you all right?"

"Yes, I'm fine. Uncle Mitch wants to see you."

She let out a sigh. "Maggie, I don't think I can move."

"Of course, you can." Maggie pulled her to her feet and led her down the stairs.

When she reached the bottom, Mitch hugged Clare so tight she could hardly breathe. With tears in his eyes, he said, "To think I was about to call the cops on you! How can I ever thank you for taking care of Maggie? She's told me that if it hadn't been for you, well…"

"If it hadn't been for me, she would've never climbed in my truck, and you would've had her back six months ago!" All the sadness, disappointment, and turmoil Clare had endured came crashing in, and she burst into tears.

"No, no." Mitch's voice was soothing, and he pulled Maggie and Clare together in a hug. "We must believe God had a purpose for all that's happened. A wise priest once told me that God writes straight with crooked lines. Maybe this is one of those times."

As Blaise tried to wiggle his way into their embrace, Clare felt joy seep into her heart.

***

Clare drove them home, and Mitch handed Maggie the keys. When she went inside, Clare turned to Mitch. "Has she told you about Kevin?"

"Yes, pieces of it. It seems some of it's still fuzzy."

"What about the sheriff? You can't go to him. I don't know how, but he knows she is alive, and I'm involved. It seems he'll do anything to protect his son."

298

"Yes, that explains a lot that didn't make sense before." He grabbed Maggie's suitcase and said, "I need some advice."

Clare opened the truck door. "I'll try to help."

"Maggie is very close to our pastor, Father Brendan. I don't want to spoil this moment for her, but he's very ill. I don't want to tell her."

"Maggie is a strong and brave young woman. She'll be able to handle it, but I don't see the harm in waiting."

She was about to get in the truck when Maggie ran out. "Dr. Clare, where are you going?"

She replied, "I won't be far away if you need me," her voice choking on the words.

"But you can't leave me." Maggie clung to her.

"Maggie, it's all right. I'm just five minutes away."

"No. Uncle Mitch, don't let her go! Please stay, just until I get used to being home again. I don't think I can remember everything without you here to help me." Maggie was frantic, and Clare's eyes teared up.

Mitch replied with a note of surprise in his voice, "Maggie, I'm sure Dr. McGuire has things to do in her office. We can't assume that she can drop everything…"

"Please, Dr. Clare, it's almost Christmas." Maggie started to cry. "You won't have to do anything now, will you? No one works over the Christmas break."

Mitch looked apologetically at Clare and said, "I know this is asking a lot, but if you can spend Christmas with us, we'd love to have you."

She looked at Maggie, whose eyes begged her to stay. But while shaking her head, Clare answered, "I would love to stay." She turned to Mitch. "And please call me Clare."

Maggie hugged her, and when Clare looked at Mitch, she read thank you in his eyes.

"Okay, it's settled. Clare, how about you tie up any loose ends at your office and collect what you need to stay for a few days? Maggie and I can come get you when you're ready. Does that sound like a plan? I don't want the sheriff to see your truck in our driveway."

Clare was relieved that he believed her suspicion about the sheriff. "Great. Yes, that sounds like a good plan."

Mitch wrote down his telephone number.

As she reached for the paper, his hand brushed hers, and warmth shot up her arm. She wondered if he felt it too.

CHAPTER 42

Therefore I tell you, whatever you ask in prayer,
believe that you have received it, and it will be yours.

—Mark 11:24

C lare stopped at Reed's Pharmacy and used the pay phone
to call the telephone company. She learned that a techni-
cian was in her area, and her line could be restored as soon as
he checked in. She called Frank's office, but could only leave
a message.

I'll call him tomorrow, as well as the gas and water companies.
What was Greg thinking by turning off the utilities? The pipes could
freeze! Great doctor, but not a lot of common sense.

She dismantled the tent and put it in the shed, finished
sifting through the mail, made a small pile for immediate
attention, and tossed everything else in the trash. She looked
at Greg's crumpled note and delighted in tearing it up and
throwing it away.

Clare went upstairs, looked at the deserted room, and waited
for her heart to collapse.

Wait! What is that sound? Clare Anne McGuire, are you humming?
She smiled.

And you're smiling too!

Yes, and it feels good. It's been a long, exhausting six months, but there's a happy ending.

She showered, fixed her hair, and put on makeup, a ritual she had not bothered with for six months. She had lost weight, and her clothes fit very well. It would feel good to slip into a dress, but the occasion called for a more casual look, so she settled on a sweater, slacks, and boots. She packed some items for a few days but hesitated to pick up the phone.

Clare knew from her upbringing it was wrong to test the Lord or ask for signs, but…what the heck? *Lord, if they have restored my dial tone, I'll consider it a sign that calling Mitch is the right decision.*

She closed her eyes and slowly lifted the receiver to her ear. She never knew the sound of a dial tone could be so glorious. Clare smiled, thanked God for an answered prayer, and dialed the number written in perfect architectural penmanship.

***

Mitch built a fire in the two-sided fireplace as Maggie set the table. He foraged in the refrigerator for dinner and apologized to Clare for the eggs-and-bacon meal.

"Don't be silly." She smiled. "I enjoy sitting by a fire, drinking wine with breakfast." She winked at Maggie, who was now in her own clothes, the ladybug pinned to her sweater.

Their conversation was light and focused on Advent and Christmas. Mitch thought it best to keep Maggie's reappearance quiet. He knew he would have to go to the police to report Kevin's death as a murder, but he wanted Maggie to have time to remember everything. Her testimony would naturally send shock waves throughout the town.

After dinner, Maggie put her head in her hands.

Clare put her arm around her. "All is well; you're home now."

"I know, but I'm starting to remember all the people I miss, like Father B. and Father James, Aunt Marge, Sam, Beverly, and my friends from school." She closed her eyes and started crying. "I'll never see Kevin again."

Clare felt Maggie's forehead. "You feel warm. Mitch, do you have any aspirin?"

"Yes, in the medicine cabinet."

They all went upstairs, and Maggie went into the bathroom.

Clare said, "It's been a long day, and it's wise that you didn't mention Father Brendan. It would be one more thing to upset her, and she needs a good night's sleep."

Clare's jaw dropped when she saw the castle in Maggie's room. "I presume this is your handiwork?"

"I guess I got a little carried away. I wanted to change it when Maggie turned thirteen, but she insisted on keeping it. She said she had lost so much of her childhood when her parents died and didn't want to give it up just yet." Mitch's eyes teared up. "Believe it or not, all her girlfriends love it!"

"It's lovely, like a fairy tale. This tapestry over the bed is beautiful. Is that Mary Magdalene meeting Jesus at the tomb?"

"Yes, it was a gift to Maggie from her mother. You probably don't know this, but Maggie's parents named her after her mother, Mary, and my wife, whose full name was Magdalene."

"So Maggie is…"

"Mary Magdalene."

Clare nodded. "The name suits her. What is this over here?"

"It started as a doghouse but has morphed into a fancy bookshelf since Blaise refused to sleep in it."

Clare smiled.

Maggie entered the room in her flannel pajamas and lay on her bed.

Mitch bent over to kiss her. "You'll feel better in the morning. This has been challenging, but you're home and safe now."

"Uncle Mitch, I need to go to Confession. Do they still have it on Tuesdays?"

"Yes. We'll talk about it tomorrow."

"Dr. Clare, can you stay for a while?"

"Sure, but it's time you started calling me Clare too."

Maggie said her prayers, and Clare recited them along with her. It didn't take long for Maggie to fall asleep, after which Clare went downstairs to say good night to Mitch.

He poured her another glass of wine and refilled his glass.

"You know," she said, "I became accustomed to Maggie's nighttime prayer ritual. She would pray for the impoverished people at the camp and then follow it up with Hail Marys and Our Fathers."

Mitch looked down at his wineglass. "Clare, I have no idea what to do next. I'm so grateful you're here. I never lost hope, but feared she might be gone forever. Maggie helped me see life through my tears. I don't know how she did it, but she showed me things I might have missed if my eyes had been dry. The tears were like a magnifying glass that gave me a new perspective on the important things in life."

Clare smiled. "I know what you mean."

They were silent as they watched the flames dance, crackle, and sputter around the logs. "Maggie ran away once in West Virginia."

Mitch looked surprised. "How come?"

"She thought she was a burden." Clare swirled the wine in the bottom of her glass. "I can't imagine what these past six months have been like for you. Josh and I were so frightened that we would never find her, and that was just for a couple of hours."

304

Mitch looked concerned. "Do you think she'll need some professional help?"

"I had her seeing a therapist, but it didn't help much. She told me that God would help her remember when it was time. She was right." Clare thought for a moment. "She wants to go to Confession. Do you think it's something that can help her emotionally?"

"It can be cathartic to talk things out and know God forgives you."

"She feels responsible for Kevin's death."

Mitch sighed. "I suspected that from what she shared. I know Father James can help her with that. He's been a good friend to me through all this. I haven't seen him since Father Brendan's relapse. I know Maggie will take it hard when I tell her. They're very close." Mitch continued, "I called the rectory this afternoon, but there was no answer. I'm sure their attention is on Father Brendan right now."

"I'm here to help. Do you think Maggie should be seen at church? Doesn't everyone know her? The news will get out. We must keep her safe until you go to the police."

"Good point."

"I wonder if we can get her to church without anybody recognizing her."

"You mean like a disguise?"

"Yes. We could make her look like a middle-aged woman, and no one will suspect it's Maggie."

Mitch looked at her skeptically.

"I'm serious.

"Yes, but I don't see how…"

"Leave it to me. I can do her makeup so she looks forty years older. I was involved in drama in college. I think I still have some tricks up my sleeve."

They talked for another two hours, but it seemed like minutes to Clare. Mitch shared stories about Maggie and his wife. Clare was amazed at his honesty and openness. There was nothing measured or contrived in his words, only warmth.

She yawned. "Oh, Mitch, excuse me. I'm drained from the emotional roller coaster and not used to drinking wine. I haven't had it for six months. I need to get some sleep."

Mitch stood up when she did, and he took her hand. "I'm sorry for rambling on so much. It's just…" He looked into her eyes. "Thank you again for taking such good care of Maggie. I can tell she's grown quite attached to you."

"Well, the feeling is mutual." She smiled. "Now, I better get to bed while I still have enough energy to climb the castle wall."

CHAPTER 43

To one who has faith, no explanation is necessary.
To one without faith, no explanation is possible.

— *Saint Thomas Aquinas*

Sheriff Wilson was tired of driving around aimlessly but didn't feel like going home. He headed to his office. The building was empty except for a new deputy on the night shift.

"Evening, Sheriff."

Sheriff Wilson nodded but said nothing. He couldn't remember the deputy's name.

He opened his office door, flicked on the light, and slumped into his desk chair. He'd been the sheriff for almost two terms now. The office walls displayed his awards, along with photos of prestigious figures, and they meant nothing to him anymore. His decision early on to pour everything into his career had cost him his wife and now his son.

I should've taken more of an interest in Chuck. Instead, I looked the other way or made excuses for him and forced his mom to be the disciplinarian. It got to the point where I didn't want to be around the kid. It was easier to go to work than deal with him. I wasn't much of a father, and now the chickens have come home to roost.

He reached into his bottom drawer and pulled out a bottle of Crown Royal that he had reserved for special occasions. He polished off the bottle, put his head on his desk, and wept.

***

The next morning Maggie wiped the frost from the bedroom window, and her raspy voice announced, "It looks like someone spread diamonds across the snow."

Clare felt Maggie's forehead and cheeks.

"It's just a cold," Maggie announced in a frog-like voice. "I don't want anything to spoil the day."

"I agree."

Maggie and Clare dressed and hurried downstairs to find the room toasty warm, thanks to the fire Mitch had rekindled in the fireplace. They found fresh bagels, cream cheese, croissants, and sweet buns on the dining room table.

The front door swung open, and Mitch wrestled a newly cut blue spruce through the front door. "Well, I hope you found the results from my trip to the bakery satisfactory."

"Uncle Mitch, where did you get that tree?" Maggie's hoarse voice made him smile.

"Don't tell anyone, but I found it just beyond Len's garden. You know, the one you and the girls brought back to life."

"But that is park property!" a croupy voice advised.

"Like I said, Miss Froggy, don't tell! Clare, may I pour you a cup of coffee?"

Clare smiled. "So you're a mind reader and a tree thief."

They sat and ate and talked for hours.

Mitch loved hearing about the DOW mission. It seemed to him that Maggie had matured exponentially these past six months. He became more grateful for and impressed by Clare with each passing hour.

"The works you two performed were certainly corporal works of mercy." He added, "I can't wait to meet Josh."

After clearing the dishes, they trimmed the tree. Mitch played his Frank Sinatra Christmas album on the turntable; he and Clare sang along while Maggie hummed.

After they lit the tree for the first time, Maggie, undaunted by the croupy rasp in her voice, offered a prayer. "I thank You, Lord, for Uncle Mitch"—she took his hand—"and Clare"— and reached for her hand—" and for bringing me home in time for Christmas."

Mitch looked at Clare and saw she had tears in her eyes. He cleared his throat. "Thank You, Lord, for returning Maggie home"—he squeezed Maggie's hand—"and for bringing Clare too."

Clare blushed, and there was an awkward moment until Maggie reminded Mitch, "I want to go to Confession. I need to see Father James and Father B. My memory is returning, making me miss Aunt Marge, Sam, and my friends."

Clare spoke up, "Maggie, I have an idea and wonder what you might think." Then she explained her plan to have Maggie be incognito at the church.

"It sounds like a truly wonderful idea! I'm sure the priests will know me."

Mitch winced. "Maggie…" he began but then hesitated. *Should I tell her about Father Brendan?*

"How about we go to Clare's and get you dressed for Confession?"

***

Clare sifted through some boxes in her closet and found one marked "Stage." She placed a black wig over Maggie's golden-blonde hair and gave her a dress and orthopedic shoes she had purchased at a secondhand store for a costume party. She then went to work on her makeup and finished off the disguise with Mitch's overcoat.

Even Mitch was surprised. "She looks very mature indeed."

Mitch drove to Saint Paul's two hours after confessions had started so the church would be less crowded. He figured it would be better for Clare to accompany Maggie since no one knew her.

Clare decided she would follow Maggie's lead and do whatever she did. Maggie dipped her fingers in the holy-water basin and made the sign of the cross when she entered the church, then genuflected before she knelt in the pew, and Clare followed suit. Maggie hung her head in prayer, but Clare was so fascinated with the decor that she could not help but look around.

The altar was beautiful. It looked like marble or alabaster. There were statues everywhere—one of the Blessed Mother and (she guessed) another of Saint Joseph. The most striking figure was Jesus, who hung on the cross above the altar. In the church where she had grown up, the cross was bare. The crucifix made an impression on her. Jesus was born to suffer and die for the sins of the world. Christ's image on the cross made that very clear. There was an empty wooden manger on the altar under the crucifix.

Oh my goodness, now I see the significance of Jesus in a wooden manger…and years later nailed to a wooden cross. The manger was a feeding trough for animals, and Maggie said that Jesus feeds the world with His Body and Blood in the Eucharist.

Her eyes drifted to the tabernacle. It was just as Maggie described it, with the lit candle to show Jesus was present. Clare had an overwhelming feeling of God's presence in this church, a sense of awe and wonder, something she'd never experienced in the church where she grew up.

Maggie got up, stood by a curtain, and motioned for Clare to stay in the pew, and then she disappeared behind the curtain.

Clare saw a little green light over the curtain turn red. *I wonder what's behind that curtain.* She focused on the spot where Maggie had disappeared and didn't like that she was out of sight. *Does that curtain lead to another room?*

Clare thought about getting up and going to the curtain, but soon Maggie emerged and headed out the side door of the church. *Is this all part of Confession?*

A minute after Maggie left, a priest scrambled out a door opposite the curtain. He appeared disturbed and frantically looked around the church. "Oh, sorry!" he said to the parishioners, who looked startled as he rushed down the aisle and out the front door.

Clare sat there just as perplexed as the rest of the people in the church.

***

Earlier that day, the sheriff hit the intercom button in his office. "Miss Gorman, can you get hold of Deputy Marks and have him come over as soon as possible?"

Miss Gorman jumped at the intercom's command. "Sheriff? When did you get in? Marks is right here." She motioned for him to go in.

The deputy entered and looked down at the sheriff's swollen eyes. "Hey, you look terrible. Are you feeling okay?"

The sheriff didn't move from his desk, but handed the deputy an evidence bag. It held a baseball bat.

"What's this for?" He looked at the pitiful man behind the desk. "Sheriff, are you gonna be sick?"

"Listen, Marks, I need you to take this bat up the street to Police Headquarters. I told them I would call when you were on your way." He finished writing a note, folded it, and handed it to the deputy.

As the deputy turned, he unfolded the note and saw three names and addresses shakily scribbled on the paper. "Sheriff, one of these addresses is yours, and your son's name's on it."

"I need you to deliver the bat and note to Captain Morse."

"Sheriff, I don't understand. What's going on?"

"You'll know soon enough. On your way out, ask Miss Gorman to come in." The sheriff picked up the phone, dialed, and said into the receiver, "Captain Morse, please."

Marks left and advised Miss Gorman the sheriff needed her.

She entered the room and found the sheriff with his head in his hands.

"Miss G-Gorman," he said, choking on her name, "I need you to type a letter of resignation for me."

She sat—or, rather, plopped down—in the upholstered chair in front of his desk with a look of bewilderment.

The sheriff cleared his throat and began to dictate.

CHAPTER 44

At the end of our life,
we shall be judged by our love.

—Saint John of the Cross

T he priest who had left the church in a panic did not return. Clare sat in the pew a few more minutes, listening to parishioners murmuring about the priest's hasty departure. It occurred to her that this was an unusual situation. She slipped out of the pew and left through the same door as Maggie.

It took a moment for her eyes to adjust, but the full moon caught Maggie's blonde hair cascading over her shoulders. She held the black wig in her hand, and the priest who had hurried from the church had his hands on her shoulders.

Clare heard the priest say, "I can take you to him."

"Where are you taking her?"

Maggie and Father James looked in Clare's direction.

"Father James, this is Dr. Clare. She saved my life."

Father James said, "Please join us."

They walked past a beautiful, life-size creche that shared the garden with a Blessed Mother statue, up the garden stairs, and across the parking lot to the rectory. Mitch was waiting outside the front door. Clare wondered how he knew they would end up there.

When Father James drew close and saw Mitch, the priest grabbed and held on to his arm for support.

"James, are you gonna be okay?"

"Yes, I'm just overwhelmed at the moment."

Mitch patted him on the back. "I get it."

"I had asked Sam to hang a wreath on the door if Father Brendan passed. He didn't hang it, so Maggie has time to say goodbye," the priest said as he unlocked the door.

Maggie followed him inside; Mitch waited for Clare to enter before him.

Father James softly said, "Maggie, I administered the Apostolic Blessing to Father Brendan a few hours ago. He's ready to go home to Jesus, but I think he was waiting for you. I know he'd love to know you're home."

Tears filled Maggie's eyes. "I have to get this stuff off my face! I don't need the disguise now." Her tears erupted into a full-blown sob, and she ran to the powder room and slammed the door.

Mitch started to follow her, but Clare took his arm. "She'll be okay. Give her this moment."

Father James asked Mitch, "Why is Maggie dressed up like that?"

"Kevin's death and her disappearance were not accidents, and we're trying to keep her reappearance quiet until it's safe."

"Safe! Oh no! Is she in danger?"

"I'll fill you in later."

The powder room's door slowly opened as Father James whispered to Mitch and Clare, "Father Brendan has slept all day. He may not recognize her anyway."

Maggie entered Father Brendan's bedroom to find Aunt Marge sitting at her brother's bedside. Sam stood beside her. They both took a deep breath when they saw Maggie in the doorway.

"Oh dear Lord"—Marge exhaled—"if this is a dream, please don't wake me." She stood up and held out her arms.

Maggie ran to her, and they embraced as Sam enfolded them both.

Fatigued, Marge looked down at her brother. "He's been like this all day. He hasn't opened his eyes, and he labors to breathe."

Maggie sat down on the chair and took Father Brendan's hand. "Father B., it's me, Maggie. I found my way home." Amazingly, her normal speaking voice had returned. "I was gone a long time, but you were always with me. I remembered all the things you taught me." She raised his hand to her cheek.

Mitch stood next to Clare in the doorway of the room. She felt like an outsider but knew she was the only one who could attest that Maggie had remembered everything about her faith.

"I love you, Father Brendan. I'm sorry I wasn't here for you these past months—" Then she could speak no more.

The room went silent except for the sound of Father Brendan's breathing. His steady exchange of labored air kept time with the flicker of the candle flame burning by his bedside. Slowly, his eyelids fluttered, then opened ever so slightly as Maggie hovered over him, her crystal-blue eyes filled with tears.

The hint of a smile brushed lightly across his lips as Father Brendan whispered, "Lord, now let your servant go in peace."

CHAPTER 45

God judged it better to bring good out
of evil than to suffer no evil to exist.

—*Saint Augustine*

M itch and Clare nervously sat on stools at the breakfast bar as Maggie met with the police detectives in the den. She was giving an account, to the best of her recollection, of the events on the evening of June 21. After forty-five minutes, Maggie escorted the detectives to the front porch, closed the door behind them, and ended that chapter of her life.

Needing a moment to catch her breath, she leaned against the doorjamb and closed her eyes. Mitch and Clare went to console her, but Maggie burst into tears and ran up the stairs with Blaise in pursuit.

Clare and Mitch looked at each other. "What should we do?" Mitch asked.

"Usually, I suggest giving her space, but now she needs our support."

They entered Maggie's bedroom to find her in the fetal position on her castle bed, Blaise beside her.

Clare sat on the bed and said, "Do you remember the night I found you stretched out on a blanket, looking up at the stars? You said you were listening to God. Do you remember what He said?"

"Be still and know that I am God."

"Then I said that doesn't seem very helpful."

"Yes, I remember," Maggie tearfully answered.

"Well, today, I take it back."

Maggie slowly sat up and sniffed. "I relived the night Kevin died as I told the detectives what happened. I thought the boys would kill me too." She closed her eyes. "Then I remembered something Father Brendan taught me. He said, '*You can't enter heaven with a grudge on your heart.*'" The tears poured down her cheeks, and Mitch handed her a tissue from the box on her desk. "The storm got quiet, and I looked into Chuck's eyes. They were wild but frightened." Maggie put the tissue to her eyes. "Then the words *I forgive you* just slipped out... I don't know how, but I meant it."

"That was very brave of you."

"As soon as I said it, the weirdest thing happened. A sense of peace came over me, like mercy had tamed the chaotic storm."

Mitch and Clare exchanged a look of amazement as Maggie glanced around her room.

"Uncle Mitch, I think it's time to dismantle the castle in my bedroom."

***

The December 21 *Baltimore Sun* newspaper landed on the front porch. Mitch opened it and found the story of the arrest on page 2. He breathed a sigh of relief and entered the house to recap the article for Clare while she scrambled eggs.

"Chuck and Jimmy were charged with armed kidnapping, Jimmy with second-degree murder, and Ben as an accessory to the crimes. Page 4 talks about the sheriff resigning from office."

"Well, the story is out now. Maggie is safe," Clare reassured Mitch. "She is emotionally exhausted, but hopefully this will bring her closure."

***

The next day, Father James presided over the Mass of Christian Burial for Father Brendan. The church overflowed with parishioners, clergy, and friends. Maggie sat sandwiched between Mitch and Clare and tried not to let her heartache overpower the words of the Gospel.

> *Truly, Truly, I say to you, unless a grain of wheat*
> *falls into the ground and dies, it remains alone,*
> *but if it dies, it bears much fruit.*

Maggie knew this verse was more about self-sacrifice than physical death, but today she wondered how the passing of the people she loved could bear fruit. She was no stranger to death or goodbyes, and Father Brendan's fatherly care had helped her through her younger years.

At Communion, it all came together for her. *Here is where we are united in the Body of Christ. I miss you, Father Brendan, Mom, Dad, and Kevin, but I know we are all together when I pray at Mass. Whenever a priest raises the host, the Body of Christ, and says, 'Behold the Lamb of God,' heaven and earth kiss.*

The congregation's shoes crunched up the snow-covered hill to Saint Mary Cemetery, where Father Brendan found his resting place. When the ceremony ended, Maggie and Mitch visited Len's grave as they had done so many times before.

Then Mitch said, "Kevin is just down the stone steps and to the left. Would you like me to come with you?"

Maggie looked up at Mitch and shook her head.

As she walked down the steps to Kevin's grave, Clare slipped in from behind and took Mitch's hand. It eased the immense pain welling up in his heart. He squeezed her hand in gratitude.

Kevin's headstone had an angel carved on it with the epitaph:

Always in My Heart
Kevin Francis Jackson
October 4, 1954–June 21, 1972

"Kevin, you were my first love, and I will never forget you." She pulled the ladybug rock from her pocket and smiled. "Remember how you bought this for me at a craft show?" She kissed the ladybug and placed it on his headstone. "I will hold you in my heart forever."

***

Maggie woke on Christmas morning to the church bells ringing louder and longer than usual. It brought to mind the poem "Christmas Bells" by Henry Wadsworth Longfellow. The poem always made her melancholy, but the last stanza inspired her to appreciate this Christmas morning as she recited the words from memory.

> *Then pealed the bells more loud and deep...*
> *God is not dead, nor doth He sleep!*
> *The Wrong shall fail, The Right prevail,*
> *with peace on earth, goodwill to men!*

The Christmas Mass drew a crowd ready to celebrate both the birth of Jesus and Maggie's return. She was a welcome gift to many. Like the stable in Bethlehem, the Hartman home overflowed with love and contentment; there was not an armload of gifts to open, but loads of open arms to welcome Maggie home. Visits from friends and Clare's presence helped lessen the ache in Maggie's heart. Marge and Sam showed up with figgy pudding for Christmas dinner.

Marge said, "I make it every Christmas because of the symbolism. I put in thirteen ingredients that represent Christ and the twelve apostles. I put the sprig of holly on top to represent the crown of thorns."

Father James said, "Yum." But when he went to touch it, Marge playfully slapped his hand.

Marge said, "Clare, make sure Father James eats his vegetables before the figgy pudding! I have to get home to my family, or I would police him myself." She laughed.

Marge took Maggie aside. "When I emptied Brendan's desk, I found this sealed envelope addressed to 'Mary Magdalene Hartman, aka Maggie.'"

Maggie's eyes filled with tears as she tucked the letter inside her sweater.

Marge hugged her tight. "I miss him too."

More guests arrived. Beverly and her mom stopped in, and Beverly wrapped her arms around Maggie with tears and smiles and said, "Don't you ever disappear again!"

Mrs. Gosling brought a beautiful evergreen centerpiece from Caplan's Department Store. "Maggie, I hope you'll return to work as soon as you feel up to it."

Fran Jackson also visited. "Maggie, I want you to meet my daughter, Katie."

"You're Kevin's mom," Maggie said, holding back tears. "He had your eyes."

"I read about Kevin's funeral in the paper. I was there when Father James laid him to rest." Katie took Maggie's hands in hers. "My mother told me about your friendship and how he returned to the church because of you. I've come home too. Thank you."

The sisters who taught her over the years, along with class-mates, came and went all afternoon.

Finally, Maggie said, "Uncle Mitch, I'd like to visit the Blessed Mother Garden before it gets too dark."

Father James said, "I'm going to church for prayer. I can take Maggie." He looked at the clock that displayed it was the three-o'clock hour. "I'll have her back before the dinner bell, and we'll bring Father Mateo with us. He's been working all afternoon on his mother's famous Mexican recipe for buñuelos. I can't pronounce it correctly, but the kitchen smells like cinnamon."

When they got in his car, Father James asked Maggie, "How are you holding up?"

Maggie answered, "Father Brendan once told me that every time I go up a staircase, I should repeat the words of John the Baptist, 'He must increase.' When I go down a staircase, I should recite, 'I must decrease.' That little prayer helped get me through that first year I came to live here after my parents died. It helped me not be so self-absorbed. It will help me again."

After Father James parked the car, Maggie sat and stared out the windshield with glazed eyes.

"What is it, Maggie?"

"I know you told me that I'm not responsible for the actions of others. But I still believe, if Kevin had never met me, he would be alive today. I can't let that thought go." A tear slid down her cheek.

Father James raised his hand to wipe her tear but decided it should remain.

> *He will wipe away every tear from their eyes,*
> *and death shall be no more, neither shall there*
> *be mourning nor crying nor pain anymore, for*
> *the former things have passed away.*

"If it hadn't been for you, Kevin may never have found his way home to Jesus."

Maggie attempted to smile, then opened the car door. He watched as she walked down the steps of the Blessed Mother Garden. He felt her prayer in his heart—*I must decrease.*

She stepped inside the stable Kevin had built, knelt by the manger, and lowered her head. The descending sun sparkled on the snow around her like thousands of twinkling lights. Father James thought of how at home she looked there with the Holy Family. A Scripture passage came to his mind: *"In Him was life, and the life was the light of men. The light shines in the darkness, and the darkness has not overcome it."* He unlocked the door and entered the church.

Maggie bent down, kissed the head of the Baby Jesus, and whispered, "In all those months I was away from home, I carried You in my heart, just like Your Mother carried You. I may have been missing, but I was never lost."

She rose and went to stand before the Blessed Mother statue. She reached inside her coat and pulled out the letter Father Brendan had written on December 12, the Feast of Our Lady of Guadalupe.

> *Dearest Maggie,*
>
> *I knew you would find your way home. The Lord often sends us on missions that we least expect, but when we hold on to Him, His grace finds us. I have held you in prayer these months, asking the Lord to bless all you touch with the tender heart of His humble Mother and the tenacity of Mary Magdalene.*
>
> *I missed your laughter and quiet, calming voice, but little ladybugs, who found their way to my*

windowsill, kept me company. The little ladies enlightened me about the work God called you to perform. I would love to hear your stories many years from now when you are called home to heaven. We will have an eternity to share them.

Remember your Spiritual Work of Mercy and pray for me.

Love and peace, my child,
Father B.

Epilogue

Friendships begun in this world will be taken up again, never to be broken off.

—*Saint Francis de Sales*

Six months later…

M arge stood in the office doorway. "Father James, the new seminarian is here. By golly, they look younger every year!"

"Really? I didn't expect him until tomorrow. Send him in."

Father James stood up and shook the seminarian's hand. "Well, I was just reading your profile the archdiocese sent over. Happy birthday! Your parents must have been thrilled when you were born on the Feast of Aloysius Gonzaga."

"Yes, they were. They are really into the lives of the saints. Please call me Al."

"I'd have thought you'd take this day to celebrate before beginning your assignment tomorrow."

"I wanted to get a feel for the parish. You know, walk around on my own."

"Of course, make yourself at home." Father James opened his desk drawer. "Here's a skeleton key that'll open any door on the grounds. I'm glad you're dressed in your clerical clothing. If you run into Sam, he'll know you are the new seminarian.

He's around here somewhere, fixing something or other. I'll let Marge know you'll be here for dinner and talk her into one of her famous chocolate birthday cakes for dessert."

"Please don't have her go to any trouble."

"It's no trouble. We make it a point to celebrate birthdays here." Father James chuckled. "When you taste her cake, you'll see why I insist. If you want to join Father Mateo and me for evening prayer, we meet at five in the church, and the dinner bell will ring at six."

***

Maggie bent down to examine a still pool of water along the edge of the Patapsco River. She was captivated by the tiny tadpoles flitting around just below the surface, until a splash of water hit her in the face. Blaise had disrupted her quiet moment by dropping a tennis ball in the formerly tranquil water.

Then Mitch called from the newly reconstructed swinging bridge, "Maggie, have you found one yet?"

"Not yet," she yelled back and threw the ball for Blaise. She looked up and saw Uncle Mitch and his wife standing on the bridge, smiling down at her. He had his arm around Clare's waist. You couldn't tell yet, but they were expecting their first child.

"Take your time," he said, "we're enjoying this beautiful June weather." Then, they strolled hand in hand across the bridge.

Maggie resumed her search as Blaise returned dripping wet. She stooped down and found the perfect stone, about the size of a small lemon. *I wonder how many years this rock had to spend in the river to become so smooth.* She climbed up the riverbank to join Mitch and Clare as they walked along the path.

Clare put her arm around Maggie's shoulders. She now believed what she had learned from Maggie, that trust in

God's plan was the best way to navigate life's journey. Her disappointments, shattered dreams, and detours on broken roads were what finally led her to true love. Prayer had become a mainstay for Clare, and with support from Mitch and Maggie, she revived her medical practice. Maggie painted and framed a verse from Proverbs for Clare's desk that read:

> *Commit your work to the Lord,*
> *and your plans will be established.*

Clare knew in her heart that it was Maggie who had saved her, not the other way around. Maggie's love for Christ drew Clare into a new relationship with Jesus. She learned that a father's love comes in many forms and found this to be so in the gift of Father James. Through the Sacraments of the Church, he helped her recognize her need to forgive herself, which supplied the grace she needed to forgive her father and Greg for their failings. Greg's ego had led her to Maggie and Mitch…and the new life growing inside her.

They walked through the park and took turns throwing the ball for Blaise. When they reached their home, Clare and Mitch sat on the porch swing while Maggie went inside.

She sat at her desk and moved a stack of letters from Josh to make room for her acrylic paints. She painted the smooth rock to look like a ladybug, held it up to the light, and blew on it to help it dry. She had taped a photo of Josh and one of Kevin to her mirror. She grabbed one of the photos to place in the family Bible, then tucked the Holy Book under her arm.

She was happy to find Clare fast asleep with her head nestled in the curve of Mitch's shoulder as the porch swing lightly swayed. Maggie held up the painted rock, and Mitch smiled and nodded. She picked a few wildflowers as she walked with Blaise to Saint Mary's Cemetery and placed them on Aunt Len's grave. She then walked over to visit Father Brendan and said a small prayer. The breeze whistled a light lullaby through trees as if to say, "All is well."

Walking down the stone steps to Kevin's grave, she whispered, "I must decrease," and then sat on the grass. She sighed as the church bells chimed three times, marking the Hour of Mercy.

"It's June 21," she said while looking at the freshly painted ladybug rock in her hand. *The river smoothed this rock like God's grace eased your rough and jagged heart.* "This morning at Mass, Father James read the Gospel of Luke, chapter 9. He said we must take up our cross to follow Jesus. When we do, we are not promised earthly success and should not expect it. The most important thing is to be faithful. We should begin each day with the end in mind. Heaven is our goal."

She looked up at the sky. "I've been praying for Chuck and Jimmy, that they would turn their lives around like you did. I thought you might like to know that Ben is coming to Mass now. He didn't have to go to jail. I believe your advice to Ben put him on the right path." Maggie sighed. "Your life made a difference, Kevin. You knew there would be conflict when you took up your cross, but you didn't waver. You led someone to God's Mercy.

"I've been praying that God would send me an answer about why you had to die. I try to shake the thought that it was my fault. Father James told me that bad things can happen because God gives each of us free will. Chuck and Jimmy willingly chose evil rather than good. But my heart whispers that you would still be here if our paths had never crossed."

Blaise rose from his resting position and started to wag his tail.

Maggie raised her eyes and saw a young priest looking down at them from the hill. He walked to where she sat, stopped, and studied her. She had never seen him before and thought he seemed too young to be a priest.

Blaise jumped up on the young man, who seemed undaunted by Blaise's size.

"Hello, boy! You're a big guy," he said as he ruffled Blaise's ears and looked around. "I think this is where I am supposed to be, but I'm not sure."

"You sound mysterious."

"Oh, I'm sorry. I don't mean to be. My name is Aloysius Gonzaga Jones, but everyone calls me Al. I'm the seminarian the archdiocese sent to Saint Paul for the summer."

Maggie's face lit up. "Today is the Feast day of Saint Aloysius Gonzaga!"

"Yes, I know." He laughed, and then his face became somber. "I see by the date on the gravestone that Kevin Jackson passed away last year on this day. Was he related to you?"

Maggie looked down and picked a blade of grass. "He was my friend. I was with him when he died."

"I'm so sorry."

She looked up. "Why do you think you are supposed to be here?"

He sat down next to her. "If I tell you, please promise you won't think I'm crazy."

Al was a perfect stranger, yet she felt at ease. Even Blaise was not wary of him. "Go on," she said.

"I keep having a dream where this guy brings me to a grave-yard, but it is more like a garden"—he looked around—"like this one. There's always a woman there. Somehow, I know the woman is Saint Mary Magdalene. You know, like when she stood in the garden outside the tomb and met Jesus."

Maggie's heart started to pound, and she became very hot and weightless. She thought she might faint and was grateful for the cool breeze across her face.

Al continued, "Every time I have this dream, the guy says, 'Genesis 50, verse 20.' I've been racking my brain trying to figure it out. I was walking the church grounds and saw this graveyard with woods and wildflowers. It reminded me of my dream. Now, I find the grave of a guy who died on my birthday, exactly one year ago, which is when the dreams started. Do you think there could be a connection? I mean, it is a coincidence, don't you think?" Al looked at the painted ladybug rock in Maggie's hand. "I just remembered; the guy in the dream always has a ladybug in his hand."

Maggie's eyes filled with tears. She opened the Bible and handed Al the photo of Kevin.

He took the photo and carefully examined it. "That's him! The guy in my dream!"

She slowly flipped the pages to find Genesis, chapter 50, and read verse 20. "As for you, you meant evil against me; but God meant it for good, to bring it about that many people should be kept alive, as they are today."

Al said, "I've read that verse many times, trying to figure out why it's in my dream. We learned in seminary that God never wills evil but can use sinful behavior to accomplish something good. That's what that verse in Genesis is about. Joseph's brothers sold him into slavery, but God used his misfortune to redeem many people."

Maggie's heart slowed to a comfortable rhythm. *Al's dream was for me. Chuck and Jimmy meant to harm Kevin, but God turned their evil action into something redemptive. God sent Al here to help me understand.*

Maggie closed the Bible and her eyes. It had all come together for her. She still didn't understand the mystery behind suffering, but she did realize that the tragedy that took Kevin's life had provided her with the affection and security of Clare. Their bond was as deep and loving as any mother and daughter.

In a peculiar turn of events, the suffering Aunt Len offered up in prayer for Mitch to become a dad was answered the day Clare knocked on his door. And Clare, after fighting it for so many years, finally opened her heart to the love of God the Father. Ben had returned to church, and Kevin's mom, Katie, had come home after sixteen years.

She thought of the tapestry of Mary Magdalene greeting Jesus at the tomb that hung over her bed. She was amazed that a chaotic bunch of loose threads and knots on the back of the fabric created such beauty on the front. It finally made sense. God weaves His gold and silver threads among the dark, loose, and broken ones that the world places there. God's tapestry creates our story. It seems messy because we only see it from below, but God weaves it from above.

Al interrupted her thoughts. "Miss, are you all right? I can't tell if you're happy or sad."

"Maybe I'm a little of both." She opened her eyes. "I don't think it's a coincidence; it's a God moment." Maggie put the photo of Kevin back in the Bible. "Aloysius Gonzaga Jones, my full name is Mary Magdalene Hartman, but everyone calls me Maggie. I'm very pleased to meet you."

"Is that really your name?"

"Yes, and your dream of the graveyard has revealed to me that God has a plan for everything that happens."

"I believe that too."

Al extended his hand and helped Maggie to her feet. As they walked up the stone steps, Maggie's heart quietly prayed, *Jesus, You must increase.*

She handed her new friend the rock she had painted and asked, "So, Al, have you ever heard the legend of the ladybug?"

For God so loved the world that He gave his only Son, that whoever believes in Him should not perish but have eternal life.

—John 3:16

Book Club Questions

1. Nine-year-old Maggie caresses the feet of a statue that depicts the Blessed Mother as she crushes the head of the snake. Later in the story, Kevin crushes a poisonous snake with his hammer. When Kevin was killed, did you feel that evil had the last word? Did the book's ending change your mind?

2. A legend is a traditional story sometimes regarded as historical fact but unauthenticated. The ladybug legend is such a story. The ladybug appears throughout the story, almost as a character in her own right. Why is the ladybug significant in the story? Blaise (named after Saint Blaise) saved Maggie when Chuck's hands tightened around her throat. Do you see any symbolism in this event?

3. Saint Thérèse of Lisieux (canonized in 1925) is a saint of childlike wisdom and trust. She impacted Maggie's life through her "little way." Do you think learning about the lives of saints can help your spiritual journey?

4. Mitch decided to give his heart to Jesus during adoration but then tried to take it back. He didn't want to let go of his emotional attachment to sadness, anger, and unforgiveness. He had lived with them for so long that he didn't know how (or want) to let them go. Is this a common weakness for people? Is it difficult to let go of the past?

5. What reaction did you have to Father Brendan's statement that freedom does not mean we can do anything we want, but it gives us the ability to do the things we are called to do by God?

6. Ben is afraid of Chuck. Do people often make poor choices out of fear?

7. Father James assures Maggie that prayer is not magic, but it helps one to view life differently. Do you treat prayer as if it were a spare tire or a steering wheel? Has this story called you to pray differently?

8. In Scripture, storms and raging waters are a sign of chaos and to be feared. Is it significant that Maggie's ability to forgive Chuck occurred when the eye of the storm brought a quiet calm to a horrific situation?

9. When lightning strikes the ground, the earth collapses, and Maggie is swept into the raging river, worsening an already-dire situation. Have you ever experienced an awful circumstance turning into a blessing?

10. Dr. Clare discovers Maggie in her truck at three o'clock, the hour of mercy. Where else in the book did the three o'clock hour play a significant role?

11. The sheriff is a good man who has placed his career above his duty as a husband and father. He's generous in helping Kevin's grandmother turn Kevin around, yet hesitant to confront his son, Chuck. Is it unusual in life to be so conflicted?

12. Do you believe Clare's difficult relationship with her father affected her vision of God the Father?

13. Do you think Clare would have felt God's presence in the church so powerfully if Maggie had not openly shared her faith?

14. Since heaven is a place of perfect love and happiness, do you agree with Maggie's statement that you cannot enter heaven with a grudge on your heart?

LET'S CONNECT

Email Mary at:
thehourofmercy1972@yahoo.com

.